A Novel of Life

Churchmouse

James S. Wamsley

DIAMOND BOOKS ◇ **Austin, Texas**

Dust jacket art by Robert Brown

FIRST EDITION

Published in the United States of America
By Diamond Books
An Imprint of Eakin Publications, Inc.
P.O. Drawer 90159   ★   Austin, TX 78709-0159

ISBN 0-89015-766-9

Quotes from Osbert Lancaster (p. 56) reprinted from Lancaster's *Cartoon History of Architecture* (London: John Murray
(Publishers) Ltd.)

Quote "We are the music-makers . . ." (p. 60) from poet Arthur
William Edgar O'Shaughnessy (1844–1881)

Library of Congress Cataloging-in-Publication Data

Wamsley, James S.
     Churchmouse : a novel of life / by James Wamsley.
          p.   cm.
     ISBN 0-89015-766-9 : $15.95 ($18.95 Can.)
     1. Mice — Fiction. I. Title. II. Title: Churchmouse.
PS3573.A476C4   1990
813'.54--dc20

89-71455
CIP

For
Hubert and Evelyn

CHAPTER 1

DEEP IN THE ORGAN CASE I LAY BESIDE THE WIND chest, dreaming of a plump and rubbery uncut Edam. Round, red-waxed, delectable, the animated dream cheese evaded my grasp, playfully darting here and there, accelerating as I chased it down the silent streets of an unknown city. We reached the edge of town. Bounding like some lost and half-inflated children's ball, the cheese found a meadow spangled with wild daisies and buttercups. I chased it joyfully but — as my dream pursuits always go — in extreme slow motion. Higher and higher we gamboled until in a last heroic leap I caught the cheese. We fell to earth amid flowers and vines. And as my incisors brushed that elegant skin, the cheese shimmered and dissolved, and my teeth clashed together in strident clicking. Then the meadow itself fractured like a kaleidoscope's shifting glass. The scene was irretrievable.

I wakened to familiar darkness, the safe though faintly melancholy setting of my home. But there was a disturbance. The clicking sound of my dream had persisted, bridging sleep and wakefulness. Someone was at the organ console.

I heard the familiar snap of the hand switch, just to the right of the manuals, but there was something else: a clattering, a thwacking, deep in the machinery. It was that which had mocked my dream, or vice versa. Something was wrong. Flicking the switch should produce a gentle hum in the blower motor, but the motor did not start. Someone tried the switch again, and yet again. Each time there followed the curious, strident clatter.

"The motor's shot, Mr. Hudson," said an unfamiliar voice outside the case. As if to corroborate the news, the hand at the switch set off a fresh flurry of clicks and thwacks.

"Hear that?" the strange voice asked. "Yonder's a little solenoid, trying to start things up, but the blower won't budge. It's probly the motor brushes. That's a mighty old motor. I can replace the brushes, but . . ." he paused portentously, "it seems to me you got to ask yourself, is it worth spending a nickel more on this unit? How much longer are you folks going to be here, two or three weeks? You can move the portable electronic in from the annex and do the job for three weeks."

Fully awake, I looked through a thicket of spindly wooden rods toward the console. Faint beams of light filtered through the organ's manuals, sometimes called keyboards, and gleamed softly in assorted cracks and seams in the ancient case. A delicate refulgence brightened the dust-fuzzed tracker board. All around me the gray banks of mighty pipes soared upwards into blackness, like the battered monuments of some forgotten civilization.

"Oh, shoot." It was the familiar voice of Mr. Hudson, the organist. I recalled his watery blue eyes roaming fecklessly behind thick bifocals, the gentle and uncertain mouth and chin, the hair that for want of a more precise expression I can describe only as mouse gray. "But you're perfectly right; it's not worth another sou. I had hoped it might stay the course. Sentimentally I pictured something like the one-hoss shay, collapsing at the proper dramatic moment when its work was done. This seems so piddling. What are brushes, anyway?"

"They make the armatures turn," the technician replied.

"I can't imagine how brushes could turn anything," Mr. Hudson said. "But no matter. I'll speak to the sexton and have him move the little portable over to the front of the nave. Oh! And I was to close out the last service with Handel. How can I possibly play Handel on that — that *accordion?*"

"Beats me," the stranger said. "But I guess this old wheezer has played its last tune."

I heard the crash of a closing tool box lid and then the whisper of footsteps departing on threadbare carpet. How intimately I knew each limp and raveled inch of it. Somewhere a heavy door creaked and slammed. Then the rumble of distant motor traffic was the only sound in Main Street Presbyterian Church.

So this is the way it ends, I thought, *not with Handel but the clatter of a solenoid, its command rejected by a big and dirty electric fan.* From the mouths of hundreds of pipes a silent reproach thundered upon me, as if I had betrayed them. Was I their guardian? I, Charles Churchmouse?

Recalling that day, as I try to compose my thoughts for this memoir, apologia, confession, call it what you will, I conclude that Mr. Hudson's renunciation of the organ was a critical fulcrum in my life. That may surprise you. If you can imagine yourself in my shoes, so to speak, for the merest trice, it should be plain that being a churchmouse is a precarious game at the best of times. Marching toward an end all too often defined by its wretched dispatch — traps, poison, starvation; the ultimate horror, cats — you'd say the mechanical failure of a pipe organ seems trivial or certainly harmless against such authentic perils.

But no. The organ's failure, like the seed of a cudzu vine, bore beneath its banal surface a cargo of genetic dynamite. To set the record straight about it is my goal. And as one good excuse is better than a dozen, I will advance no further rationale for my story than this: The world needs a clarification of those press accounts which refer, with a despicable touch of low melodrama, to a "mystery" called the Phantom of the Organ.

On the morning I have recounted, I had no sense of precognition of bizarre events to come. The future was decently veiled. I was merely depressed by the apparent fate of the old organ, as I lay there in its tomblike silence smelling of ancient metal and long-dry wood. The organ was more than a residence. To the hard and Spartan life of a churchmouse, a pipe organ brings precious, fleeting beauty and excitement. Was that now snatched away? And a still greater calamity had been casually broached in the conversation just concluded between Mr. Hudson and the repairman. I had learned about it earlier,

3

under circumstances which I will explain shortly. The congregation of Main Street Presbyterian had built a new church, miles away in the suburbs, and was abandoning the old building here in the very center of Byrdport. What would happen to my home? Would it be demolished? Suddenly, my future seemed even more endangered than usual.

In times of loneliness and gloom I draw comfort from inspirational figures I have met or heard about, and one who steadfastly recurs in that role is my grandfather. It was he who came now, in spirit, as I lay there in the silent organ. Grandpa was the bravest mouse I have ever known.

His name, roughly translated, was Virginius.

Grandpa had his imperfections, chiefly garrulousness and a propensity for cackling and whooping. He was always very certain about things. Those are qualities appropriate to grandfathers but trying to others in shared close quarters. I recall in pain how he fretted my father, a dignified and gentle mouse who could always see both sides of every question. Father was especially annoyed by the way Grandpa smacked and chomped over his food.

It was Grandpa Virginius, characteristically whistling off-key through his incisors, who first awakened me to music. He had no truck with "high church flapdoodle," scorning the baroque marvels of Bach and Handel. He rejected the redoubtable Reformation canticles of Luther and Buxtehude, and the still older cantatas with roots in the Gregorians. Grandpa insisted that the only church music worthy of the name was "the old-fashioned kind," and he was untroubled by the paradox that such works were relatively modern; he loved uncritically each fountain filled with blood, every call to lapsed and dissipated sinners, all visions of gold-cobbled streets. "What a Friend We Have in Jesus," "There is a Fountain," and "When the Roll is Called Up Yonder" whistled incessantly through Grandpa's age-stained gnashers. I think he was attracted by strong and gripping melodies. I should explain that to us as mice, the theology involved, as with all abstractions on the human side of the aisle, was normally beyond our interest or understanding.

There came a Sunday when the complete Churchmouse

family — Mother, Father, my brother Chester, Grandpa, and I — waited in the organ case with almost feverish anticipation. It was communion Sunday, one of the few days on which we churchmice could enjoy a square meal. In Main Street Presbyterian, church elders passed silver trays of bread chunks through the pews. In their efforts to detach small bread fragments, and transport them to their mouths to be consumed in pious rumination, humans dropped many crumbs. The dark pine floors of Main Street Presbyterian held a rich quarterly harvest for the Churchmouse family.

On that communion morning the organist, Mr. Hudson, completed the recessional and switched off the organ blower, which was our signal that soon the church would empty. Then Father led us from the organ (which was in the west gallery choir loft) down through the floor and walls, along the convenient footing of the laths, and through an opening in the baseboard on the main sanctuary floor.

"Take care," Father said. "Some people are still in the narthex. Stay under the pews and you'll be safe."

We foraged and dined happily. Chester, scarcely more than a baby, clung close to Mother.

"Will the cat be here, Mama?" Chester piped.

"Hush." Her eyes widened. "No. At least we haven't seen it for a time."

Stereotypes are rooted in truth, and there is verity in every cat-and-mouse cliché. I suppose to humans it is all a joke, a subject for low slapstick, and I have even heard of moving pictures burlesquing the plight of an innocent mouse named Jerry. The core of truth is, however, as hard as stale Gruyere. The feline malefactor of great stealth is the eternal dark shadow crossing our lives.

Despite Mother's assurance to Chester, I knew that we did have a cat problem, although, like Chester, I had never seen the creature. That was soon to change.

Grandpa and I saw her first. The shock paralyzed me. I shuddered; my mouth dropped open and a fragment of bread fell out. The cat, an ogre of reddish-orange fur moving in liquid malevolence, her vertical pupils gleaming like candle flames, was stalking Mother and Chester, who had not seen. In my terror I crouched on the floor and did nothing.

5

But Grandpa! With easy insouciance he strutted—there is no other word for it—strutted from a position of relative safety to a point on the threadbare carpet directly in the cat's line of vision. He had intersected the creature's stalking course toward Mother and Chester, and now he stood about three feet away, staring levelly at the cat. His expression was almost pleasant.

"Hello, Alabama Ruby," Grandpa said. "You devil. I been hoping you got run over in the street."

"Oh, Virginius," the cat said. "You talk so *awful*. And to me, just a poor old striped tabby, tryin' to get along. I've missed you, though, Virginius. Let me demonstrate how much . . ."

As the cat pounced, my last view of Grandpa was one I shall remember forever. Standing his ground, he slashed back with tooth and claw until he disappeared under a heaving mass of red fur.

Should we have gone to Grandpa's aid? I cannot say. We mice are not expected to waste time mourning life's might-have-beens. I merely report that we bolted en masse for the baseboard, and scrambled through the hole around a radiator pipe. We climbed upward through the walls, and in less than a minute we four survivors were back in the choir loft, safe in our organ case sanctuary.

We huddled together silently until Father spoke.

"The cat is too fast and too mean," he said. "We can't stay here. We must leave Main Street Presbyterian and seek shelter elsewhere."

I was too young to understand that cats are much the same everywhere, and that leaving a tested environment for unfamiliar quarters almost always magnifies the hazard. Better the devil you know than the devil you don't. Father must have known that. But once calamity strikes it is natural to avoid its locus. Besides, Father had been raised in an Episcopal church and I don't think he was ever truly content in a Presbyterian environment. He told me once he missed all the kneeling and rising and chanting of prayers. But, as I have explained, human talk of abstract matters is irrelevant to mice. For some reason Father just liked the Episcopal action.

Yet when we moved that night, it was to a Baptist church.

I remember the alternating thrills and terrors as we tip-toed through empty streets about 3:00 A.M., hearing the fitful grunts of distant vehicles. Our journey was only two blocks, but in other, perhaps more human terms, it was a very long way from Main Street Presbyterian. To Triumphant Mt. Horeb Baptist we repaired, and quickly found quarters within a kitchen wall.

"There should be plenty to eat," Father said. "Food is more important than ritual."

Indeed, there was food: We feasted on fried chicken and pork chops at least once a week. I will treasure the memory always, yet my matchless recollections of Triumphant Mt. Horeb are of its music, by which Professor Tyrone Washington and the Celestial Messengers enchanted that shabby, dingy interior. The Messengers were a large choir with the most astonishing ability to improvise. As I had heard little but Presbyterian music to that point, the contrast was absolute.

There was an old organ in the church, but it was rarely used. Organ music was not the Mt. Horeb style. The chief musical instrument was the piano, and not a great deal of that was heard. Occasionally, Professor Washington would take the bench and detonate syncopated gospel riffs like an overture hurled from some rakish Sinai, his giant hands easily spanning ten-note chords. When the piano feeling was on him, Professor Washington could cover more ground than any musician I have since observed. But my best memories of the church are of the Celestial Messengers and their magical vocal combinations. Ah, the reedlike contraltos and baritones and tenors; the sopranos brushing the upper limits of control, roughening out on the edge of a shriek and gliding into icy purity; the basses grumbling like distant cannon. *That* was music. When the Messengers were in full cry with "Give Me Jesus" or "I'll Take the Wings of the Morning," I was stunned by the glory of it.

That period was all too brief. Call it an intermezzo. Perhaps Father, who in his quiet way was always searching for something, had been rendered incurably and increasingly restless. Ecumenically we moved on through a variety of churches, synagogues, and cathedrals. It was dangerous, but often exhilarating. I suppose we were happy, although my parents began worrying about Chester and the early traces of streetwise swagger marking his demeanor.

The most boisterous phase of our gypsy period found us traveling with a tent evangelist, the Reverend Delbert Loudermilk, and his musician wife, Lorena. In the back seat of their 1976 Pontiac Bonneville we rode with Reverend Delbert and Lorena to a procession of small towns and dusty fields, where the air smelled of crushed grass and leaking transmissions.

I developed a singularly maladroit weakness: a reaction to sawdust, which covered the tented ground for each weeklong revival. Often I sneezed uncontrollably as we foraged in the wood chips for peanuts and breath mints. One night, just after a particularly furious oration by Reverend Delbert, my allergy erupted in a violent seizure. It came during that numb, reverent moment just before the congregation is exhorted to come forward and consecrate itself. I unleashed a fortissimo sneeze that blew a puff of sawdust into the tent's still air. A sweating fat man spied the four of us. I recall that seconds earlier, I was fascinated by the cardboard fan he twitched under his face. It bore a portrait of Jesus on one side, in blue, yellow, green, and purple, and on the other the picture of a funeral home. The fat man shifted the fan to his left hand, picked up a hymnal with his right, and hurled it at our family group, flattening Chester.

"Hey, Doris, I got one," the man said to his companion.

As Reverend Delbert Loudermilk implored the flock to come forward, Lorena struck up "Just As I Am" on the electric organ. Soon the sawdust churned with the shuffling feet of the almost-saved. Chester's lifeless forepaws extended from beneath the hymnal, frozen in a supplicating gesture dreadfully mocking the minister's outstretched hands. The rest of us darted frantically to escape the nightmare of plodding shoes, but there was no place to hide. A gaunt woman in a flowered cotton dress trampled my mother without even seeing her. Father almost reached the cheap plywood altar at the front of the tent, but became confused by the lights and allowed himself to be knelt upon by a strapping teenaged girl in tight jeans.

"Rats!" Someone screamed erroneously. "They're everywhere!" Heads swiveled. The shuffling procession halted in confusion.

Seeking shelter in the organ, I dashed around feet, purses, and bench legs. "There's one!" a voice boomed. A mud-stained boot crashed down, pinning my tail to the ground. I wrenched free and continued running. "He's heading for the organ!" the voice roared.

"Lawd, Lawd. Jesus come down!" Lorena Loudermilk bellowed.

As the organ squealed discordantly, she bounced from the bench and plunged yelling into the crowd. It was a flawless catalyst for a stampede. The congregation turned as one and surged for the tent's single exit. Some peeled off and dove under the canvas walls. Only Reverend Delbert stood his ground, vainly bellowing from the pulpit: "Come back, O ye of little faith! Rats are emissaries of the Devil! Don't let them drive you from the temple!"

I plunged under the organ, where I spent the night in misery and mourning, my family's only survivor. My tail ached; fully half its length had been severed by the boot.

Next morning, although I had no enthusiasm for it, I remained with the traveling evangelists as they packed up and moved on. There seemed nothing better to do.

Dispiritedly, I continued the evangelistic odyssey for three more weeks. Finally there came a day when the Loudermilks raised their tent on the outskirts of Byrdport, and Lorena announced she was going into town for shopping. I recognized my native city at once when we parked near a familiar steeple. A sense of comfort and welcome descended on me. Despite my fear of Alabama Ruby, I knew I had to return. Main Street Presbyterian was home. Home is where the door must always open.

That was in the fall. Apparently, I was the only mouse in residence: Alabama Ruby had done her job well. But now, fully grown, and battered by experience, I had no difficulty avoiding the cat. An old church stacks the safety odds in favor of a clever mouse. Construction methods of former centuries were generous with hidden space. Hollow walls and ceilings, traversed by mighty joists, afford an infinity of sanctuaries. I glimpsed Ruby on occasion — she was definitely aware of me, and tried to stalk me — but I was alert.

I had never paid much attention to humans except when their activities aided, pleased, or threatened me, having learned to accept them as a necessary part of the environment, aliens in the same existential plane. My own crossover knowledge of human thought and affairs came gradually, in a fusion of events perhaps unique to me. Being alone now, and thus often lonely, I commenced observing people more closely. And as the months began to pass, and I developed more sensitivity to human talk and action, it seemed that something was different, if not actually wrong, about the church's daily routine.

I noted it first at the organ itself, which was where I lived. From a supply of old paper I shredded the materials for a comfortable bed beside the organ's wind chest, thus residing, as far as I was concerned, at the very heart of the church. So I was sensitive to any change in organ routine, as in the gradual abatement of Mr. Hudson's practice sessions. The weekly choir practice seemed to grow perfunctory. There was excited talk about "new facilities."

After a struggle for comprehension I pieced together the story's essentials. On the day before the blower failed, the last bit of information dropped into place. I had wandered into the church annex, an adjoining wing containing the pastor's study. The annex, I once heard, was added in 1869 "at the height of mid-Victorian excess, in overripe Gothic revival style." (That is typical of the human assertions which I merely pass along in these memoirs. I may not fully understand their meanings, and you must judge if they are relevant.) In any case, the study's walls bristled with intricately formed and darkly varnished wood. From a corner crack behind the crown molding, I could emerge from the wall and climb down the Gothic paneling to the picture rail, where I could lie in perfect safety, yet see and hear everything in the room. That day, two people were down there: the Reverend Angus Christie, D.D., minister of the church, and a woman whom I recognized as a sometimes member of the congregation.

I had listened to the decanting of many heartbreaks, guilty consciences, fears and frustrations in that room, but somehow this conversation did not seem to fit the usual pattern. The minister seemed somehow defensive. "Do you think I

10

haven't loved this old church?" Dr. Christie demanded with some fervor. "How could I not be awar-rr-re of its significance?"

Never underestimate the value of a Scottish brogue in an American Presbyterian pulpit, I have heard it said, and although Dr. Christie had left a place called Aberdeen forty-two years before, he could still say "church" in a way that flirted cunningly with "kirk." In private, as in talking with the sexton, Jackson Ward, he often dropped the accent entirely. But in public oratorical flight his r's rolled like the purrings of a giant cat, a simile painful to acknowledge, as otherwise I had no complaint with Dr. Christie. "Do I not rr-r-recognize the enormity of what we're doing, you ask," he continued. "My dear Miss Tebell. Perhaps you should explain."

"How disappointing that an explanation is necessary," she said. "But here it is. If plans to demolish this building proceed, we shall have a large preservation flap in Byrdport. It may even create a national cause célèbre. The architect of this building was a major talent, after all."

Miss Tebell had an exceptional timber to her voice. From my days at Triumphant Mt. Horeb, I could tell a good contralto when I heard one. I looked over the picture rail to study her appearance more carefully. It is hard to tell human age, but I would learn later that she was in her middle thirties.

"So I think it's fair to ask," she continued, "if that's the sort of legacy you wish to bequeath."

"Legacy?" Dr. Christie said coldly. "I'll tell you the sort of legacy that will be transmitted by Angus Christie. Ser-rr-vice to the Master. The Gospel pr-rr-roclaimed. Duty per-for-rr-rmed."

"All that, I'm quite sure," the woman said. She paused. "But you may need to add one more qualification. 'Under his stewardship, a historical architectural masterpiece destroyed.'"

"That, I am persuaded, you clearly believe," Dr. Christie replied uncontentiously. I discerned his ruff of silver, curly hair, halolike against the afternoon light from the study's windows. His features, normally arranged in a state of some pugnacity, seemed tired and old. He continued with no rolling of r's:

"One man's architectural masterpiece is often another man's nuisance, Miss Tebell. The value may be debatable. And each case is different. I — wait a minute please, let me finish — I concede that in certain cases a building may be of exceptional interest, so far above the average that many sensible people — by no means just rabid preservationists — would like to see it saved. I am quite aware of all that, Miss Tebell. This building may fall in that category. But sometimes preservation just isn't possible."

"But if there's a chance, it must be pursued. And there is a chance," the woman said.

"There isn't. There's absolutely nothing I can do about it. The church sold the building, at least two years ago," Dr. Christie said.

"I know that," Miss Tebell said. "When Byrdport University got it they had no specific plans; nobody considered, really, what the building's value was. The preservationist climate here was weaker then."

"The church building represented a valuable property directly on the edge of the campus," Dr. Christie said. "And the school said something about remodeling the interior for a student activity center."

"That would have been acceptable, a reasonable adaptive use," Miss Tebell said. "Now they're tearing it down."

"Yet consider, Miss Tebell, it is not being replaced by a parking garage or fast-food outlet. I remind you that what's going up is a thirty-million-dollar health education complex, a badly needed addition to the university's general medical center."

"A building they could put on at least three other sites," she countered.

"Be that as it may. What can I do? What can the church do?"

"Stand up and be counted. Fight the destruction of this old building. Talk. Mobilize opinion. It works," Miss Tebell said. "There's one thing about demolishing a building. Once it's gone, it is gone. Forever off the earth. The movement to save it dies with the structure. It's one of the few perfect ways to eliminate a cause, as well as an architectural gem. To say nothing of part of the city's heritage."

An awkward pause. Then: "I'm sorry, Miss Tebell."

"Thanks for the time, Dr. Christie," she said, her rich contralto voice flat and distant. She reached for her purse. "My membership here is fated to be brief, it seems. I certainly shan't accompany the church to its new home."

She walked out. Dr. Christie sat motionless until a second door to the study opened, admitting the squat figure of the church secretary, Maude Pope. She walked to the other door and looked down a hall toward the street exit. I heard a door's faint thud as Miss Tebell left the church.

"Miss Tayloe Tebell," Dr. Christie said reflectively. "A formidable person, Mrs. Pope. I'm afraid she has the capacity to cause a great deal of trouble."

"Pah. Why should you think that?" Mrs. Pope asked.

"She has a cause, a quick mind, and a strong character. Combine those with her fatal curse of beauty, and one has quite an . . . adversary."

"Beauty?" Mrs. Pope's jaw, shaped like the coal scuttle beside the study fireplace, jutted forbiddingly. "I couldn't see it at all. These young women today . . ."

"I wonder though, Mrs. Pope, if she will prove to be an exception to Petrarch's rule. The one where he said, 'Rarely do great beauty and great virtue dwell together.' "

"Who can find a virtuous woman? For her price is far above rubies," Mrs. Pope snapped. "Proverbs, thirty-one ten."

"Thank you, Mrs. Pope," Dr. Christie said, with sudden weariness.

CHAPTER 2

WOULD YOU CARE TO KNOW THE MAINSTAY OF MY DIET at the time of these events? Soap. Soap, from the church washrooms. Some soap is not bad, such as the more expensive, fragrant, fatty varieties. But Main Street Presbyterian had a flat, one might say institutional or ecclesiastical, taste. I was sustained but not inspired.

It was not always thus. There had been Business Men's Prayer Luncheons and family covered dish suppers in the Sunday school portion of the annex. There I had reconnoitered for tuna casserole, meat loaf, and cold spaghetti. But those banquets were phased out as the church approached moving day. Soon even the soap disappeared. Clearly, I had food supply trouble.

I wasted no energy anathematizing Jackson Ward, the sexton, for his shiftlessness on the soap detail. It was time for productive action.

I determined to visit the Rib Cage.

Understand that Main Street Presbyterian lay on the very edge of the Byrdport University School of Medicine (BUSM), the campus portion of a fourteen-block medical complex in the city's old downtown. In our neighborhood few structures remained that pertained neither to the medical center nor to the state government, concentrated across Main Street. The Capitol itself, a Roman Revival structure of 1790, stood directly across Main Street from the church.

Even medical students and state employees must eat, and so the neighborhood supported establishments like the Rib Cage, an untidy den combining the worst features of a delicatessen, pizza parlor, hamburger joint, and place of assignation. Conveniently for me but to the regret of the church members, the Rib Cage was separated from Main Street Presbyterian by nothing but a cobblestone alley. A desire to escape the Rib Cage may have been a factor in the church people's decision to move to suburbia.

Close though the Rib Cage was, I always dreaded crossing the alley because of the Ratsoff.

That seductive rodent poison was keyed to the taste of rats. But for mice, too, Ratsoff exuded a heavenly aroma that exploded in the brain like visions of a Camembert mountain. The Rib Cage management scattered Ratsoff frequently across the cobblestones. I am not sure how effective it was on its designated victims. Rats are notoriously cunning, and most of them probably learned how to avoid the poison. The only recent Ratsoff casualty to my knowledge was a nearly tame Capitol Square squirrel. Cruelly served bourbon by a political reporter, he became disoriented and staggered across Main Street, miraculously avoiding traffic. Entering the alley, he drunkenly mistook Ratsoff pellets for bar snacks.

As I left the church the alley reeked of an odd effluvium: Ratsoff, garbage, and those human derelicts called winos. Three of the latter sprawled on the pavement, cradling brown paper bags. Despite my haste in crossing the alley, one of them spied me and hurled an empty bottle with surpising strength. There was a musical crash and a bright cascade of glass shards just behind me as I dived for a familiar hole in a basement window of the restaurant building.

It was good to visit the Rib Cage.

Often, you see, I secretly envied the lifestyles of my more affluent kinsmen.

I had cousins who dwelt in split-level homes, growing fat on Roquefort and Smithfield ham. I had a connection with some raucous mice who lived in a theater specializing in Xrated films, and who subsisted handsomely on popcorn. But at this time my closest confidantes were Sidney and Rebecca, resident mice at the Rib Cage. I found them easily in the kitchen walls.

"Have some feta, Charles. Eat. You look terrible," Sidney said. "Some Polish sausage, maybe. Here. There's plenty of cheesecake when you want. Blueberry topping, strawberry . . ."

"Try some of this red wine," Rebecca commanded, "and tell us how you are."

"I'm being evicted," I said. "They're tearing down the church. Perhaps you've heard."

"There's talk on the street," Sidney said. "I heard it among the doctors and med students from BUSM. So, you have to find a new place. That's no calamity."

"I just like it over there," I said. "It's home."

"Merely a roof. Home is safety, love, family, food. You can't think of home as a building, Charles. The building doesn't matter." Sidney insisted on waxing philosophical. "Charles. It might be actually better if you got away from churches for a while. Move in here. Plenty of food, music, company, action . . ."

We were in a wall behind the kitchen and a row of booths, where generations of mice had blazed food-producing trails. The view from assorted cracks and holes was none too good — human feet and legs, grimy floor, and the undersides of tables lumpy with chewing gum — but the ambience seemed warm. I could see why Sidney and Rebecca liked it.

I started thinking over their offer. And as I did, I met Serena.

She came into the wall from a corner booth, a stranger with sparkling eyes, dragging a segment of pizza half as large as she. "Anchovies and pepperoni!" she laughed. "Help me eat some of this. Look at the mozzarella. I'm all gummed up in it!"

You may talk all you please about the superiority of a love that grows slowly. It goes something like this: Two creatures meet, with no inordinate excitement, yet after one thing and another their lives begin to intertwine. They share experiences. Their thoughts become parallel. One day they look at each other and say, "Is this love? It must be love." I know it works that way sometimes. It is said that in societies where parents arrange marriages for their children, such a process often occurs, with salutary results. All I can say is that as far as Serena and I were concerned, it did not work that way.

Understand that she was the most beautiful creature I had ever seen. She intoxicated me like too much of Sidney's wine. I ached with the splendor of her, as meanwhile a mysterious refulgence enchanted the Rib Cage's squalid interior. Love at first sight? Ask me. One minute a conservative, controlled, skeptical mouse; the next, a raging obsession masked by fur and big ears, a colossal love rocket fired by blazing hormones.

I loved; therefore, I was insane. Sidney and Rebecca certainly believed it, and when I moved in they exchanged tolerant smiles. I see now that as the days passed, my madness over Serena began to tire them, although I was too distracted then to notice.

Late one night Serena whispered "Come," and gently touched my forepaw. At that, while I would have followed her into the mandibles of Alabama Ruby, my spine softened into creme caramel. She led me along a power conduit in the wall behind some booths. Then we followed a connecting cable through the wall, and into one booth's remote control unit for the jukebox. There, in brilliant illumination, Serena and I were dwarfed by the tall flaps that displayed the song titles. She waved at the inventory.

"What do you like?" she asked.

I said I knew nothing of popular music.

"I'll pick one," she said, and disappeared. I heard clicking sounds. Then she returned, and led me down to the table, where amid dirty dishes a candle stub flamed in the neck of a Spanish rioja bottle.

"I selected the latest by a group called Southern Cross," Serena said. " 'The Song Nobody Knows.' The Cross is the only group to fully blend redneck soft rock with medieval English minstrelsy."

Wondering how she knew so much, I surrendered to the magical moment. Serena was gazing into my eyes. Have you ever looked, hardly blinking, into the candlelit eyes of a new love? Looked and looked until it seemed you could swim over and enter those enormous pupils? That is how it was.

I was scarcely aware of the song that she played, but since then I have come to know it well. Here are some of the lyrics:

> *There was a song somebody played*
> *When I was young, before I paid*
> *For all the scores, and all the strings;*
> *Before the silence heartache brings;*
> *I can't remember how it goes,*
> *It's just a song nobody knows.*

After those early days with Serena, you should understand that a piece of my heart remained permanently affixed, like ineradicable tomato paste, to the battered booths of the Rib Cage.

But through my giddiness there persisted a faint, nagging ambiguity in our relationship. In rational moments I began to suspect a problem was concealed somewhere offstage. Were there subtle signs that unlike me, Serena was holding some emotional territory in reserve? Inexperienced with females, I wondered if perhaps I was missing certain unspoken signals. All would be well. And yet . . .

Late one morning Sidney found me in a rare solitary moment. He appeared serious and ill at ease.

"Charles. I'm your friend, right?" he began.

"I have none better, Sidney. You know that," I said.

"And I know you for a serious mouse. Restrained. A gentleman. My God, Charles, you're a . . . a churchmouse."

"By name and by trade," I admitted.

"So you should now remember who you are, and get a grip on your foundations. They are strong foundations, Charles," Sidney said.

"What are you trying to tell me?" I asked.

"Rebecca and I, we had always hoped you would find someone of approximately the same heritage and culture, and upbringing. To settle down with, you understand. We did not realize how seriously you might become attracted to Serena. No, no, Charles. Don't get that stuffy look. It is unbecoming," Sidney said.

"Are you implying that Serena and I are ill-matched?" I asked, in some pique.

"Like Billy Graham and Dolly Parton," Sidney said. "Now understand me, Charles, I am very fond of Serena. A beautiful, smart, fun-loving mouse. Complex. Very complex. And someone like that always has somebody, er, in her life."

"Somebody else, you mean," I croaked.

"She didn't tell you. I knew she hadn't." Sidney waggled his head in disapproval.

"Somebody . . . serious?"

"Oh yes," he said. "Although the way she's been acting with you, I'm not as sure exactly how serious. Yet in some manner he must be reckoned with. His name is Earl. A playboy, a wastrel. He lives in a Mercedes convertible. He could make chopped liver of you, Charles. He has been to Atlantic City twice."

The news from Sidney produced an acute spasm in my diaphragm, followed by a sensation of weakness, as though my vitality were flushing out through some invisible leak. I thanked Sidney, whose swarthy, intense features — doubtless reflecting his concern for me — seemed contorted in clownish melancholy. How gauche Sidney was. And his solicitude left me untouched: How strange what little comfort there is to be had from even the closest friend when one's great love seems lost. Or, as in the present case, seriously in question.

I wandered off to ponder my burden of news. The darkness in the walls seemed oppressive, and I sought light and air, climbing to the ledge of a window that overlooked the alley. The gray stuccoed wall of Main Street Presbyterian loomed in massive reproach. I realized that in the four days I had sojourned in the Rib Cage, not once since meeting Serena had I thought about my imperiled home.

Nor, hardly, did I now. Down in the alley was distraction of another kind, a glistening torpedo in black lacquer and cream convertible top. I have nothing against cars, but you must understand the instant dislike I felt for the Mercedes, which I knew instantly was the fateful car of Sidney's allusion, even before I saw the small silver-gray figure of Serena leap gracefully onto the rear bumper, trot over the rear deck, climb the fabric top, and like a gymnast swing down its edge and wriggle past a raised window, her adorable legs giving a kick as she disappeared inside.

So it was true. Should I dash down, enter the car, and confront Serena and her Mafioso? The prospect of facing Earl somewhere in the viscera of that glossy tonneau sent signals of unsteadiness to my own bowels. Such bravado would be stupid and probably pointless, I reasoned furiously. Perhaps Serena was, even now, telling Earl goodbye. "I love Charles," she was saying, "and it is only fair to tell you it's over between us, Earl." After all, what could I do? Challenge Earl to a duel? Wait this out, I told myself. She will return. She will explain.

Until that happened, I had to occupy my mind. From the window ledge I looked restlessly back into the main dining room of the Rib Cage, aclatter with the luncheon crowd. A man and a woman approached and occupied an empty booth far beneath me. I felt some faint cheer on recognizing Miss Tayloe Tebell, the lady who had argued with Dr. Christie. *Why,* I wondered, *was she so committed to saving the church?*

I descended through the wall to the jukebox control unit in Miss Tebell's booth. *Some music might go well,* I thought. Serena had taught me how to trip the internal levers. I made a selection and waited beside a trough of coins.

I heard Miss Tebell's voice. "What are you going to play?" she asked.

"B-Seventeen," the man said. "The Song Nobody Knows."

"Please don't play B-Seventeen," she said. "It's too sad."

"Okay, I'll . . . how about that? Somebody's already played it."

Sorry, I thought. *Sad is what I wanted.*

"It's okay, I want to talk anyway," she said.

"Fine. Where shall we begin? How about: It's been a long time, Tayloe."

"Not very original. Once you said that you and I transcended time, Caleb. Have we transcended fourteen years? Are my crow's tracks imaginary, like those bifocals you're wearing? Hey, but you know what? The difference is that fourteen years ago I didn't know what 'transcended' meant. You used so many words I didn't know. Half the time I didn't know what you were talking about. It was one of our main troubles."

Through a small crack beside A-Seven I looked cautiously from the control box.

How can a mouse evaluate human beauty? You may well ask that, and I would respond: as well as a human can judge a horse, a dog, or a mouse. There are standards. They begin with the bones. In females, there is that cunning distribution of an extra layer of subcutaneous fat. There is pelt color and texture, a quality admittedly vestigial in humans, but in the case of Miss Tayloe Tebell magnificently represented in a short, careless mane the color of ripe wheat. Eyes: large and gray, flecked with iridescence. Nose: short and straight, except at the tip, where a slight upward beveling was chiseled with restraint. Jaws and teeth: strong and symmetrical. Once I heard of a sculptor named Praxiteles, who lived in ancient Greece. He would have taken one look at Miss Tebell and bawled for fresh marble.

But if Miss Tebell was beautiful, it must be acknowledged that across her softly curving brow were tiny harbingers of time's erosion gullies.

"You said, if I remember right, I was a pompous ass," the man called Caleb said.

As for him, what can I report to you? Rather gaunt and professorial he might be limned, with a somewhat narrow, craggy face, dark brown hair going gray, owlish glasses. Not your garden variety matinee idol, I decided, but possessed of a certain grace and intelligence.

"Yes," she said. "But I may have been wrong. Or hyperbolic. Who could remember, after all these years?"

"It was September of seventy-two," he said. "We had that awful scene in the parking lot . . ."

She nodded. They contemplated each other as the Southern Cross clanged to a big falsetto finish. I won't say their eyes gleamed like Serena's and mine a few nights before, but they were not unhappy to see each other.

"I always felt so ignorant," she said.

The man called Caleb looked down, fiddled with his drink, did not speak.

"Sorry," she said quickly. "All that's behind us, Caleb, so long ago. Well. 'How did she know where to call me?' Dr. Caleb

Old might well ask. And I would reply, 'What the heck, Byrdport isn't all that big.' I haven't been keeping tabs on you but word gets around. You do make the newspapers once in a while. I even heard that you and — Rita, was it? — were . . ."

"All finished."

"Final papers done?" she continued. He nodded. "Mine too," she said.

They looked at each other for a long moment, almost blankly, each apparently lost in personal reverie.

"*Au revoir* yesterday," he said at last. "By the way, congratulations on the job. I saw the newspaper story. You're — executive director, is it? — of the Historic Byrdport Foundation. Very impressive and surprising. You never had any interest in that kind of — "

"Highbrow stuff? I'm as surprised as anybody," Miss Tebell laughed. "Pretty good for a high school grad from the country, huh? Funny how it worked out. After you and I . . . after our parking lot scene, the big farewell . . . after that, I married Foster Biggs right away. But soon it was clear I had to do something or lose my mind. Foster's chief interest was in making money. When you own one-third of a brokerage house you can make a lot. So while he tended to futures and options, I tried other things. The Junior League, the Red Cross, the United Way. I took up bridge but soon I could beat everybody. No fun there.

"Foster did care about something else: collecting," she continued. "Art, armor, tapestries, porcelain, you name it. What passion he retained after a day of shaking out the short sellers, he lavished on his hobbies. He really was a connoisseur, and was always around other big collectors and dealers, so I got a glimmering of how it might be fun. I studied antiquities a little. Then one day downtown I saw some commotion on the sidewalk. It wasn't far from here. Just over on Canal, where that beautiful block of ironfronts used to be. Remember the ironfronts, Caleb?"

"Er, vaguely. Where they built the First and Planters Bank?"

"Yeah. Designed by a Los Angeles architect. A duplicate of one he did for Minneapolis. Anyway, I had never paid any attention to the ironfronts; I had never heard the name. They were just dingy old buildings to me. But here I was, suddenly in front of them. A demolition crew was just starting to unload some barricade stuff. Greeting them were about half a dozen pickets with signs that read, 'Save the Ironfronts.'

"This was in early February, Caleb, all misty and freezing like it gets. Most of the picketers were young or middle-aged, but there was this one very old lady with a wonderful face: strong, classic, patrician. She had on a big duffle coat, but she was trembling with cold, and her nose was running. She handed me a brochure and I moved on.

"Next day, the paper had a big four-column photo of two cops hustling her away from the site. One was on each elbow. I guess they weren't being rough, and she had asked for it as she had personally tried to block the demolition guys. So the cops moved her. That was hours after I was there. Her name was Judith McGuire, I learned, and she was — still is — a legendary figure in the preservation game. I've been trying to meet her.

"It all made a huge impression on me, Caleb. I grew up with the ERA movement, even marched in some demonstrations, but to lay it on the line for some old *building*? I dug her brochure out of my pocket and read it. The block of ironfronts dated from 1866. It was a new type of commercial building, an early form of fireproofing. They had been designed and cast right here in Byrdport. And they were famous: architects and historians everywhere knew about Byrdport's last surviving block of ironfronts. So Byrdport tore them down to build an L.A.-Minneapolis bank. Hey, let's have some music."

I plied the levers and gave them a triple selection of Pat Benatar, John Prine, and Merle Haggard. *It's on me, Miss Tebell.*

"So from that point on you — somebody got his quarter in ahead of mine again — you were interested in historical preservation?" Dr. Old said.

"Really hooked. That was about seven years ago. I took some courses in architectural history. Joined preservation societies. Met the most interesting, intelligent gang you can imagine," she said. "I got a job with the state government's landmarks department. Then I switched over to the Historic Byrdport Foundation, a private group with a good endowment. One thing we do is buy threatened buildings and then resell them to new and sympathetic owners. And — "

"And now I know what's coming," Dr. Old interrupted. "You're about to paint a picket sign that says, 'Save Main Street Presbyterian.' "

"How did you know?" Miss Tebell asked.

"There was talk at the hospital that some preservation group had the wind up. As you talked, I could see it coming," Dr. Old said.

"When I start painting picket signs, Caleb, may I paint one for you?" she asked.

There was an awkward pause as Dr. Old looked increasingly stern.

"Tayloe. Do you know what you're asking? I am a staff physician at Byrdport University Medical Center, and a faculty member of the school of medicine. In fact, I am assistant provost. Our highest priority, our consuming preoccupation, is the construction of a new health education building. I'm sorry you covet the old church now on the site, which indeed will be torn down. But after all, the church sold it. They were delighted to have it off their hands."

"Caleb, let me tell you something," Miss Tebell said. "Civilized people don't wreck landmarks like the church. And I happen to know the medical school owns two other equally good building sites. The main reason you guys are sticking to this one is — apart from the sheer stubbornness of refusing to admit a mistake — that you've spent half a million bucks on preliminary plans. Taxpayers' money. I understand how awkward that is."

"Awkward! To change the plans now would be insane. No. No." I could see him shaking his head. "We're light years apart on the issue, Tayloe. I'm sorry our reunion comes down to this. Until I got the drift of things, I had hoped that when you called it was because you wanted to see me. To *see* me. Not to ask for something. I think I'd better leave. There's just one other thing I'd better tell you."

"What's that, Caleb?" she asked in a flat voice.

"You have a piece of tomato skin on your teeth," he said.

I watched him go. Down the cluttered aisle of the Rib Cage, his erect carriage and expensive clothes reproached the cheaply groomed habitues who let him pass.

Miss Tebell sighed, ran her tongue over her teeth, ordered a cup of coffee, and before I could play another selection on the house, shoved a coin in the slot. It caused a meshing of levers that painfully pruned another half-inch from my tail. I did note that she played B-17.

Miss Tebell's mission to save the church excited me, but Serena remained my chief preoccupation. Some time had passed since I saw her enter the Mercedes, I realized. Perhaps she had returned. I left the control box to seek what news there might be.

I encountered Sidney and Rebecca.

Sidney's mobile face told me everything. But he said, superfluously: "She took off with Earl, Charles. In the car. Serena is gone."

CHAPTER 3

A MAN NAMED CAPT. CARTER BYRD FOUNDED THIS city, or so I have been told. It could not have been much when he laid it out around 1730: the sheds of a trading post, some rude huts for the rabble, slightly better shelter for the Scottish factors, a grandiose home for himself. Actually, Captain Byrd spent most of his time downriver at his favorite plantation.

Byrdport might have remained rustic and small had it not been for the pusillanimity of the state legislature during the Revolution. Fearful that their capital — a place to the east called Hummeltown — might drop, along with their skins and necks, into Redcoat hands, the legislators fled to Byrdport, bearing only the irreducible necessities of government: the Speaker's chair and the tax records. Byrdport seemed so agreeable that they made it the permanent capital.

When the Revolution ended, one of our American diplomats in Europe was Carter Byrd, Jr. He engaged the great British architect Robert Adam to plan a new Capitol in the classical revival style. It was a primeval event in that rising architectural movement. From the new Capitol's pure front porch, like some Corinthian, Doric, or Ionic virus, columns fructified rapidly outward. Gaining momentum, columnmania exploded like a Canadian logjam in the spring, hurling white trunks from Maryland to St. Louis. The movement would not abate until 1861.

In 1839, at the peak of this passion, the congregation of a Presbyterian church in Byrdport was aflame with the Holy Spirit and solvent with the donations of new-rich tycoons prospering in the flour, iron, and tobacco businesses. They voted to erect a new sanctuary. Church elders purchased the finest available site, a location across from the Capitol. Church and state would thus be within hailing distance of each other, but separated by Main Street, down the middle of whose broad thoroughfare now sparkled that miracle of the age, the steam railway to Washington, D.C., about 140 miles away.

To build their church, the Presbyterians showed the good sense to engage Thomas Ustick Walter.

He was thirty-five and in the dawn of a brilliant career. Walter's ambitious classic revival designs were causing an architectural sensation. He would go on, in 1851, to design new Senate and House wings for the United States Capitol, as well as its present dome, thus becoming responsible for much of that national symbol as we know it today. For much of his long production, which ended at age eighty-three in 1887, Thomas Walter was justifiably regarded as the top pen of American architecture.

"I will build you a church for the ages," Walter told the Byrdport Presbyterians.

That summary of early Byrdport history is based on hearsay. I gleaned most of it chronologically later in the events of my story, by listening carefully to the assorted actors. Yet already I knew something of the church's history, and that, blended with my anxiety at losing my home, could explain my growing affinity for Miss Tayloe Tebell and her cause. That she seemed to be the only person in Byrdport trying to save the church was enough to cement our relationship.

And now that I knew the full compass of Serena's defection, it would be intolerable to dally further in the raffish luxury of the Rib Cage. I thought of returning to the church, to live as a churchmouse should, yet what kind of future lay there? The congregation would depart in a few weeks. Already the great organ was broken. Insipid tweets from the portable electronic instrument would pipe the congregation to its new home in the suburbs. Would I then follow to that virgin building, doubtless a tight, mouse-resistant structure whose walls were crammed with styrofoam and fiber glass? Or would I remain in the old church like some pathetic ghost, waiting for the demolition crew? I liked neither course. Yet how can I, normally the most circumspect of mice, account for what I did next?

With a hasty goodbye to Sidney and Rebecca, I ran back to the booth occupied by Miss Tebell. She was still there, lost in thought, drinking coffee. With a cheeky stealth that amazed me, I climbed to her seat, calculated the distance to her handbag (its mouth ajar), and in a flash I leaped inside.

You don't know it, Miss Tebell, but we're in this thing together, I thought.

The exhilaration of reckless élan, always a short-lived thing, soon decomposed. I had voluntarily committed the animal kingdom's maximum error: I had trapped myself. The realization dawned, with panicky hindsight, as Miss Tebell snapped shut the exit. With a sickening lurch the purse became airborne, in a clatter of lipsticks, compacts, keys, and ballpoint pens. The crackling of mint wrappers disconcertingly simulated fire. I can certify that compared to the first journey of a mouse in a woman's purse, the Oregon Trail was a promenade for weaklings.

I felt her sling the big bag's strap across her shoulder, and we set forth into the unknown. Her heels tapped the pavement in a reaching, athletic stride; she was a tall young woman and she stepped long. The bag swayed slightly, but seemed secure. Soon the progress grew less terrifying. I bit off a small piece of chewing gum from a half-stick she had economically saved. It calmed my nerves. I heard the random beeping horns and rushing tires of traffic. By the time we walked about five minutes my courage had returned. I was about to enjoy purse travel when we entered a building, and the trip was over.

"Any excitement, Thelma?" I heard her ask.

"*Only* a call from Flemmons R. Slemp," a strange voice said, with the air of one who is bursting with news held too long.

"Hmmm. With a name like that I assume there is only one," Miss Tebell said.

"Indeed, chief. The original Flem Slemp, and he wishes to see you. In fact, he sought an appointment in the morning.

Being a nosy and officious sort, I gave him one," the woman named Thelma said. "I'm dying to know what he wants."

"God, Thel. That man is president of Hygeia Pharmaceuticals. No, board chairman. One of the authentic high tomcats. Big rich. And he's up to his ears in the new medical building that BUSM wants to plop down on our church site. He's a big BUSM donor, I think," Miss Tebell said.

"Shall I arrange to have him kidnapped, or just kneecapped?" Thelma asked.

"We'll see. How interesting." There was a giddy drop as Miss Tebell carelessly flung her purse. Amid the general crashing of female artifacts, I received a heavy blow from her tightly stuffed maroon wallet. *Poor Chester,* I remember thinking. *I know how he felt.* Yet the blow, which knocked me unconscious, was not the fatal crusher that I feared. I awakened soon with nothing worse than a headache and sore ribs. Light bathed the purse interior. She must have snapped it open for something and left the mouth ajar. Now I could look around.

I saw a tall-ceilinged, old-fashioned room and a mixture of furniture: a shiny roll-top desk, a big cupboard filled with books, and a sofa with carved flowers and nuts. I have learned that the style is called Renaissance revival. It was, I correctly assumed, Miss Tebell's office. Through an open door I saw a larger room where a man and a woman worked at desks. I remembered that Dr. Caleb Old and Miss Tebell had talked about her job running the Historic Byrdport Foundation. That's where I must be, I decided.

Soon the others said good night and departed. Miss Tebell remained at her desk, stabbing with a pen at assorted papers. She seemed to fume restlessly. Finally, she muttered aloud, "That's it. Another day closer to the tomb. Damn that Caleb Old," and marched around snapping off lights. I braced for the lurch as she snatched up the purse. We were off again, and I anticipated another street venture. Instead, she began mounting steps inside the building!

We climbed one flight. There, I would debark into an apartment of the same construction details as downstairs: double-hung carved doors, fancy moldings, arched marble fireplaces with coal grates. I would learn that the apartment's antique furniture represented the Georgian age through the Victorian. I would, in sum, come to know this apartment very well, for it was Miss Tebell's private residence, here above her office in the group of 1850-ish buildings known as Live Oak Row. And I would come to love this place, her home, her den, her nest, as I came to love Miss Tayloe Tebell.

How quickly I adapted to life on Live Oak Row! That evening, while Miss Tebell dined alone and performed domestic chores, I scouted the walls, floors, and ceilings, disclosing a labyrinth of hidden cavities in the glorious tradition of nineteenth-century builders. I checked out the pantry and dined on corn chips. Late that night, when my hostess had retired to her massive four-poster, an American Empire piece with carved plumes twined around its columns, I ventured to a front window sill for a look outside.

It explained instantly the short walk from the Rib Cage. The window overlooked one of the streets that bounded Capitol Square. Just across that square, beyond the floodlighted oyster-gray bulk of the Capitol, lay Main Street. And on the other side of the street were the church and the Rib Cage. The orientation comforted me. Relaxed, I sought out a pile of Miss Tebell's used laundry and, amid its now-dear scents, enjoyed my best night's sleep in weeks.

And how I dreamed. Flown backward to childhood in the church, I returned to our family nest in the great organ, with Mother and Father and Chester and Grandpa. It was Sunday morning. Mr. Hudson, with a brilliant attack, commenced Bach's "Prelude and Fugue in E Flat." Great arpeggios rushed through the pipes, nearly veiling the theme; stormy pedal passages, like the laughter of a playful giant, roiled an ocean of sound. Mr. Hudson, so feckless off the bench, was a tiger upon it: his jaw firm, his shoulders square, his eyes no longer in watery wandering but riveted fiercely on the score. In the dream I heard Grandpa yelling: "Godalmighty, play it, Hudson," above the roaring pipes.

By 7:30 A.M., when Miss Tebell's clock radio switched on and a voice announced the time, I was already awake, performing my morning ablutions in her leaky sink. It was hard to remember that I must avoid her, efface myself, remain forever invisible. Yet I suppose this implicit frustration appealed to my chivalric streak. In the affair's bizarre hopelessness, I was the Don Quixote of mice. So be it, I agreed. Let us face the day together, Miss Tebell.

Getting to the office was even more convenient for me than for her. While she descended long stairs, I simply dropped a foot or so through the ceiling above her office, shinnied down the chain of a gas chandelier of brass and German silver, and made myself comfortable in a tulip-shaped, frosted glass chimney. No espionage microphone was ever more perfectly sited to record the speech of the unsuspecting.

At midmorning, Thelma the secretary escorted two men into Miss Tebell's office. The elder was short and past sixty. His head was large and bald, deeply tanned, and spattered with brown spots. No visible neck joined that formidable head to its squat, muscular body. But despite his gnomelike proportions there was a quality of businesslike grace and power about him, like a Civil War cannon shell, indicating that in action the man introduced as Mr. Flemmons R. Slemp would zoom through an accurate trajectory to a potent detonation.

The other man looked less than half the age of Slemp, and though he was probably no taller than six feet, he appeared to tower over his associate. While the elder man was packed into a double-breasted gray suit, the younger wore a blue blazer of continental cut and gray slacks, projecting a jauntier image. He puzzled me. His features were certainly Caucasian, but about his dark skin and black hair was an Indian look, by which I mean some progeny of Varanasi or Delhi. But that seemed unlikely, for the secretary gave his name as a very American one, Granville Zebulon.

The pair conveyed friendliness and composure. They did not seem in pursuit of anything.

"Maybe we should have met before, Miss Tebell, but we can't change that now," came Mr. Slemp's opening words. His voice, pitched rather high, whined forth in a peculiar lilt. "This is where we start from. Now, from what little I know about it, I admahr what you folks here are adoing. You aim to preserve historic buildings. That about it?"

"That does sum it up," Miss Tebell said.

"I should have learned something about the subject," Mr. Slemp continued. "A man in my position, he makes a sight of waves sometimes, whether he wants to or not. Whether he does something, or does nothing. That's why I need people like Zebulon here," he grinned at the younger man.

"I am Mr. Slemp's director of public affairs," Granville Zebulon said. "It's a nice way of saying publicity, lobbying, benefactions, affiliations. Putting the best corporate face forward. With over four hundred million in sales last year, Hygeia Pharmaceuticals is a major economic force. We are also a good corporate citizen."

Mr. Zebulon's speech reminded me of people I had heard in North Carolina, while traveling with the evangelist. Except that he sounded more polished. They seemed an odd pair, the millionaire drug manufacturer and his assistant.

"The point is, we see a big wave acoming about that old church, and I'm not sure what to do," Mr. Slemp said.

"I guess you mean Main Street Presbyterian," Miss Tebell said.

"It come up on my blind side. Understand, ma'am, the only reason BUSM can afford a new medical building is because of me. I made a ten million dollar challenge grant to dare the legislature to cough up the other ten million. It looks like they're going to come across. The governor has recommended such an appropriation in his budget; the finance committees of both houses have approved, and it's ready to hit the floor. The votes are probly there. I've had all that on my mind, you see, not some old church," Mr. Slemp explained.

"I see," Miss Tebell said. "And now . . ."

"I owe everything I am to Byrdport University," Mr. Slemp churned on. "They took me in, a kid from the mines, with one of the few scholarships they had in the Depression. It was 1934. I got me a degree in chemistry in three years, and then I kept going through pharmacy school. Started a little pill-rolling operation."

"The beginning of Hygeia Pharmaceuticals?" Miss Tebell asked.

"The creation. My friends said I was boring with a mighty

big augur — taking on too much — but I made it. Me and Evac-uall. That was a laxative I cooked up; nothing but a little so-dium lauryl-sulfate and danthron. I packaged it right and com-menced distributing all over the South. There was a sight of people blocked up in the Depression, and they could always find money for workin' medicine, as we called it then."

"Evacuall was the company's flagship, as it were," Gran-ville Zebulon said.

"Today we have forty plants and subsidiaries around the world. Not as big as Merck and Upjohn and Lilly, but not far off. We make all kinds of complicated stuff I can't pronounce."

"I'm totally positive that Hygeia Pharmaceuticals is a roaring success," Miss Tebell said with a touch of irony.

"But why am I telling you all this? Here it comes. This city has been good to me. Here I found a civilized home. You'd have to come from the coal creeks in the Depression to know the meaning of that, Miss Tebell. Oh, I been snubbed, of course. Even though I married a Byrdport girl I guess I'll never be ac-cepted here socially. But in spite of that, I love this old city and its history."

"That's wonderful!" Miss Tebell said. "Some of the most ardent preservationists come from outside. They see things with a fresh . . ."

"I ain't going that far. Let's say I may have a slight awak-ening. The point is, I don't want me or the company to get a black eye. We have built us a great name as easers of pain and curers of the sick. We don't want to be known as destroyers of a valuable landmark — *if that's what it is.*"

Granville Zebulon raised a graceful finger. "Unwittingly," he said, "we have come into a situation where, if the new med-ical college building goes up, it seems the church comes down, and we could be in bad odor preservationwise. It's Mr. Slemp's money, of course, his personal money, the ten million, but he and the company are practically synonymous around Byrd-port."

"I compliment your sensitivity," Miss Tebell said. "The campaign to save the church has hardly started, and here you are . . ."

"Young lady, I didn't build Hygeia by waiting for things to

happen, and then playing catch-up. Here is a case where I'm going to think everything through again. First I'm getting some help from Mr. Zebulon here. I rely on Granzeb's judgment. Seems like it might be a good idea if he was to see the church. I ain't got the time right now."

"I'll be happy to show Mr. Zebulon the church," Miss Tebell said.

Mr. Slem nodded once sharply. Then, in another quick snap, he rose to his full prominence, a fireplug in pin-striped gray flannel. He marched to the office door as Miss Tebell and Mr. Zebulon followed. As Mr. Slemp opened the door, he started to turn and say goodbye. But he froze at what he saw waiting in the outer office.

"Son!" Mr. Slemp exclaimed.

"Hey, Daddy, hey Granzeb. Your office told me where you were. I got good news."

Did the old man seem touched by sudden weariness?

"May I present my son," he said. "Flem Junior, Miss Tebell."

"Hey, Miss Tebell. Daddy, I just came from the commissioner's office in New York. He told me I could have the franchise. So I bought it, Daddy."

The four remained bunched at the door. I could hear them from my perch in the light fixture.

Flemmons R. Slemp massaged his forehead with a stubby, powerful hand. "That's just grand, son." I could not understand the note in his voice. He turned to Miss Tebell. "It's the high calling of Flem Junior to bring professional basketball to Byrdport," he said.

I studied them side by side. Flem Junior had not exceeded his father's five-foot-five. He was, in fact, remarkably like the elder Slemp. Comparing them revealed an astonishing, almost ludicrous, similarity. The years would render Flem Junior an exact image of his father. They were twins, a generation apart.

The meeting and its irrelevant postscript had broken up. Beyond the door the Slemps were saying their goodbyes. Miss Tebell and Mr. Zebulon stood framed in the dark fluted moldings of the door.

"Set for a look at the church?" she asked brightly.

My heart sagged. I wanted to follow them, but how? How could I have prepared for this?

CHAPTER 4

"JUST A MINUTE," MISS TEBELL SAID. "I LEFT MY PURSE upstairs. Meet you at the front door."

Faster than an Olympic gymnast I clambered up the chandelier chain and into the ceiling. When Miss Tebell arrived I was waiting in the purse. She snatched it up, headed back to the apartment door, changed her mind, and diverted to the bathroom. Crash! My conveyance struck the countertop. There was a sound of chiming waters.

Then we were down the stairs and on our way.

"While you're here," she said outside to Mr. Zebulon, "notice how perfect the neighborhood is. All these row houses were built in 1858. If you took away the cars, the blacktop, and the utility poles, this block wouldn't have changed a bit. Nor has Capitol Square. Let's cross over and walk through it."

I knew instantly when we had entered the square. Traffic sounds diminished, and I heard the mincing chatter of those pampered gourmands, the Capitol Square squirrels.

Mr. Zebulon spoke. "I'm down here all the time — after all, I'm a lobbyist — but I hardly stop to look around. I suppose it is rather beautiful."

"Probably the nicest twelve acres in the state," Miss Tebell said. "Where are you from, anyway?"

"North Carolina," he said. "Don't expect wild enthusiasm from me."

They laughed, but I did not understand the joke. We walked until the sounds of traffic returned.

"Back to the twentieth century," Miss Tebell said. "Main Street. But over there, in its own time capsule, is the church. Can you imagine anybody wanting to tear it down?"

"It looks a bit lonely, surrounded by all the university high-rises," he replied indirectly. "Perhaps I'm seeing it for the first time. Really looking at it. Actually, the place is rather like a Greek temple with a steeple. Tell me about the architecture, Miss Tebell."

"Reckless to assume that a Carolinian can absorb all this," she said. "But since you ask, Main Street Presbyterian's design is based on a Greek temple form of the Doric order, stuccoed over brick, with portico and two fluted columns. On the portico's sides are bays framed by pilasters. The entire building is crowned by an entablature with triglyphs and metopes. The broad, massive front steps, of granite quarried locally, create the impression of a stylobate. Got all that, Mr. Zebulon?"

"It'll do for basics. I may want to talk to a real scholar for the erudite minutiae."

"How dare you," Miss Tebell said. "Come on, we've got the light."

The purse rocked giddily as we crossed the eight lanes of Main Street. *I could develop motion sickness,* I thought.

But how good it was to inhale the church's old familiar smells! They penetrated even the medley of scents native to Miss Tebell's handbag, soon after we entered by the massive walnut doors.

"Now jes' remembah, lady, I'm a Nawth Carolina Baptist who don't have no truck wi' dis high Presbyterian stuff," Mr. Zebulon said.

"Oh, Presbyterian isn't 'high,' " Miss Tebell laughed. "But I guess this is about as uppity as Presbyterians ever got in the South. Seriously, isn't it beautiful?"

"Yes, and furthermore it looks older than I thought it would," he said. "I mean there's none of that Gothic stuff. It's kind of light and pleasant and restrained. Not churchy at all, if you get my drift."

"Hey, you're sharper than you let on," she said. "Actually, the inside relates more to the eighteenth century than the nineteenth. Paneling is classic. The windows are big but rather plain, with clear glass. The gallery goes around in a full horseshoe. See? Like a theater balcony. Even with white paint it all seems warm. There's not a whiff of that fake cathedral stuff that came on so strong in the next decade, the 1850s."

"Is the congregation going to walk out and leave everything?"

"No. Almost all the furnishings are so fine that much of the movable stuff will go to the new church. Take the chancel. An English woodcarver worked three years on that; it's black walnut. Look at the cherubs' heads and acanthus leaves. You couldn't get work like that today. The pews will be left behind, but antique dealers are already bidding on those. In a few weeks everything will be cleaned up. The university bought only the building," Miss Tebell said.

She was leaving out the most important thing!

"I almost forgot the organ. You'll have to see it."

We climbed familiar stairs to the gallery.

"I can't tell you much about this," she continued. "Those who know organs claim it's quite special. The maker was Henry Erben, supposedly the best of his day. I've heard this was the biggest one he ever made. More than 2,000 pipes. But it's said to be in terrible condition now, and won't play at all."

"What will happen to it?" Mr. Zebulon asked.

"Nobody seems to know. Usually in a case like this they just get junked. There are some organ freaks around; they try hard to save the old instruments, but actually what do you *do* with something this big? No house can hold it. Sometimes a poorer church will buy one, and patch it up for a few years. But these days, most smaller churches prefer electronics."

"Look at the carving on the case. And way up there, around the top of the pipes, more carving," Mr. Zebulon said.

"We think Erben employed the same carver who did the chancel, to make it conform," Miss Tebell said.

She was sitting at the console. She put her purse down beside the pedals.

"Want to walk up front? You get a good perspective from the front of the horseshoe," she suggested.

As the sound of their footsteps diminished, I could not resist a quick look around at my old home, the scene of so many happy days. I squeezed upward through the still-latched purse until with some difficulty my head emerged. The handbag's pressure on my neck made me lightheaded from improper circulation, but at least I could see.

I saw droppings, beside the pedals. They appeared fresh.

I had been gone, I calculated, approximately one week. As far as I knew, I was the only mouse in the church when I departed for the Rib Cage, yet it was not possible that these unsightly signatures were mine. I was tidy by nature, and also, in the cause of personal security, I was careful not to advertise my presence. Even if in a fit of absentmindedness I had fouled the floor, it would have been vacuumed up. Dr. Christie was implacably strict with the sexton about a careful weekly vacuuming. In that, Jackson Ward was thorough and methodical.

Therefore, another mouse was around. On leaving the church, I had abdicated any territorial claim. Yet I was curious. I struggled up a bit higher for a better look.

A faint whistling sound came from the organ. I listened intently. Someone was rendering an off-key whistle of "What a Friend We Have in Jesus."

"Who's that?" I said sharply. "Who's in there?"

The whistling stopped. Then came the tart reply, "Who the hell wants to know?" A pair of old mouse eyes peered suddenly from between two of Mr. Erben's sadly eroded pedals. Then a gray head emerged.

"Grandpa!" I yelled in happy recognition. "I can't believe it. Is that really you?"

"None other, kid," the patriarch said. "How've you been?"

"But Grandpa, you — you're *dead*! I saw the cat, Alabama Ruby, she . . ."

"Naw, she didn't kill me. She gave me one hell of a pasting, though. Cut me right to the jawbone." He thrust one side of his face upward, and I saw the jagged scar on his cheek, where the fur had regrown imperfectly. "Knocked me cross-eyed. But she got greedy; thought she had me, then stopped to look around for the rest of you. Meantime I drug myself into the wall. By the time I come around, you all had lit out from the church. What happened to the family after that, Charles?"

Painfully, I described our subsequent wanderings, and the final calamity in the evangelistic tent.

Grandpa adjusted to the news. Finally, he said: "They have gone to that far bank on the starry shore, where parting shall be no more forever. Amen."

"I guess, Grandpa."

"Seems like it's just you and me now, Charles. Except . . ." He seemed to brighten up, and his incisors bared in a grin, ". . . there just might be another mouse who wants to move in. Although it appears to me that church soap would be mighty poor truck after living in the Rib Cage."

"Who . . . who . . ."

"Not that I would complain, kid. Not about a good-looking mouse like that. She kind of pesters me, though, coming around and asking for you."

"Grandpa. Her name?"

"Oh, name of Serena. Look, why don't you git out of that purse? You're downright comical looking."

"I can't, Grandpa. I have some unfinished business with the purse's owner." My brain was in turmoil, intensified by the tight squeeze. I now realized that I had missed the old church more than I had found it convenient to admit. And how could the chivalric attachment I felt toward Miss Tebell ever replace my natural passion for another mouse, i.e., Serena? And furthermore . . .

"They're coming, Charles," Grandpa rasped.

It was too late to think it out. But before I wriggled back inside Miss Tebell's purse, I told Grandpa, "I'll be back. Tell Serena."

When Miss Tebell retrieved her purse, and we resumed strolling through the church, I felt — let me face it clearly — the first real stab of jealousy. She and Mr. Zebulon seemed to enjoy each other's company. But I? I was the mouse with the impossible dream. No kiss from Miss Tayloe Tebell, in the unlikely event that one could be procured, would ever transmute this three-ounce rodent into a handsome prince. Compared to me, Cervantes' Knight of the Rueful Figure was the dullest pragmatist. But despite all that, I did not dislike Granville Zebulon, who seemed a decent enough sort, possessed of a certain wry good humor and apparent intelligence.

They were discussing where to have lunch.

"Ever been to the Canal Boat?" Miss Tebell asked. "No? Let's go there. We can walk from here."

Blam! A collision between them on the church stairs squashed the purse and fetched me a pain in the ribs. They seemed to be laughing and enjoying themselves more than the situation required. That demeanor continued out on the streets, where we walked about four blocks. I could tell by the pauses at intersections, and the ups and downs at curbs. I also judged by Miss Tebell's stride that the route was downhill.

"This was the Civil War commercial district," Miss Tebell said. "Now it's filled with restaurants, specialty shops, even condos and apartments. Terrific adaptive use. People love it. See the river? Here we are. The Canal Boat Restaurant is in one of the oldest warehouses. They decorated it with authentic relics of the canal days. Charming, huh? Here's a table."

The purse slammed down.

"Why are you looking at me like that?" Miss Tebell continued.

"I was thinking of how wrong I was," Mr. Zebulon said.

"About what?"

"About preservationists. I thought they would all look like warthogs," he said.

Miss Tebell giggled. "I'm a closet warthog," she said.

"Sure. But really, I did have preservationists pegged as, well . . ."

"Odd? Absentminded fuddy-duddies? How do you know I'm not? Once I read where a psychiatrist explained people who are interested in saving and restoring. Anything from buildings to cars to jukeboxes. He said it was all very simple: they're afraid of growing old. They are trying to reverse the aging process. When they restore something, they are symbolically rolling back the years."

"Do you buy that?" Mr. Zebulon asked.

"Partially. Like a lot of what the shrinks say, it's part truth and part twaddle. I just know that for me, preservation is more than a cause, or a job . . . it's fun."

"I believe," he said.

"Well, there's something I *don't* understand," she said, more businesslike now. "That is Mr. Slemp's position. I mean, what's going on? Can he control whether the old church stands or falls? Will you make a recommendation to him? If so, what will it be? And will be listen?"

"Preservationists certainly ask a lot of questions," Mr. Zebulon sighed. "Yes, I will make a recommendation. But it may be academic. Things have gone so far that even if Mr. Slemp decided to help preserve the church, there's little he could do. Look. Review the bidding. He made a ten million dollar challenge grant to Byrdport University School of Medicine, a state institution, to help build a new health education center. The state bought the church site for that purpose, and spent half a million in preliminary building plans. The governor has put the remaining necessary ten million into the budget. The House and Senate finance committees have approved, and floor action will come any day. If the legislature nods okay, and the governor signs the omnibus appropriation bill, that'll wrap it up."

"But the university has two other sites. Just as good," Miss Tebell said.

"True."

"What would it take to get the legislature, the governor, and BUSM to change their collective minds and put the building on one of the other sites?"

"The Second Coming. Something so dramatic I can't conceive it," he replied. "Wait! We'll get Flem Junior to buy the church at a huge profit to the state, and convert it to a basketball arena for his new team. Adaptive use, I believe you said."

If Mr. Zebulon meant to be humorous, I believe he failed.

"Not funny. What is it with him, anyway? He may look like his father, but . . ." she paused.

"But not, perhaps, of the same kidney? Actually, he tries very hard to go his own way, and he's been rather successful," Mr. Zebulon said.

"The basketball thing — is he that much of a sportsman?" Miss Tebell asked.

"He went out for every varsity sport in college. Never

41

made a team, but he tried. Changed his major every year, looking to find something he liked," Mr. Zebulon said, with a slight laugh.

"I get the feeling you think he's a lightweight, but loyalty to Mr. Slemp precludes your saying so," she said.

"He's not so bad. We just don't seem to have much to say to each other. He's quite unlike like the old man, however much they look alike. About the only thing they ever agreed on was to be reasonably liberal in social causes. They're both big in promoting racial harmony in Byrdport. And that pleases me, of course," Mr. Zebulon said, "as you can probably understand."

"Understand, er, exactly what?" Miss Tebell asked in puzzlement.

He sighed. "Sometimes people say they have difficulty telling. Look at me carefully, Tayloe. Do you realize you're gazing at one-eighth of a West African?"

"No, I do not. Well, maybe now I do. A little. Who . . . who cares?"

"Almost everybody, to a degree."

"I don't," Miss Tebell retorted.

News that Granville Zebulon bore a cargo of African genes neither surprised nor interested me. I infer that among humans, a touch of the tar brush, as I have heard it rudely described, is some kind of bigoted, artificial handicap. If that cast Mr. Zebulon as underdog, he got no sympathy from me. A mouse knows the meaning of real handicaps.

Back on Live Oak Row, I made myself comfortable, plundered Miss Tebell's store of food, and puzzled over what to do next. I had left Grandpa at the church with a promise to return. Serena might be expecting me. I could scarcely lollygag around Live Oak Row without so much as a visit to Main Street Presbyterian.

But getting there? Even if I waited for Miss Tebell to make another trip across Capitol Square to the church, the handbag coordination was chancy. No, I would have to walk. It was a dismal prospect, but I steeled my mind to it.

In the kitchen I fortified myself with french fries. When the Capitol Square Bell Tower chimed 4:00 A.M., and city traffic was at its lightest, I set forth.

No vehicles whatever moved along Live Oak Row, and I crossed easily to Capitol Square. There, I felt, was the most dangerous segment of the journey, not from those voluptuary squirrels and pigeons who were doubtless sleeping off another day's welfare gluttony, or from any human agency, but from stray cats searching for mayhem to commit. In such an encounter, I would have little chance to escape Capitol Square.

But luck favors the vigilant and prepared. Remaining always in shadow, along brick pathways, under coal-black hollies, beneath ninety-foot magnolias, through periwinkle and ivy, skirting ghostly marble monuments, I did not meet another living creature in Capitol Square. At Main Street, I saw the firefly lights of a few distant vehicles. That was all. I crossed over easily, and disappeared into the blackness of Main Street Presbyterian.

CHAPTER 5

I HAVE HEARD THAT EARLY IN THE NINETEENTH CEN-
tury, Byrdport went pleasantly insane over the beauty of local
belle Maria Gallego. Among the eligible bachelors who
swarmed around her was musician John Howard Payne, who
serenaded the spectacular Maria from every available piano.
Alas for Mr. Payne, Maria decided to marry a young army officer, a hero of the recent War of 1812. Payne resumed a life of
feckless wandering, filled with disappointment and failure.
Maria's beauty soon faded. Her husband was killed in the Mexican War.

But John Howard Payne wrote "Home, Sweet Home."

Was he thinking of some Byrdport parlor, with Maria
standing by the piano? I cannot answer. But in the silence of
the great old church, Payne's sentimental masterpiece played
softly in my brain. This was home.

At the organ, I greeted Grandpa joyfully. Through my
careful eavesdropping, I had learned a great deal more than he
about the church's evident fate, and I recounted to him the various statements of Mr. Hudson, Dr. Christie, Dr. Old, Mr.
Slemp, Mr. Zebulon, and Miss Tebell.

"Seems to me there's nothing to be done," Grandpa said.
"All the preservationists in the world ain't going to prevail

against a combination of politicians and doctors. Remember that the doctors are behind this whole thing. They want their new medical building, and by God they're going to get it. Ain't nobody going up against doctors and winning. Humans hold 'em sacred."

"Miss Tebell may find a way," I said. I almost said Miss Tebell and I. "Grandpa, is there anything to eat around here? I'm starving. That long walk and all this conversation has done me in."

"Jackson Ward left part of a baloney sandwich on the little organ. He was trying to play it at lunchtime yesterday."

In my absence the electronic organ had been moved to the nave, a substitute for the defunct Erben. We trotted down the center aisle to where it stood at one side of the altar. Above its keyboard I spied, on a crumpled piece of waxed paper, the remnants of the sexton's lunch.

"Go ahead," Grandpa said. "You can climb up there easier'n me. Just throw me down some. I'm hungry too."

It was an easy climb. I reached the heavy-scented sandwich fragment and began tearing off chunks of bread and baloney.

"Here it comes, Grandpa," I exclaimed. But as I tossed down the food, my rear feet — slippery with mayonnaise from the sandwich wrapper — shot from under me. I fell about ten inches, landing on the keyboard. The surprise of the slight fall was nothing, however, compared to what happened next. A merry treble note pealed through the church! Jackson Ward had forgotten to switch off the organ!

Stunned by the volume of sound rocketing through the church, I saw Grandpa down below, gesticulating wildly. I suppose he was yelling at me to get off the key, but I could hear nothing above the organ. I regained my feet and took some tentative steps up the scale. By the time I had spanned an octave my fright had vanished, replaced by emotions of such power and beauty that I was moved to ecstasy. First on white notes, then black, I touched the magic keys and reveled in calliopean tumult. Reluctantly, fearing that Grandpa, who was now dashing in circles on the floor, would suffer a stroke, I stepped off the keyboard.

"What's the matter with you, boy?" Grandpa squalled. "You'll wake the dead."

Organ echoes still reverberated in the dark recesses of the church. And nearby, a new voice spoke.

"Maybe not the dead," the voice said. "But you sure did a job on me."

The owner of the voice sauntered out from the front pews. I could not see her expression in the dim light of the church, but I could see who it was.

"Serena!" I blurted.

"Mr. Hudson you're not, Charles, but with a little practice . . . my, is that something to eat?" Serena asked.

It was almost as though we were back at the Rib Cage, and she had not run away with Earl. I could think of nothing to say, so I picked out the best baloney portions with elaborate care, and threw them over the edge. Then I climbed down and we picnicked beside the organ's pedals. Grandpa did most of the talking.

"What you done there, Charles, playing the organ, takes the rag off the bush. Who ever heard the like? Who ever heard of a mouse playing the organ?" He ranted on in that vein.

"I didn't exactly play it, Grandpa," I said. "All I did was make noise. Yet I must say it was a great thrill. Even on such a poor substitute as the electronic. Wouldn't it be wonderful to try it on the Erben?"

"Why don't you?" Serena asked.

"The blower is broken. No wind," I explained.

"That's enough excitement for one night anyway," Grandpa said. "The old Erben may not play, but it's a safe place to sleep."

Later, as Grandpa snored from his untidy nest, I sat beside Serena. She had assumed an uncharacteristically serious, almost prim, demeanor. I sensed that she was about to speak profoundly.

"You left the Rib Cage too soon," she began.

"What? I left because you left. You drove away in that car,

the Mercedes. Sidney watched you leave," I said. "Or so he said."

"I didn't mean to. I just went out to tell a former friend, Earl, that I couldn't see him anymore. In the middle of that, the car's owner came and drove us away. It was terrible. I had to stay in the car all that day and night, not knowing what to do. Earl was upset. I was afraid, but finally he stopped arguing. I begged him to tell me how I could get back to the Rib Cage."

"And he told you?"

"Yes. He said to just wait. Slemp had lunch in the Rib Cage every day, Earl said, because he goes with one of the waitresses, Viola da Gamba."

"*Slemp*?" I exclaimed. "Which one, the father or Mr. Junior?"

"What do you mean? I don't know but one," Serena said. "A little short man, young as humans go. Perhaps about thirty."

"Mr. Junior," I said. "You mean it's his car?"

"Exactly. And next day he drove back downtown, right to the Rib Cage, and I got out. I was so glad to be home. But then I learned from Sidney and Rebecca that you'd left . . ." Her eyes blurred and glistened.

"Oh, Serena. I should have had more faith. But we're back together now. Let's keep it that way," I said.

"I hope we can, Charles. Come here."

Her dear paws reached out to me, there in my once-lonely paper nest inside the quiet Erben.

When I awoke it was fully light, revealed by dim shafts penetrating the organ case. Serena still slept. What a night, I thought: Reuniting with Serena and Grandpa, and playing the electronic organ too. The enormity of it! I gave hardly a thought to Miss Tebell. Instead, lying there that morning, my brain was filled with fortissimo melodies.

I have explained how childhood events imbued me with a reverence for organ music. But I had never dreamed of playing the instrument myself. I was merely a dilettante, like many fanciers of pipe organs. Such dedicated hobbyists form organ historical societies, spend their weekends seeking out old churches where interesting antiques might survive, and try to preserve them for posterity.

By listening to Mr. Hudson give lessons at the Erben, I had learned much organ lore. Already I knew that the pipe organ was invented more than 250 years B.C. I knew something of its medieval development. The first modern organist was Francesco Landino of Italy, who played at a place called St. Mark's in Venice in the fourteenth century. By then the pipe organ had assumed much of the mechanical form it has today.

I had even learned about the sinister associations that sometime defame the noble instrument. When the Phantom of the Opera finally whirled to the camera, exposing his ghastly face, it was not from the keyboard of a harpsichord. When radio suspense dramas like "I Love a Mystery" needed a few bars of music to heighten an atmosphere of dread, they did not call on the studio accordionist. When the mad professors of Grade-B horror thrillers sought to relax at twilight after a day of degenerate experiments, they did not reach for their guitars. No. It was the organ, piping some sepulchral theme like Schubert's "Valse Triste," that triggered the appropriate spectral chill.

I can explain some of this slander against the pipe organ. It is the most complicated and mechanical, therefore the farthest from human (excuse me; sentient) expression, of all musical devices. Its subtleties are those of a machine. There is a paradox here, however, for this machine's voice is based on one of earth's most natural, original sounds: the moan of turbulent wind. A whistle, in fact. A stream of air blows over a lip or across a metal tongue; the air vibrates, and is qualified by resonance in the pipe.

An ancient sound. A sound made by wind striking obstructions for millions of years before man, or mouse, arrived to hear it.

For all its complexity the organ does not play itself, except in tricked-up mechanical player versions. Normally, there is a human agency. And here is another facet in the special image: *The organist is often unseen.* In many large churches, the congregation never sees the musician at all. High in the gallery, hidden in a cockpitlike cavity hollowed from the base of the instrument itself, the organist plays in solitude. In some churches he is more visible; at the console of certain modern organs he may be glimpsed far off like the captain of an airliner, faintly bathed in reflected light. Even then, he is faceless.

Compare such a musician with the pianist, the cornetist, or the violinist. Twitching, grimacing, swaying like storm-blown Lombardy poplars, they are in the limelight. Presumably, they enjoy it. The organist receives no such scrutiny. Isolated, enigmatic, veiled, recondite, he plays on, unseen.

Is there any wonder that the organ should be touched with mystery?

I've heard Mr. Hudson say that even in ancient literature one finds macabre references. In 1598, an organist named Girolamo Diruta assembled a book of compositions and dedicated it to Sigismond Batori, prince of Transylvania. The book was called *Il Transilvano.* Already you picture a grisly castle surrounded by howling wolves, eh? And there was an M. Praetorius who in 1619 wrote a book called *De Organographia.* Why was one of the memorable villains in a 1930s horror movie named Dr. Praetorius? Why does the name reek of menace? It is all miserably unfair.

There is also a connection with funerals, particularly via certain mournfully sentimental funereal music dating from the last century. Played slowly and murkily on wretched parlor pump organs, that helped fix a connection between organs and death.

Such were my thoughts and recollections, as I lay there beside the Erben's tracker board stroking Serena's glorious pelt. One simply must accept that to some uncouth minds, I concluded, organ music may weave a spell of mystery. The noble pipe organ with its thousands of rich tones and effects can, as well as a symphony orchestra, bring to its listeners the song of heaven itself. It can also bring them a shriek from the grave.

"Hey, Charles. You awake?" It was Grandpa.

I exited the nest carefully, leaving Serena undisturbed, and found Grandpa near the blower. He was looking thoughtfully at the old electric motor, woolly with dust, protruding from one side the hopperlike fabrication of sheet metal comprising the air pickup and primary duct. An organ blower is little more than an enclosed electric fan of exceptional force. Originally, the Erben was powered by foot pumps, requiring two strong men to keep it in wind while the organist played. Addition of the motor-driven blower, late in the nineteenth century, was a commonplace event when reliable electric motors were developed.

"Is this the thing you said was broke?" Grandpa asked.

"Maybe," I said uncertainly. "All I really know is that the repairman told Mr. Hudson the motor had failed."

"Look at these old wires," Grandpa mused. "Fabric-insulated. So old it's all cracked. Fallen off in places. What if the motor just warn't getting power?"

"I don't think so, Grandpa. I distinctly heard clicking in a thing they called the solenoid."

"That still don't rule out bad wires. A partial short could sap off enough juice to keep from switching the solenoid, but let enough through to make it rap."

I looked at Grandpa with fresh appreciation. "How did you learn so much about electricity?" I asked.

"When you've spent as much time as me in the walls, dodging bad wires, you'll know too," he said. "And I've watched lots of electricians work. Ha. Look here." He pointed to a brittle-looking wire resting on the motor housing. A section of insulation had fallen completely off the wire. All around it on the dirty housing, for a space about the size of a coin, there were burn marks. Electrical fire had cleaned off the dirt, exposing gray metal.

"That's where she's been shorting. Now we'll see if I was right," Grandpa said. With exquisite care he raised the wire so it would not touch the motor. Then he bent it upward in a slight arc so that it remained clear.

"Now go switch her on," he commanded.

I ran to the console and found the switch. I had seen Mr.

Hudson do it a hundred times; I knew what to do, although I found the toggle a bit stiff. I put my back into it and shoved until the switch clicked. Simultaneously, I heard the low rumble of the blower cutting on.

"It works, Grandpa! You did it!" I yelled.

Grandpa sauntered out. "Like I tried to tell you, I've heard the owls hoot in a sight of places," he said.

"Now we must see if it'll play!" I cried. I began climbing from the console's side down to the manuals, or keyboards.

But Grandpa was quicker. With a malicious grin he leaped astride one of the foot pedals. A sixteen-foot principal pipe spoke with a basso honk. I jumped to the floor, and Grandpa and I pummeled each other in excitement. Neither of us saw Serena emerging from the organ case.

"That does it," she said. "Every time I try to get some sleep in this church, somebody decides to give a concert." Then she, too, laughed happily and joined our celebration.

But soon our innate caution interrupted it.

"The time must be getting on to eight, eight-thirty in the morning," Grandpa said. "Best we quiet down. You can't tell who'll come around now."

"True," I agreed. "I've been looking for Alabama Ruby ever since I returned, but I haven't seen her. Nor have you mentioned her, Grandpa. Is she still around?"

"Ain't seen her in a week or so. That don't mean much. She's probly still around."

"We must assume so," I said. "Grandpa, I think it would be well, for now anyway, if we fixed the Erben back the way it was, so it won't play. Can you do that?"

"Well, sure. But why?"

"I just think it's a good idea," I said.

"Okay. Just make sure the console switch is off. I ain't anxious to ride the lightning."

Together we recrippled the Erben. The knowledge that we alone could determine when, and if, the organ would play was intoxicating. I think that was why I wanted the wire short-circuited again. For the first time in my life, I knew the feeling of

51

power! The three of us enjoyed a naive little caper of self-congratulatory excitement.

Soon, however, the sounds of people downstairs imposed caution. There came a multiplication of the shufflings, bumpings, and whisperings that occur when humans enter a church.

"I forgot it was Sunday," Grandpa said.

So had we all. As for me, I felt some rekindling of the old Sunday morning excitement. I told Serena: "What we'll hear when Mr. Hudson plays the electronic will be less than the real thing, but better than nothing. There's an ideal listening post up in the ceiling. Want to come?"

Serena shrugged good-naturedly and followed, with Grandpa in the rear. We climbed through the walls and into the attic, a low, unlighted expanse where the shallow triangle formed by the roof was filled with supporting beams and trusses. The spot I was heading for was a beam of light, leaking through the ceiling from the sanctuary; a long walk, for it was the point directly over the pulpit far below.

You have met the Reverend Angus Christie, D.D., in the relative solitude of his study. His public persona naturally diverged from the private in some respects. Like many successful ministers, he had a strong histrionic streak. I have personally observed that most big preachers are excellent actors. That they use such talent for divine motives is doubtless true, but they are still hams. Dr. Christie in particular was an ecclesiastical Edwin Boothe.

And like most actors, he was not averse to the supporting tricks of stagecraft. Therefore, the Christie Control Panel was installed.

That electronic marvel had been operating for about six years at the time of these events, and had added so much flair to Dr. Christie's already solid services that membership soared, even in the inconvenient old downtown location, where few people still lived. The Christie Control Panel's manifestations were polished and subtle. The congregation seemed to accept as divinely inspired the celestial chimes, the superb amplification of the minister's brogue, and the adjustments in sanctuary lighting. For certain occasions when the choir was not performing, Dr. Christie played tapes of the Mormon Tabernacle Choir. According to Dr. Christie, only a few austere, old-school Presbyterians complained that he had been infected by something called the Oral Roberts virus.

The minister's lone solid-state fiasco occurred in striving to enhance the Erben organ. The sound engineers, ordered by Dr. Christie to set tiny microphones in the organ loft, never got it right. The Erben rewarded their labors by broadcasting roars, grunts, and squeaks of outrage. That part of the project was dropped.

I admired the skill with which Dr. Christie's sensitive fingers played over the control panel (hidden just below the great pulpit Bible), touching switches and twirling knobs, without muffing a word of one of his prayers or sermons.

That summary is relevant because our destination in the attic was the location of the pulpit spotlight.

Lights had been recessed at several points in the ceiling, but only this one had the key role of shedding a high-intensity ray directly downward onto the silver head of Dr. Christie. With the other sanctuary lights dimmed, the effect would have been coveted by Moses himself, had it been available. The spotlight was fixed to a beam just above the ceiling hole, about ten inches in diameter. The hole was our observation deck. I had spent so much time there that once, in the vicinity, I fixed a secondary nest of shredded paper. From the edge of the hole, we could peer straight down about fifty feet. Serena was giddy at her first look into the void, but she adjusted to the experience and enjoyed watching the foreshortened humans.

We could see the small organ on the floor far below. Mr. Hudson, stately in a black robe, marched to the console bench and seated himself, shifting and tilting. He interlocked and massaged his fingers as he contemplated a score on the organ's rack. He shifted and tilted again. Then he exploded a series of introductory arpeggios, followed by galaxies of chords as his polished black shoes twinkled at the foot pedals. Warmed up, he paused for the congregation to compose itself, and then launched into the day's prelude. To my intense satisfaction, it was Purcell's "Toccata in A."

"So beautiful," Serena said afterward. "I feel like applauding."

"You should hear it on the Erben," I said. "But Mr. Hudson gets a lot out of an electronic organ."

When time came for Dr. Christie's sermon, I warned Serena not to be startled when the spotlight came on.

"And don't look up at it," I said. "It's like looking into the sun."

The minister's text was taken from some solemn lines written by a prophet named Isaiah. "All flesh is grass, and all the goodliness thereof is as the flower of the field. The grass withereth, the flower fadeth, because the spirit of the Lord blowest upon it; surely the people is grass. The grass withereth, and the flower fadeth, but the word of our God shall stand forever."

With a stab, the awesome words brought Miss Tebell to my mind. What was it she had said? About preservationists seeking to escape their destiny of growing old?

A congregational meeting followed the service. What seemed to be routine matters were discussed, and we were ready to leave the ceiling hole when I heard Dr. Christie ask if there was more business to be brought up before adjourning.

There was.

An old man asked to be recognized. Tall and skeletal in his frailness, he walked slowly to the front of the nave and stood before the altar. Dr. Christie nodded at him with a faint smile.

"I am pleased," the minister said, "to recognize my distinguished predecessor in the pulpit of this church, Dr. Cotesworth Stirling." Was there a jot of asperity in Dr. Christie's tone?

The old man turned to the congregation. Even from the ceiling I could discern the strength and intellect shining from that ravaged face. Dr. Stirling! He was a legendary figure at Main Street Presbyterian. I had never seen him, but from snatches of conversation I knew he had served the church for decades, and was quite old when he retired some ten years ago.

"My friends, thank you for hearing a few wheezes and

gasps from this extinct volcano," he began. The audience stirred with polite chuckles. The old man paused.

"I ask you," he said, more serious now, "to cast your minds back some three years, when you made an important decision. I felt it was inappropriate for me to speak upon it at the time. And I have regretted my silence ever since."

A wave of fluttering and coughing ran through the congregation.

"I will not have many more opportunities to rectify that sin of omission. Sin of omission: a favorite expression among us Presbyterians. We're a stubborn lot, and don't like to admit mistakes. Yet the hourglass is running out for me, as well as for . . ." he stopped and pointedly looked around him at the sanctuary, ". . . this grand old building.

"Yes, I should have spoken three years ago. I should have told you what John Ruskin said. That the greatest glory of a building is not in its stones, or in its gold, but in its age; in its sense of mysterious sympathy, its lasting witness, its quiet contrast with the transitional nature of things, its strength through the lapse of seasons and times.

"Only in the golden stain of time, Ruskin said, can we find the real light, and color, and preciousness of architecture. Only when a building has been hallowed by the deeds of men, until its walls have been witness to suffering, and its pillars risen from the shadows of death, can we appreciate it properly."

"Godalmighty," Grandpa said. "He talks purtier'n you, Charles."

"I should have told you," the old minister continued, "about an Ostrogothic king named Theodoric. Remember how we ministers are prone to talk about the fall of the Roman Empire, and the barbarians at the gates, and assorted other oversimplifications? They're among our favorite clichés. But here was this barbarian king, this so-called plunderer of civilization, visiting the fallen Rome in 500 A.D., and speaking thus: 'These excellent buildings are my delight, the noble image of the Empire's power and the witnesses of its grandeur and its glory. It is my wish that you shall preserve in its original splendor all that is ancient and that whatever you may add will conform to it in style.' Thus from a barbarian who helped topple the Roman Empire. Some barbarian, my friends.

"And I should have conveyed the thoughts of a modern English artist and critic, Osbert Lancaster. To the young, he said: perhaps you feel that preservation is not only ridiculous in itself, but embodies 'a reactionary backwards-looking ethos positively reprehensible; that faced with today's problems we should think only of the present and the future and relegate the past, along with all its architectural manifestations, to the dust heap.' To those who think thus, Mr. Lancaster said, 'no matter how contemporary you strive to be, scratch as a starting point is forever unattainable.'

"And he talked about churches, old and historic churches, and what may befall them. 'It is a far, far better thing,' he said, 'for the House of God to fall into the hands of the infidel than to pass into the keeping of a government department.'

"Those are a few of the things I should have brought up. And I would have — should have — added some localized sentiments of my own. I should have talked about those long-vanished churchmen of the 1840s who built this mighty fortress and dedicated it to their Almighty God.

"I should have talked about my own grandfather's experiences here when this church became a hospital in 1861–65, when the pews were removed to make room for the stretchers brought daily from the battlefield, when these old pine floors ran red with Confederate blood. Look down. You will see the stains there yet."

Dr. Stirling paused. He took a few steps to one side, then back.

"I know. We sold our church. It is no longer ours. It is to be demolished, for a worthy cause. Yet the worthy cause may yet find another accommodation.

"I beg you to consider: As long as this building stands, it is not too late. There is a movement afoot to save Main Street Presbyterian. You — we — of all people have the most to lose. Not from our purses, but from our consciences. Or to use an old-fashioned word, from our souls."

Dr. Stirling looked down at the floor, clasping together

bony, misshapen hands. His thumbs made a tremulous rotation around each other. Then he shuffled back to his seat as silence gripped some 500 people.

Dr. Christie regained his feet and said in a subdued voice: "If there is no further business, the congregational meeting is adjourned."

High above the rest of the congregation but precisely like them, we made our way slowly to the rear of the church. As we descended through the portico wall we could hear, sputtering like an ill-tuned automobile trying to start, the first spoken reactions to Dr. Stirling's words.

"Wha'd you think?"

"He's right. I feel terrible."

"What's the use of bringing all that up now? The decision's made."

"I'm at the age where more good doctors are worth a heap more than a worn-out building."

"My great-grandfather died in there in 1864."

"We ought to do something."

"We sold it. And bidnes' is bidnes'."

CHAPTER 6

WITH THE PATIENCE BRED INTO UNTOLD GENERATIONS of churchmice, we waited for the building to empty. And like the rest of the congregation, we dissected Dr. Stirling's speech.

"Don't expect any results," Grandpa warned. "Like everything spoken in a church, they'll forget about it in twenty minutes."

I did not altogether agree.

"Presbyterians are unaccustomed to being aroused," I said. "They may be therefore affected deeper and longer once you get their attention. I have also heard that they have strong consciences. Perhaps what happened today was so unusual that someone will be stimulated to action."

"But what action, Charles?" Serena asked. "What can anyone do?"

"I don't know. Some powerful person could do something. Who has the most power?" I wondered.

"The governor," snickered Grandpa. "Governor Jack Pine. But he's a Baptist."

"How do you know that?" I asked.

"Shoot, I know a lot about Governor Pine. I practically lived with him."

That was news to me, and I said so.

"Where do you think I was for all that time after the cat

58

nearly got us? After I healed up, and decided the family was gone for good, I went across the street to the Capitol. It's a nice place when the Assembly ain't in session. Then it's too busy. I come back here just a few days before you showed up in that woman's purse. Sure, I know the governor. I got to know him better than I cared to."

"You didn't like him?" Serena asked. "Why not?"

Grandpa puzzled over the question. "Who can say, with humans? There's just something . . . that ain't there. He's got some big, hollow place where humans are supposed to have something important. I don't know what it is."

I had heard Mr. Zebulon say the governor must sign something before construction could begin on the new medical building school. But if Grandpa's judgment was accurate, placing hope in such a man seemed unwise. My elation at Dr. Stirling's address began giving way to depression.

"Such a sigh, Charles," Serena said. On her beautiful face a look of gentle teasing mingled with concern. "Why don't we go over to the Rib Cage and watch TV? Basketball may be on."

"I don't care much for basketball," I said. I remembered Mr. Junior and his dream of bringing professional basketball to Byrdport. It seemed a massive irrelevancy. "And I certainly couldn't enjoy TV for thinking about the church. If only there were something we could do. It's hard, just waiting for them to tear it down."

"We'll find another," Serena said. "Meanwhile, I'm not going to sit around crying about it."

"Nor me," Grandpa said emphatically.

I felt an implied rebuke.

"You're right," I said. "Let's have no sniveling. In fact . . ." I felt my spirits lifting as a great thought dawned, ". . . if we can't save the church, then at least we'll have the time of our lives every night until they tear it down."

"Doing what?"

"Playing the organ, Serena." Even as I spoke I felt a new stirring of resolution, and the controlled excitement that flows from the vision of a worthy goal. And I recalled some lines Mr. Hudson had uttered to one of his students long ago as I lay listening in the organ case. They meant nothing to me then, but now I began to understand.

We are the music-makers, he had said, *and we are the dreamers of dreams . . .*

It was 9:00 P.M. by the Capitol Square Bell Tower when we entered the organ. I judged by the expressions of Serena and Grandpa that they felt the same excitement as I. Here was the old familiar Erben, a noble if rickety mass of dirty pipes and boxes and levers, but we were seeing it in an entirely fresh and different way.

Grandpa disappeared into the machinery. I noted that Serena was studying an untidy heap of sheet music scores, some of them yellow with age, stacked inside the organ case just behind one of its ornately carved, cabinetlike doors.

"Look at all this," she said. "Too bad we can't read music. There's surely a lot of it around."

"They're Mr. Hudson's," I said. "Although he rarely touches them. Occasionally, I shred one for a nest."

"I fixed the wire," Grandpa yelled from the rear of the organ. "You can cut her on."

Here is the picture of the Erben organ. Imagine, rising at the console where the organist sits, a central case of black walnut, paneled with graceful moldings, and measuring twenty-eight feet wide and fifteen feet to the rear wall. Surmounting the case, and soaring up to a height of thirty-seven feet, were three great clusters of pipes, topped and bound together by carved walnut fretwork. Inside, hidden by the case and the big pipes out front, resided many ranks of other pipes. The Erben spoke with more than 2,000 of them.

You might think of the organ as occupying the same space as a good-sized room, which is crammed with pipes and machinery. Even that was not all: There was a satellite organ. Behind the console, hanging onto and over the church balcony, was the so-called choir organ, a miniature version of the major instrument, with its own self-contained mechanism and pipes. All this was made by Mr. Henry Erben of New York City in 1842. That was long ago, even in human terms, but I have heard Mr. Hudson say that high-quality modern pipe organs are still made in much the same way.

"Why are there three keyboards?" Serena asked as we clambered up the console.

"They're called manuals, not keyboards," I said, dipping into my memories of Mr. Hudson instructing his students. "The top one is for the swell organ. That's the part whose pipes connect to a swell chest, which is the one way an organist can control expression. It's done by changing the air pressure in the swell chest. The swell organ's pipes are the smaller ones, up on top."

We reached the manuals. I threw the switch, and heard the exciting low rumble of the blower.

"The middle manual is the heart of it all. That's for the great organ. Its pipes are grouped in the middle; there are more of them, and they work in more combinations. The organist gets the basic job done on the middle manual.

"The bottom manual," I continued, "works the choir organ, there behind us on the balcony. The organist varies his effects by playing combinations, and sometimes coupling the great manual to the others."

"What about the pedals?" Grandpa asked.

"They cover two octaves," I said. "And they play those big pipes to the left and right of the great organ's pipes."

Serena was studying the knobs that bristled from either side of the console. "They're the stops," I said. "The organist pulls and pushes them to make more pipes speak on a particular note, or to stop them from speaking. I think they work on the principal pipes, or diapasons. The principal pipes make the pure organ sound. But other pipes make other sounds, like flutes and reeds. I especially like the flutes. Their high notes come from tiny pipes the size of pencils. They make a sound like the tinkle of little bells."

"Okay, Charles, class is over," Grandpa said. "From here on it's put up or shut up."

"Amen," Serena said. "There are those who talk, and those who act."

"And some who do both," I yelled, leaping onto the great manual in the center.

How many supreme events can a lifetime hold? Three or four? However many life may hold for me, that first night on the Erben will never be surpassed, although musically speaking it began as pure cacophony. How we pranced over the yellowed ivories and chipped ebonies of those battered manuals! How we tugged and shoved the knobs marked bourdon, gedekt, and gemshorn! How we pushed and pulled the stops for bassoon, hautboy, and clarionet! It was a time and a mood for wild experiments, and we conducted them. We made daring high jumps from bench to pedal. We formed ourselves into balls and rolled from the music rack across all three manuals. We caromed off each other like antic demons.

After two hours we paused to rest. Serena was charmingly breathless and disheveled. After composing herself, she turned thoughtful.

"What would you think if, instead of just jumping around making noise, we actually tried to make music?" she asked.

Grandpa and I exchanged superior smiles.

"Sure," he laughed. "Let's play some Beethoven."

"Serena," I lectured, "it takes years for humans to play the organ. And we have certain practical limitations. How do you propose that — "

"Oh, I know we can't read notes," she said impatiently. "But we might learn. And it doesn't make much difference what pushes a key down: a human finger, or a complete mouse. The air still comes out of the pipe the same way, doesn't it? Why don't we pick some simple hymn — a melody we all know — and see if we can play it?"

We thought it over.

" 'Sweet Hour of Prayer,' " Grandpa said. "The melody don't jump around too much."

But the effort to play a melody soon underscored the enormity of our handicaps. A depressed organ key continues to sound its pipe's voice, unlike a piano key. The piano key generates a plink and lets it escape. Similarly, with the guitar, pluck a string once, and the sound soon dies. The organ stays with you, tooting away as long as the key is activated. Obviously, the human hand, raising and lowering fingers at will, was better designed for controlling an organ than a three-ounce rodent.

We practiced "Sweet Hour of Prayer" in several arrangements. Serena, about half an ounce lighter than Grandpa and I, encountered some difficulty in actuating the keys by just stepping on them, so she created a technique of leaping briskly onto an individual key with her entire weight. Her notes thus registered a superior vigor and precision of attack. Grandpa and I tended to step from key to key, and thus created a rather murky effect.

"If we could just get a hymnal up on the rack," Serena said, "we could try to figure out how to read music. Wouldn't it be wonderful if we could learn to pick out three parts of a four-part harmony!"

As it developed, we reached a point where I improvised the melody on the center manual, Serena bounced through an ad-lib tenor on the top keys, and Grandpa worked at the baritone on the bottom. The old fellow was dead game, but I concluded he was partially tone-deaf.

Soon after midnight, exhausted and emotionally spent from the excitement and unfamiliar activity, we ended our first concert on the Erben, and returned to our nests in the case.

Grandpa was unnaturally subdued. "Hard to believe we done that," he said. "Much as I enjoyed it, somehow it bothers me. Seems like we may be trying to reach above our raising."

Serena and I disagreed.

"What's the harm in it?" I asked.

"None, maybe. But let's just be extra careful from now on. Mice are supposed to be quiet creatures," Grandpa concluded.

Around 4:00 A.M. I heard a cry for help.

It was strangely amplified, like a human belching in the shower stall. A musical echo lingered after the one-word plea, reverberating through darkness.

Startled fully awake, I reached to check on Serena, and found her safely alongside and simultaneously reaching for me. Grandpa snored heavily in his untidy nest several feet away.

"Help!" came the resonant cry again. "Somebody get me out of this damn thing."

Grandpa's snores strangled to a stop. "Charles? Serena?" he said.

"We're okay," I said.

"Over *here*," the voice said. "In this *pipe*."

"Pipe? Which one?" I called.

"How do I know which one?" the voice replied.

"Just keep making noise," I said. "We'll find you." By now the three of us were on our feet, seeking to locate the source of the cries.

"Okay, I'll sing. 'Th-e-re is a foun-*tayne* filled with blood, dah dah dahh, dah da-da-dahhhh . . .' "

"Right, I think I have you," I said, tapping on an eight-foot principal. "You in there?"

"Yeah," boomed the voice, a bass eructation. "Can you get me out?"

"Who are you?" Grandpa demanded.

"Save the intros," the voice said. "I'm stuck. I could die in here." For the first time, there was a quaver in the voice not altogether attributable to the pipe's resonance.

"Are you at the bottom of the pipe?" I asked. "We might be able to pull you through the mouth. That's the slit about a foot up from the bottom."

"No. I must be about halfway. I've been trying to climb up, but I keep slipping back. I'm kind of wedged in now, bracing with my back."

"Maybe we can blow him out with air," I said. "Although I don't think the pressure will be enough. A mouse is compact and streamlined, and this is a low-pressure organ."

"It's worth trying," Grandpa said. "But how do we know which note to push?"

"There's no need to even go to the keyboard," I said. "We can pull down the pallet right here." The pallet, a device at the base of each pipe, admits air from the wind chest. It is usually activated by the tracker.

I tugged at the pallet. The pipe, a flute, burbled richly.

"Hey, that may work," the imprisoned mouse cried. "If I can just get my . . . there. Try it again."

I admitted another blast of air.

"It's working," the voice said. "Keep it up this time. Don't quit."

We watched the top of the dingy, pewter-colored pipe. Although it was dark in the organ, our vision was adequate to see what happened.

A head popped into view from the pipe's crown high above us.

Serena screamed. I tried to suppress an involuntary gasp. Grandpa, even Grandpa, flinched.

"Godalmighty. That's the ugliest mouse I ever seen," he whispered.

Strange claws came forth and clamped on the pipe's rim. Burly shoulders strained to pull the creature further into view.

"I heard that, venerable one," the apparition laughed. "But the thing is . . ." Nightmare umbrellas snapped open on either side of him, ". . . I'm not a mouse!"

"Sweet Jesus!" Grandpa breathed. "It's a bat."

"En verite." The bat now stood on the pipe rim, moving his wings as if to test and inspect them. "Everything seems to be in order," he said. "Switch on. Contact. Stand back or we'll all be killed. And assorted other aeronautical jive."

With a leap, a graceful glide, and a soft insinuating flutter, the repulsive creature landed on the floor beside us. He surveyed us with glittering bright eyes. Then, with an exaggerated folding of his wings, he stretched to full height and made a mocking bow.

"Gute *eevening,*" he said.

We gaped like bumpkins.

"Whatsamatta?" he said. "Never seen a bat before? Family *Vespertilionidae.* Species *Myotis lucifugus.* Commonly known, in a patronizing way, as the little brown bat. Call me Stoker."

Finally, I found my tongue. "We've just never seen a bat close up. We knew there were some in the belfry, but . . ."

"Yeah, separate but equal," he said. "You think I'm funny looking? As far as I'm concerned, you chaps are nothing to write Transylvania about, either. I nevertheless should extend appropriate dithyrambs for getting me out of that mother. You sprung me from a fate worse than sunrise. Even though it was you who got me into that mess to start with, I must in candor add."

"How did we . . ."

"By making those sounds, baby. Mercy on us, what a rush.

Nobody ever played this thing in prime time before, or if they did, a bunch of humans were stumbling around with the lights on. In the daytime we have to hang in the belfry. So when I heard the pipes tonight I homed in like a pigeon."

"You were attracted by the sound?" I asked.

"Like the Sirens calling Ulysses to the rocks. Sound is our thing, Ace. We get around by echolocation: sending out little ultrasonic squeaks and listening for the echoes. *Eep! Eep!* Like that. Tonight was something new. I came in and listened. Then I kept cruising closer. I discovered that the veritable breath of Aeolus blew from the tops of yonder pipes. I wondered if I could hover above those gentle zephyrs, like old Cap'n Buzzard on his thermals."

"Did it work?" I asked.

"Mezzo mezzo. There wasn't quite enough breeze. I was sort of treading water over that one pipe when you yanked the air. I dropped a little and hit a wing; tried to grab the edge and slipped in. El ploppo! To the bottom like a stone! Kept trying to climb out. Finally gave up and yelled for help. When you got it together and blew, there was just enough push. I could have bought the farm, chaps." He glared at us with his ferocious, warlike eyes.

"I'll bet you won't come back for any more concerts," Serena said.

"*Au contraire,* little cabbage," Stoker said. "I still love the groovy sounds. But I shall take a safer seat for the next performance. Something in the royal circle, perhaps. Right now," he continued, "this whole trip has left me starving. How are things here provenderwise?"

"I'm afraid we can't offer you anything but a little soap," Serena said. "But you're welcome to that."

"Soap! You jest."

Serena dropped her eyes in embarrassment.

"Er, well," he continued quickly, "it shan't be long before Aurora flings her fair, fresh-quilted colors through the air, as we bats say with a certain becoming lyricism. So I think I'll just pop outside and scarf up a few moths."

"*Bugs!*" Serena exclaimed. Now it was our turn to be amazed. "You eat bugs?" Her earlier fright was gone.

66

"Nothing else, Sweetie," Stoker said. "Most bats are bugivores. A few aesthetes do fancy bananas. There's even a big hummer who catches fish. Ah, yes, and there are some . . ." he approached Serena with stagy stealth, grinning to expose hideously sharp, parted teeth ". . . oh, my dear, what an exquisite neck . . . there are some who . . . who . . ." He pulled her close.

"Drink blood!" Serena shrieked.

"I can't stand the sight of the stuff, myself," Stoker said, giggling. "Only those crazy Mexican bats go for blood. But seriously, folks, I must not be caught abroad at curfew time. Stand back and give me room."

He spread his strange wings. We stared in fascination at their spindly framework of bones, covered by membranelike ancient, wrinkled leather.

"Cleared for takeoff. Now watch me grab some sky," said Stoker.

How silently he launched himself!

But moments later, from somewhere high above us, there came a faint and not unpleasant beeping sound.

"Holy mother," Grandpa said. "See what I mean? Mice start playing the organ, and they draw bats. It ain't natural."

"Oh, Grandpa, I thought he was kind of cute," Serena said.

CHAPTER 7

IT WAS MONDAY, LATE MORNING, AND I OCCUPIED MY station in Dr. Christie's study, stretched out in the picture molding high on the wall.

"Doctor Christie." The voice of Mrs. Pope, the mirthless church secretary, brimmed with disapproval. "I have now taken three telephone calls regarding Dr. Stirling's little talk of yesterday, which I gather is all written up in this morning's newspaper. How much longer do you want me to say you're not available?"

"No longer, Mrs. Pope," Dr. Christie sighed. "I suppose it's my job to talk to them. I do wonder how the press got hold of it." The morning *Enquirer* was spread before him on the desk. Mrs. Pope snatched up the newspaper, making brisk crackling sounds as she popped it open. She read silently for a moment.

"They did get it all, didn't they? 'Former pastor, near-legendary figure in Presbyterianism . . . strong plea to preserve historic church . . . points to Civil War bloodstains on floor . . . quotes Ruskin and Theodoric,' " she snapped.

"I read it, Mrs. Pope," Dr. Christie said.

A young man entered the study. He wore an ill-favored beard and a look of gentle smugness. Unbidden, he collapsed awkwardly into a chair.

"I take it you're discussing yesterday's episode at the congregational meeting," he said.

"Yes. Now that you're here, Mr. Smeak, I . . ." Dr. Christie began.

"Call me Jerry, Angus."

"I always call my assistant ministers 'mister.' In any case, I was about to say that I want us to agree on a suitable posture vis-a-vis the controversy about this building," Dr. Christie said.

"But Angus, my feelings are well known. The church should never have been sold."

"I was not aware of the widespread currency of your feelings. I take it, though, that now you would like to see the building preserved," Dr. Christie said.

The young pastor waved a limp, dismissing gesture.

"I couldn't care less about preserving the building. What I meant was, the congregation should have remained here, and drastically altered the character of the institution. The church should have been converted to a mission to serve the city's disadvantaged — all those winos, junkies, gays, and blacks who have nothing to do but hang around the bus stations. The congregation should have become a volunteer staff to minister to such people, thus in some small tentative way expiating the crushing guilt that burdens us all."

"It was merciful," Dr. Christie said icily, "that you were not here when the decision was made to sell this building. Can you honestly see the members of this congregation, some of the elite of Byrdport . . . oh, never mind. The only issue involved now is how the fate of this building may give our church a public black eye. At the time, selling it for a worthy cause seemed justified. But now these preservationists have the wind up. There may be stormy times ahead, Mr. Smeak."

"Then I say, screw the backward-looking romantics. With all the needy causes in the world . . ." Mr. Smeak mournfully shook his head.

"We shall never run shy of needy causes," Dr. Christie said. "If the world had waited until every hungry mouth was fed, every hovel roof patched, every illiterate educated, every drunk dried out, then I'm afraid we would still be in the Dark Ages."

"Our lot, my dear Angus, should always be cast with the underdog."

"Our lot, my dear Mr. Smeak, should also pay occasional mind to the loyal members of what is sometimes ter-r-r-med, in a quaintly archaic expression, our *flock*. Do you know, sir, it is positively amazing how you and I can never manage to agree on anything. It is almost diabolical. Suddenly, I feel a great surge of empathy with the pr-r-r-eservationists. You have accomplished that, at any rate."

With a condescending shrug, Mr. Smeak rose to leave. At the study door he collided heavily with Jackson Ward, who was simultaneously entering from the hall. The young minister petulantly shoved his way past the ponderous sexton.

"Doctah Christie." Jackson Ward, overweight and middle-aged, wore pale green chinos that billowed when he moved, like a partially inflated hot air balloon. "Sump'm funny going on here, Reverend. I thought you might need to know." He paused to let the dramatic look sink itself into Dr. Christie.

"Hardly anything you could say would surprise me, Jackson, but go ahead."

"I got this friend, a nurse. Work over at the big hospital they call BUSM, you know? Well. Last night, she get off about eleven o'clock, and she hustle over to Main to catch the las' bus. So she come right by the church. You with me, Reverend?"

"I am, Jackson."

"Now. As she walk by the church, she hear awgan music comin' from inside," the sexton said.

"Hm. That seems an odd time for Mr. Hudson to be . . ."

"Wan't Mr. Hudson," Jackson Ward continued. "I done axt him. He say he wan't closer'n ten miles to this here church. And that ain't all. Mr. Hudson say, ain't nobody playin' the awgan, 'cause the awgan broke."

"But the little electronic organ is in there now," Dr. Christie said. "Undoubtedly, it was that one that your friend heard."

Jackson Ward smiled in the knowledge of superior information.

"Naw, Reverend. I done poosh the little awgan back in the annex, right after church yesterday. And my friend Rosetta, she *sho* the music coming from the main church. It were the old

70

awgan, all right. I axt her was she *sho,* and she say, 'Yeah.' Rosetta know her music. I say, 'Could that music have been comin' from that little awgan?' And she say, 'Naw, it had to be the big pipe awgan.' What's more, she say whoever was playing, he made a mighty botch of it."

"The performer was unskilled, you mean? I mean, she meant?"

"Rosetta say it was more like just noise than music. She stood out yonder maybe ten minutes, waiting for her bus, listening. She say after a while it did begin to sound like maybe they was trying to play 'Sweet Hour of Prayer.' But it were powerful rough."

"Well, Jackson, I agree it sounds peculiar. I assume the church was locked," Dr. Christie said.

"Tight as a tick. And no sign of nothing jimmied. I checked all the doors, all the windows. Everything was shut tight and locked. Tight. No tamperin'."

"And did you look around inside to see if there was anything unusual?"

"Everything look okay to me, Reverend," the sexton concluded.

"Then," Dr. Christie said, "it does seem that you have discovered a mystery, Jackson. But I'm sure it will do us no harm. Perhaps it will take our minds off some of our other problems."

Jackson Ward rippled ponderously from the study. Dr. Christie looked at Mrs. Pope.

"If the truth were known," she barked, "what the woman heard was one of those tape deck things, coming from a parked car. Perhaps in the alley between us and that awful Rib Cage. The Lord only knows what goes on out there after dark. I will be so *glad* to get away from here."

"No regrets, Mrs. Pope?" Dr. Christie asked.

"None. This old place has long since served out its usefulness."

She clumped away on thick-heeled shoes. Dr. Christie put a hand to his forehead and closed his eyes. High on the wall, I sensed the passage of a prayer, like a silent speeding rocket, on its heavenly trajectory.

71

"Somebody heard us," I announced back in the choir loft. Then I related the news as decanted by Jackson Ward.

"Maybe we should wait until later at night before we start playing," Grandpa said.

"Why?" Serena asked. "There will always be a few people around. Somebody's going to hear us. And I think it's neat if they do. What's the point in performing if nobody hears?"

"I thought the point in doing it was for our enjoyment," I said. "But I agree it's rather exciting, to know that we have played before strangers."

"Hush. Somebody's coming," Grandpa said.

We retreated into the Erben.

The visitor was Dr. Christie. He marched to the Erben's console and flicked the switch five times. He poked at the keys. He jiggled the pedals. But thanks to Grandpa's careful restoration of the short circuit, the blower did not stir. No pipes could speak.

Satisfied, Dr. Christie walked away. We heard him mutter: "Organ music indeed."

That night, we added "The Old Rugged Cross" to our repertoire.

Tuesday night, at Grandpa's urging, we attempted "Nearer, My God, to Thee," with some surprising improvement in our three-part harmony technique.

And on Wednesday morning, we learned the world had listened.

"Good Lord," cried Dr. Christie, spreading out the morning *Enquirer* on his study desk.

"Exactly," snapped Mrs. Pope.

He read aloud the headline:

PHANTOM OF THE ORGAN
PLAYS TO EMPTY HOUSE

"Excessively melodramatic, I'd say," Mrs. Pope said.

" 'Main Street Presbyterian Church, soon to be demolished for the construction of a new Byrdport University School of

Medicine (BUSM) high-rise, apparently has a phantom organ-ist,' " Dr. Christie read.

" 'For the past three nights, witnesses say, the unmistakable sounds of organ music have been heard coming from the locked, totally dark sanctuary.

" 'First allegations of the nocturnal concert came from an off-duty nurse, Rosetta Stone, who was unimpressed by the talent of the mysterious organist. "It sounded like somebody just playing around, especially on the first night," Ms. Stone said. "The second night it came a little better."

" 'Last night, a small crowd gathered on the sidewalk around midnight. Quentin Brightstone, a hairdresser who told police he was on his way to the bus station, said he listened for fully ten minutes before being assaulted and robbed by others in the audience. He described the organist's playing as "hardly expert," but recognizable as "Nearer, My God, to Thee." "

" 'The alleged organ music came as civic interest was apparently building for a late-blooming preservation battle to save the old church. In a related development, Mrs. Fitzgerald Randolph, president of the statewide Pocahontas Garden Club, announced yesterday that she would meet Thursday with officials of Historic Byrdport Foundation to discuss possible mutual action.' "

Dr. Christie put down the paper and cradled his chin in his hands.

"It's insane," he said. "The whole affair is becoming a circus. I don't know why we can't be permitted to pack up and leave in peace and dignity."

The assistant minister walked in talking.

"It's either (a) some divine revelation which we must interpret, or (b) a certifiable fruitcake at work," Mr. Smeak said. "As I don't believe in divine revelations, or anything divine, for that matter, I conclude it must be (b). I only wish he had some talent. It's just our luck to draw a phantom organist who can't cut it. I'm — "

"You will keep silent about the whole situation," Dr. Christie said.

I ran through the walls to report the morning news to Serena and Grandpa.

They were sitting together, rather closely and solemnly, in the Erben. They did not interrupt as I recounted the *Enquirer's* story.

"So we attracted a sidewalk crowd, eh?" Grandpa said. "We also attracted somebody else. Inside."

"Alabama Ruby," Serena said. "We saw her this morning, just after you left."

"She was layin' up on a chair in the choir," Grandpa continued. "She was watching the organ, all right. I wonder if she was here last night. It's enough to give me the shakes, just recalling how we was jumping around on the keyboards like who last the longest."

This was serious, even alarming, news.

"I'd hoped she was gone for good," I said. "We'll have to be more careful. When we play the organ, somebody will have to be lookout. No more three-part harmony."

"I'll do it," Grandpa said. "Watching for cats comes more natural to me than playing the organ."

"But tomorrow," I said, "I'm going to be leaving the church for a few hours, and you must both promise me not to break cover for so much as a moment. It worries me that Alabama Ruby would have returned at just this time, but you'll be safe if you stay inside the organ and the walls."

"What's so important that you must leave, Charles?" Serena asked.

"There's a meeting. The newspaper talked about it. A meeting between the Historic Byrdport people and some big garden club people."

"Oh. I didn't realize you had been invited," she said coldly.

"I guess he ain't showed us his invitation," Grandpa said.

"Look, you two," I said. "This could be a critical point in whether the church and the organ are saved. In whether we'll still have a home in a couple of weeks. We need to know what's going on. I simply must go."

"Do you know where the meeting is?" Serena asked.

"No, but I will find out."

"He'll just telephone the president of the garden club," Grandpa said.

"Actually, I have good connections with the Historic Byrdport Foundation," I said. "Their office is nearby. That's where I will go to find out about the meeting."

"And once you learn where the meeting is, how do you propose to get there?" Serena asked.

"I don't know. Maybe I can't. I'm just saying that I must try." Their disapproval hung stonily in the air.

"We must do what we think is right, Charles," Grandpa said at last. "But I'll tell you something important. Getting out of something can be a heap harder than getting in."

The long daylight hours of that Wednesday generated events of more than ordinary interest.

Always in a city church, especially around midday, a small number of humans enter in search of a few minutes' solitude. I judge by the haunted expressions on a high percentage of their faces that they have troubles in their hearts.

But that Wednesday, most of the visitors wandered around with looks of simple curiosity. *So this is the place,* they seemed to say. Several climbed to the choir loft and looked blankly at the Erben. Some, more purposeful and businesslike, made notes and took pictures.

We heard animated conversation in the stairwell. I recognized the voice of Mr. Hudson.

"Young lady," he said, ascending the stairs, "I agreed reluctantly to come down for an interview, but I have made it perfectly clear that the organ will not play. It is broken; out of order. It will not be repaired. There is no way I can play it for you."

We could see Mr. Hudson and his companions now. One was a young woman whose hard, reptilian mouth spoiled what I supposed might otherwise have been good looks. Her companion was a bearded man carrying what seemed to be a big camera with a spotlight.

"I don't believe this crap," the woman said.

Mr. Hudson stiffened.

"Okay, Gary, like this," she said to her companion. "Start on me, while I intro it for about fifteen seconds. Then pan to the organ and zoom on the keys for about ten seconds. Then back to me and I'll talk to this guy, and wrap it up."

Poor Mr. Hudson. His eyes roamed desperately, as if looking for a place to hide.

A brilliant light snapped on and the woman began to talk, spewing words at a small wand she held in front of her chin. She did, I admit, present a balanced summary of what little information was then available to humans.

"... yet despite the reports of various night people, the organ apparently will not play." She walked to the console and poked at the keys with exaggerated emphasis. Nothing happened, of course. Then she stepped to Mr. Hudson's side.

"With me now is Arthur Hudson, organist at Main Street Presbyterian Church. Tell us in your own words, Arthur, what you think of these developments."

"I . . . I . . . I find the whole thing confusing and impossible to believe. The organ cannot be played."

"Is that the church's official position?" the newswoman asked.

"Official? It's just the truth. The organ is unplayable. Out of order. Defunct."

"That sums up church opinion," she said. "But questions remain. Could all this be mass hysteria? If people really are hearing something, what is it? Is it just barely possible that somehow there truly is a Phantom of the Organ?" She paused melodramatically. "And if so, will he play again? Now, returning you to Channel Seven's headline edition . . ."

The light snapped off.

"That's all?" Mr. Hudson asked.

"This ain't Issues and Answers, Arthur. Let's go, Gary, we gotta make the Welfare Mothers' Parade."

We heard them clump downstairs. In the church vestibule the television fired off a parting comment.

"Hey, Gary, I've solved the mystery. Look at the big red cat asleep on that radiator. What all those people heard was the cat howling!" She laughed raucously.

I could have told her that for all Alabama Ruby's obscene habits, the cat did not howl.

We anticipated that sooner or later, someone might enter the sanctuary during one of our performances. Although the church was locked at night, any staff member might unexpectedly surprise us, especially now in the face of the organ's sudden notoriety. Thus, from now on, we knew that we must keep lookout not only for Alabama Ruby, but humans as well.

Grandpa thought it best to cancel the Wednesday night concert. Serena was uncertain. "I love playing," she said, "but maybe it would be wise . . ."

I brushed aside their objections. I realize now that for me, playing the organ had become a feverish obsession. As evening approached, my pulse went allegro.

And I prevailed. Grandpa, reluctant but game, took a position on top of the music rack, the highest point around the console. Just before midnight Serena and I began to play, a two-part harmony of "Amazing Grace," which after three attempts sounded remarkably smooth.

Suddenly, a yellow light fanned outward from an opening door, far down in the front of the pitch-dark church. I knew the door led to the annex where Dr. Christie had his study. We fled inside the organ case, and Grandpa expertly restored the short circuit.

The main sanctuary lights flashed on. Footsteps resounded as several humans mounted the stairs.

Through a crack in the case I discerned Dr. Christie, Mr. Smeak, and a policeman. The latter creaked and jingled as he walked. He held a flashlight which, despite the brilliant illumination of the church's lights, he insisted on playing over the organ.

"There was really no need to trouble yourself," Dr. Christie said. "We could have handled this ourselves."

"But it's causing some commotion," the officer said. "So long as there weren't anybody but a few degenerates out listening on the sidewalk, it weren't so bad, sir. But now it's attracting wild kids and ordinary curious citizens. People are getting rolled. All right," he said sharply in a raised voice, "what's going on here? Who's playing this thing?" He shot the beam of light around aggressively. "Come on out, we know you're in there."

"Come out from *where*?" Dr. Christie asked. "Inside the organ?"

"Let's have a look. Open it up, sir," the officer said.

The three of us leaped under the tracker board as one of the small doors to the case opened and the light beam probed inside.

"They's as much junk in there as under my Chevy cruiser's hood," the policeman said. In a moment the door closed. "Hm. I don't see how you can say it won't play, when we all three of us heard it."

"Try for yourself," said Mr. Smeak. "Look. Here's the switch."

Click, click, click. Then we heard the gentle, fluttering sound of keys being depressed on the manual.

"I thought it was probably a tape recorder planted somewhere," Mr. Smeak said. "But where could it be, and who turned it off when we came in?"

"Maybe he's hiding under one of them benches here in the balcony. Let's fan out and look under 'em," the officer said.

They searched the church for about half an hour. Then, expressing subdued bewilderment, they exited and the lights went off.

"Mercy on us," Grandpa sighed. "That's put the spit on the apple. I'm done. No more organ music. I'm done." Grumbling to himself, he retreated to his nest.

"He'll feel better about it tomorrow night," I told Serena.

"I doubt it," Serena said. "I'm not even sure that I'll feel better about it tomorrow. For that matter, I'm not even sure you'll be here tomorrow."

"Of course I will. I told you; I'm just slipping across Capitol Square for a little while. I'll be back tomorrow night when the traffic has abated."

Serena's expression was grave.

"Charles, we learned to play the organ, and it's a thrill. But I worry that we've stirred up things we can't control. Worse, all this business about your going to meetings! I'm suddenly afraid it will bring some awful trouble on us. Just don't get more interested in the organ and the church than you are in me."

"Serena!"

"Maybe you're starting to take me for granted, Charles.

I've noticed some little things lately, like the way you always assume I'll play the harmony while you play the lead," she said.

"That's absurd, Serena," I said.

I fell into troubled sleep. About 4:00 A.M. I awakened, filled with turmoil over what to do. How could I leave Serena, so beautiful there beside me, for such an adventure as crossing Capitol Square again, a mission whose hazards I had deliberately minimized? Was not the excitement of playing the organ sufficient? Was I already crying for madder music and stronger wine? No, I decided. My desire to attend the church preservation meeting seemed reasonable and unpresumptuous. Furthermore, I had been thinking about Miss Tebell.

I would return in only half a day. Bidding silent *adieu* to Serena and Grandpa, I crept from the organ and down the walls to the vestibule, whence I exited onto the broad granite stairs of Main Street Presbyterian. The air was cold.

Directly across the street, a police cruiser waited at the curb.

CHAPTER 8

WOULD THE OFFICERS, DOUBTLESS ALERT FOR FURTHER outbreaks of organ music, take note of a mouse's progress across the pavement? To be careful I ran west to the front of the Rib Cage, so as to cross behind the cruiser. The Rib Cage! How long it seemed since Serena and I had gamboled there, without a care for Main Street Presbyterian.

The street was clear of traffic, and I ran across in seconds. My route to avoid the cruiser put me now at an unfamiliar point on the edge of Capitol Square, far from my eventual destination of Live Oak Row. Now, for the first time, I had a good view of the Governor's Mansion, which sat inside the square on its western extremity. But I wasted no time admiring the building, which like the Capitol was painted a chaste gray that glowed pearlescently in the winter night.

I wished, in fact, that the great hilly square might have had fewer lights. Mounted on poles, they concentrated their glow along the herringbone-patterned brick pathways, and spread a soft illumination almost everywhere save under shrubbery. I tried to stay in the shadows, but occasionally I had to cross a brick path.

I was within sight of Live Oak Row when a dog discovered me.

Normally, mice pay little heed to dogs, apart from a few

terrier breeds. Dogs are not too difficult to avoid. The average dog, while making a great commotion upon seeing a mouse, is really not interested in killing or eating us. But you never know. I did not like the look of this dog, a large mixed breed shorthair, a type often seen in poorer neighborhoods. He came after me with a snarl.

I had noted that along Capitol Square's winding walkways were shallow brick gutters that carried off rain water, sluicing it regularly through iron grates that led underground. I reached one of the grates just ahead of the dog's filthy muzzle. He barked hoarsely as I plunged through the bars, wondering where I would land. But I fell only a few inches into the damp opening of a sewer pipe.

The dog roared above me. I was enveloped by his revolting breath, which stank of stale grease.

"Hey," I yelled, brave enough behind my iron grate. "Get away. Let me pass."

"I hongry, buddyro," the dog bellowed.

"You wouldn't like me. Go knock over a garbage can. You'll find a selection in the alley by the Rib Cage," I said.

"Don' like that Yid food," the animal whuffed.

From my dark hole I saw him whirl around. Then I heard a human voice.

"Git!" the voice said. "Git!" Heavy shoes tramped on the walk, echoing in the pipe that connected to my opening. The dog crouched and sprang away from the oncoming human, who creaked and jingled like the officer who had visited the organ. Now, as the man stood directly over the grate, I saw an immaculate black Capitol Square policeman, whose uniform resembled that of a state trooper who once stopped the Reverend Delbert Loudermilk for speeding.

"Next time," the officer said, "I'll call the pound."

He had some curiosity as to what the dog had run to ground, and peered fruitlessly down through the grate. Then he jingled away on his rounds. I climbed out and made straight for a concealing patch of periwinkle and ivy, through which I continued to the square's eastern side. Live Oak Row and the Historic Byrdport Foundation loomed ahead of me.

A sleek, shiny automobile was parked at the curb by the

foundation's front door. I would learn it was called a Nissan Z-car. As I prepared to leap through the black iron Capitol Square fence for the last leg of my journey, the door — my very destination — quietly and slowly opened.

Through it stepped Mr. Granville Zebulon.

He walked to the car, and as he entered it he looked up to the front second-story window. As I knew well, behind it was the bedroom of the executive director of the Historic Byrdport Foundation. Mr. Zebulon raised one hand in a quick wave, and I saw, in response, Miss Tebell's graceful fingers brushing at the glass.

You may ask: Did the tooth of jealousy nip me as I waited for the sleek car to drive away? Indeed not. Was I surprised? No. Disappointed in the slightest? Don't be ridiculous. Do you believe my denials?

If I waited at the fence a moment longer than necessary, it was to retrieve my strength after the long, frightening trip through Capitol Square. But I persevered. Had you been watching that night, or that morning, for it was by now around 4:30, you would have seen a small aerodynamic shadow dart resolutely across the street, mount the stairs, and slide under the bottom of the door on Live Oak Row.

It was now Thursday, two weeks from the day that Mr. Hudson and the repairman had prematurely declared the Erben dead. So much had happened since then! And now I crawled up the stairs of Miss Tebell's apartment for my second visit with her, wondering what the coming day would bring, feeling a touch of the melancholy that comes to all creatures in pre-dawn February in an old house, in an old, old city.

I found her sitting up in bed, in her four-poster with the carved plumes around each tree-trunklike column, her chin reflectively on her knees. As her bed was near the window, and soft light from the street and Capitol Square filtered through the gauzy curtains, she was outlined as if by a halo. To me at that moment, she seemed the noble essence of what there was, such as it was, to love in human beings.

As the work day began at the offices of Historic Byrdport

Foundation, my sense of humility returned with heavy impact. Perhaps Serena and Grandpa were right: I had lapsed into unaccustomed hubris. I had so aroused myself over the fate of Main Street Presbyterian that I was thinking as a participant. If I wished to attend a meeting on the crisis, why not? Charles Churchmouse simply strolls in and asks where and when the meeting will be held. Oh, indeed. Imagine it, as a three-ounce hitchhiking fugitive.

I had to learn if the meeting would occur at Miss Tebell's office, or at the garden club mentioned in the newspaper story, or at some other place. Were it anywhere but Live Oak Row, I reasoned, I must be alert to the problem of transportation.

Yet the forenoon dragged on with no reference to the meeting. The main business at Historic Byrdport that morning was the excavation of an early nineteenth-century well, recently exposed at a construction site. Artifacts from the dig littered Miss Tebell's desk. I saw bottles, fragments of dinnerware, a china doll, and unmistakable pork chop bones.

"I'd love to go on a dig with you sometime," she said to the high-booted young man who had brought in the objects. "Do you guys ever get carried away with the romance of it all? Just think. When you dug up this doll, nobody had seen or touched it for maybe one hundred and fifty years. It was almost like somebody of that day handed it to you. It puts you so close."

"Sure," the man said. "We think like that sometimes. Archaeologists cover it up with a lot of dry, scientific doubletalk, but I never knew one of us yet who wasn't a hopeless romantic, down deep."

"It's different with old buildings," Miss Tebell said. "With buildings all the generations of human use come crowding in. We work above ground; you below. But it's all part of the same thing, isn't it?"

"Sure," the archaeologist said. "We're all trying to understand what our ancestors were all about. The difference is, you're trying to preserve existing, complete artifacts, while we're looking for broken bits and pieces which are rarely more than clues. Every preservationist is just one step ahead of the bulldozer."

"How true," Miss Tebell said. "Figuratively speaking, I

must go throw myself in front of one right now. I guess you could think of garden club ladies as a collective bulldozer. Maybe it will be a friendly bulldozer, though."

The archaeologist rose to go. I had stationed myself behind a baseboard, where access to Miss Tebell's purse was faster than from my usual post in the chandelier. I moved quickly while she walked with the man to her office door, and shot into her purse, which lay on a lowboy near her desk. As she returned, I could barely hear her words to the secretary, Thelma.

". . . wanted to have it at their club. No way, I said. I don't know what those old dowagers have in mind, but I wasn't about to meet them on their own turf. Besides, I wanted to invite the other people, including Granzeb, who'll report what Mr. Slemp has decided. Coming from him it may have more impact than from me. So we'll have a nice seafood lunch at the Canal Boat. Then we'll see what hits the fan."

She was coming closer to the lowboy. "I think I'll go upstairs and get my maroon purse," she said.

My heart thudded.

"Oh, daggone it, I'm late. This one's okay."

I lurched into the air.

"Back in about two hours, Thel," she said gaily.

In the four-block walk to Byrdport's restaurant district, it seemed that Miss Tebell's step was even springier than usual. Soon we climbed some stairs as I identified the interior smells of the Canal Boat, and we entered a room where — I judged by the sounds of clinking ice — refreshments were being served. My observations of the meeting were perhaps imperfect, for there was no opportunity to leave the purse and see anything, but I shall relate and interpret the conversations that occurred.

"Ah, my co-hostess," croaked a ravenlike female baritone. "Have a Bloody Mary. It's one damnyankee habit of which I approve." The president of the Pocahontas Garden Club, Mrs. Fitzgerald Randolph, exploded in a gravelly laugh. "I'm so glad you suggested this place. It's charming. At the Pocahontas we tend to stay in our own little world for lunch, and not get out enough."

"Your headquarters building is so wonderful, I'm not surprised," Miss Tebell said. "No wonder you prefer to stay there."

"It is a grand old pile, isn't it? There just aren't many four-story Italianate mansions from the 1850s around anymore. What a shame. We restored it in 1928, when I was just a slip of a girl. *Hoo, hoo, hock, whoop, gack!*" Mrs. Randolph tended to strangle upon her witticisms.

"Do you know everyone here, Mrs. Randolph?"

"Well, I just met that nice young man, Mr. Zebulon. What an interesting complexion. And the doctor from the university, Caleb something. I can't understand why he's here; they're the ones who want to tear down the church. And I met the little man from the State Landmarks Office. Oh, look who just came in. Little Jerry Smeak! I know his mother!"

I heard Granville Zebulon's low voice. "I ordered the seafood platter for everyone. Hope that's okay. I can't understand why I got stuck with planning your meeting. As if I cared about what happens to your old church."

"Dearest, I always use my men pitilessly before I discard them. By the way, what do you think of Mrs. Randolph?"

"She's driving me wild with unspeakable urges," Mr. Zebulon said.

"Ah. More evidence you're that way for older women. I have quite an age gap on you too, son. Note please I didn't say 'boy.' "

Mrs. Randolph returned with Jerry Smeak in tow.

"Call me Ditty," she rumbled. "How's your mother? Still batiking?"

"Beats hell out of me. What is it, some groovy perversion? If it feels good I doubt that she's doing it, but you never know."

"*Hoo, haw, gack,*" said Mrs. Randolph, without enthusiasm.

"I think we should begin," Miss Tebell said.

Feet shuffled, chairs bumped, and purses were flung. A lipstick case cracked against my head. I lost consciousness briefly, and awoke to the mingled aromas of broiled scallops, shrimp tempura, and crab parmesan. I longed to jump free and dine with the group. But I persevered inside the purse. Ultimately, Mrs Randolph began the meeting.

". . . here to join hands in a new cause. Tayloe Tebell and I thank all twelve of you for responding to our invitations."

85

"Eleven," said Mr. Smeak. "Nobody invited me, I crashed."

Mrs. Randolph explained that every year, the Pocahontas Garden Club sponsored a major restoration project. Usually it was a historic garden, but as she explained, "There's more to life than boxbushes, azaleas, and serpentine walls, and sometimes we adopt an entire building. The benefit can be considerable. Each spring we sponsor Boxwood Week, in which great homes and gardens, normally closed to the public, are opened — for a fee. The money thus collected goes to finance our project of the year.

"Our executive committee, I am happy to tell you," Mrs. Randolph continued, "held a special session and voted to adopt Main Street Presbyterian as our next project. Come next May, we shall present a check to . . . to . . . well I must say, Tayloe dear, the details elude me."

"Let me handle the fine print," Mr. Zebulon whispered.

Miss Tebell thanked Mrs. Randolph for the Pocahontas Club's "marvelous gesture," and asked Mr. Zebulon to put the matter in some overall perspective.

He succinctly explained how the state came to own the church, and how Flemmons R. Slemp had made a ten million dollar challenge grant to build a new medical education building. "Late yesterday," he said, "the Assembly approved the appropriations bill. It includes the state's ten million dollar portion. The governor favors the new building, and it's doubtful he would veto that section of the appropriations bill."

"So," interrupted Mr. Smeak, "it's all too late. The matter is academic. Let's go back to the bar."

"Not necessarily too late," Mr. Zebulon said. "Mr. Slemp thinks the university already has two other good sites. Just as good as the church location. One is a parking lot today." Mr. Zebulon paused. Then he said: "Mr. Slemp has decided that Main Street Presbyterian should be preserved."

Applause clattered in the restaurant. I, too, was thrilled by the news.

"Mr. Slemp has checked with the attorney general. There is nothing in the appropriations bill requiring the state to put the new building on any particular site. So the building may go up on another location."

More applause.

"But wait," Mr. Zebulon said. "Mr. Slemp points out that the state has spent half a million dollars already on preliminary engineering and architectural plans for the Main Street site. So if the location is changed . . ."

"The taxpayers would be out half a million dollars," said a new voice. It was cultured, aristocratic, and vaguely familiar.

"Correct, Dr. Old," Mr. Zebulon said. Caleb Old! Miss Tebell's lover of many years ago!

Mr. Zebulon continued speaking. "So Mr. Slemp — always a plain-speaking man — says that those wanting to preserve Main Street Presbyterian might pull it off, but they must get busy with more than talk. He will throw his weight to supporting another site. As he's already donated ten million dollars, his weight is substantial. But he feels it's not up to him to provide the other half-million to spare the taxpayers."

"The capitalist always shows his true colors, eh?" sneered Mr. Jerry Smeak.

"In this case," Mr. Zebulon responded evenly, "the capitalist is willing to go halfway. The property alone — the church lot, plus the salvageable materials in the church, which is how the state has figured it — is worth about one hundred thousand dollars. To cover that, plus the half-million already spent on plans, makes six hundred thousand dollars. To repay the public till, and then buy the church.

"Mr. Slemp will put up half. Three hundred thousand dollars more of his own money. He expects the preservation movement to do the rest," Mr. Zebulon concluded.

"Why, that's perfectly *grand!*" Mrs. Randolph said. "But gracious, that would leave us facing . . . a three hundred thousand dollar Boxwood Week? I'm just not sure we can — "

Dr. Old interrupted again.

"I can appreciate most of what you say, Mr. Zebulon. And while the doctors and deans of BUSM are not habituated to having their plans thwarted, it is possible that a combination of public opinion and the wishes of this generous donor, Flemmons R. Slemp, would sway them from standing pat on their present position. It is an interesting scenario. But something keeps nagging at me. The congregation abandoned its building, even though it was in good condition. Why? Because nobody lives around there anymore. At least not enough of the kind of people who support a large, affluent, metropolitan church. There is nobody left in the neighborhood to use such a structure for its original purpose. Therefore, I must ask a question that, apparently, nobody else has been crass enough to ask. What in the name of heaven are you going to do with Main Street Presbyterian Church when and if you save it?"

"Caleb sort of spoiled the party, didn't he?" Miss Tebell mused as we walked slowly up Canal Street in midafternoon.

"Not necessarily," Mr. Zebulon said.

"It's an old but often effective tactic, this 'but what are you gonna do with it?' business. The important thing is to save the building. Then there'll be time to figure out what comes next," Miss Tebell said heatedly.

"But there's nothing wrong with thinking ahead," Mr. Zebulon said. "That's being realistic. And, Tayloe . . . when you look at the church, what *could* be done with it?"

"An indoor mall of small shops, maybe. Oh, don't waggle your eyebrows at me. I know we're becoming a nation of people selling fudge and tee shirts to each other."

"A market full of fudge and tee shirts would be a sad comedown for a classic building like that. How about a new museum?" Mr. Zebulon said.

"Byrdport is crawling with them already."

"Like to sit here on the bench a minute?" Mr. Zebulon asked.

We had entered Capitol Square.

"Sure. Level with me, Granzeb. Did Big Flem really make up his own mind to help the church, or did you do it for him?"

"Both. He's a businessman and a scientist, and he doesn't know much of anything else. But he is sensitive to what's right when somebody lays out the facts. His impulse to do right was probably more important than any fears for the company's bad public relations. The PR wouldn't have been all that bad. It would be the state, the university, who's tearing down the church, not Slemp and Hygeia. Apart from that, sure, I helped the cause."

"Out of pure motives?"

"Of course not. What sort of an insipid creature do you take me for? My motives were thoroughly dishonorable. To take advantage of you."

"Swine," Miss Tebell said. "The Girl Scout manual never covered this."

They laughed. I could not understand why.

"The only time I had some faint flash of altruism," he continued more seriously, "was when I read about the Reverend Mott Gooch. To make my report to Mr. Slemp, I did some research. And I came across Mr. Gooch."

"And he was . . ."

"I'm trying to tell you. Before the Civil War, amazingly, Main Street Presbyterian had more black members than white. Of course, it wasn't my kind of integration. Most of them were slaves. They had to sit in the back and in the balcony, with your famous organ. But they were enthusiastic members, and they loved the church.

"The custom, when a church had so many black members, was to have a black assistant pastor to minister to them. That was Mott Gooch. He had been a slave, had bought his own freedom, and then the freedom of his family. This was not too long after the present building was erected. The church was thriving, and decided to send its first missionary to Africa. Mr. Gooch volunteered. He became not only Byrdport's first missionary to a non-Christian land, but he was a black man to boot." Mr. Zebulon grew silent.

"That got to you?" Miss Tebell prompted.

"A little. It made the whole thing more human to me."

"You mean it stirred one-eighth of you?"

"That's a bit unfair, isn't it?" Mr. Zebulon responded.

"Sorry. Diplomacy was never my forte. But . . . you never seemed sensitive . . . in fact you've joked . . ."

"About being black? We have to either joke or fight."

"About being one-eighth black," Miss Tebell corrected.

"According to the old laws, which were just repealed a few years ago, one-sixteenth was enough to constitute legal blackness. Period. You were black, or you were white."

"Who was the, ah . . ."

"Who in my family? Some distant great-grandmother. She had a child by a white schoolteacher who came down in Reconstruction times. One of the good Carpetbaggers. All their descendants, including my own father until twenty years ago, were considered black. They were all teachers. They taught in black schools."

"You could have been a teacher and taught anywhere. How come you broke the tradition?"

"I wanted to get into TV."

"Now I remember you!" Miss Tebell shouted. "Weren't you the Channel Seven weatherman?"

"Yeah. Later I covered city hall. Then the Capitol. That's how I met Mr. Slemp. His lobbyist was retiring, and he needed a new one."

"Any regrets about leaving the news and signing on with a rampant capitalist like Flem Slemp?" Miss Tebell asked.

"If Flem Slemp is a rampant capitalist, then it's okay with me. He is no robber baron. Businessmen are as varied as any group. I agree with Montaigne that 'the souls of emperors and cobblers are cast in the same mold. The same reason that makes us wrangle with a neighbor causes a war betwixt princes.' "

"Mr. Slemp is certainly an emperor," Miss Tebell said. "An emperor with the key to saving Main Street Presbyterian."

"No, that's your baby," Mr. Zebulon said. "All you have to do is find three hundred thousand dollars. And get the governor to declare the church surplus property."

"Granzeb, the magnitude of it just hit me. What am I going to do?"

"Charge admission to the phantom's concerts," he said.

"I may be that desperate," she said. "Do you really think there's a phantom of the organ?"

"If there were no phantom, it might be necessary to invent one."

"Then you think it's somebody's figment?"

"Why don't we go over tonight and see? Or hear?" Mr. Zebulon said.

I was relieved when she accepted the invitation, for it meant a safe ride back through Capitol Square, a scene of dangers I had no desire to experience again on foot. Yet, I told myself, I would have ventured it, as I had promised to return to Serena after the meeting.

As my companions rose from the bench, I thought of how wonderful it would be to play the organ for Miss Tebell! I could do it tonight, but only by departing Live Oak Row earlier and alone, and taking my chances in the trek across Capitol Square.

But I remembered the dog, and decided to wait and ride with Miss Tebell. How quickly we grow spoiled.

CHAPTER 9

THE MOUSE IS ONE OF FEW ANIMALS WHICH MAN HAS observed with percipience. Once I heard Dr. Christie, in a sermon, quote an ancient Roman named Plautus as having said, "Consider the little mouse. How sagacious an animal it is which never entrusts its life to one hole only." That is quite accurate as well as empathetic, and Plautus said it in 200 B.C. Man and mouse have lived together for a long time. But when imagination has filled the gap in humans' knowledge of animals, the results have been pure fiction, not science.

Consider the lion, a beast enjoying the prestige of royalty, perceived as noble, brave, and fierce. In squalid truth, Leo prefers to scavenge the provender already killed by other, more honest predators, such as wild dogs. The food that lions do kill is almost always brought down by the female, whereupon the male rushes up and eats most of it. If nothing remains when the female finishes, the cubs are left to starve.

An animal at the other pole of reputation, the hyena, is seen as a cowardly, slinking thief of others' choice cuts. In fact, he is a brave, well-organized hunter who plans his attack with the fierce sagacity of a Stonewall Jackson.

The wolf? His character was blighted forever by Little Red Riding Hood. Who could believe the truth, which is that wolves are rather timid souls who mate for life and enjoy touchingly strong family relationships? And the gorilla? An almost pathologically shy, gentle beast who eats vegetables, who as a climber is such a klutz that he often falls to the ground, and who is so diffident romantically that his libido is aroused only once a year.

By the time we returned to Miss Tebell's apartment I was so hungry that, like the slandered hyena, I could have attacked a zebra. Luckily, my first encounter in the kitchen was with a Smithfield ham.

I waited impatiently for evening. Mr. Zebulon had said he would return to the apartment at 10:00 P.M. It must have been substantially earlier when someone rang the old-fashioned mechanical doorbell downstairs, producing a sound like rocks churning in a bucket. Miss Tebell emerged from the bathroom in a heavy woolen robe, ferociously toweling her hair. Then the visitor downstairs must have seen the modern electrical doorbell connecting to her apartment, for it rang, too. Miss Tebell went to a speaker box beside her door. "Who is it?" she asked.

"It's Caleb," a voice quacked from the box.

"Oh, Lord," she muttered. Then she pushed a button, and something buzzed and clicked downstairs. Moments later, Dr. Old entered the apartment.

"I was working late and on the spur of the moment I thought I'd come by. Your light was on," he said defensively.

"It's okay, Caleb," she said.

"What a beautiful room. I must be turning soft. I always wanted nothing but modern furniture, but these old walnut and mahogany pieces look better all the time."

Miss Tebell grinned. "It happens. Did you just pop in to admire the furniture?"

Dr. Old seated himself in her best wing chair. He took off his glasses, and rubbed his eyes in fatigue. "Perhaps to admire the owner. Let's see, I forget. Are your legs Queen Anne or rococo?"

"La, sir. Don't be indecent. At the time this parlor was

built, you could have been disgraced for such talk. Even pianos had limbs, not legs. But judge for yourself." From her own perch on a sofa she extended her legs, and wriggled her feet in their furry slippers. Hidden muscles rippled cunningly down to blade-slim ankles.

"As good as ever," Caleb Old said.

"Oh, you always were a leg man. Now, quit kidding and tell me to what do I owe the honor, et cetera."

"I thought you might like to know how your preservation activities are going down with my colleagues at BUSM," he said.

"I'd guess I'm not too popular," she said.

"Were my fellow doctors making nominations for saint-hood, then Typhoid Mary and the Bitch of Buchenwald would get more votes. You have cut a colossal shine before the medical community. I suppose you were unaware that the plans of doctors are sacrosanct. We greet opposition at first with pleasant, wry tolerance, assuming that the poor lunkhead will see his error, repent, and get out of the way. You have not done so. Therefore, you have activated phase two. An icy chill. Angry, contemptuous dismissal. All I can say is, if you get sick any time soon, let me have you admitted to some other hospital."

"Oh, Caleb, I guess it doesn't matter if they like me or not. But does it mean that you guys will stonewall on Main Street Presbyterian?"

"A lot of them are saying that. There are many reasons being propounded why any slight delay in the new building would bring the end of civilization as we know it."

Miss Tebell glanced at her watch. "And how do you feel about it, Caleb?"

"I have decided, as to postponing the new BUSM building, that at worst, a change would be a slight aggravation. As to any personal, active wish to preserve the church, well, I must say that after your luncheon meeting today I walked up and took a good look. I do admit — to you and nobody else — the old building has a certain nobility. Especially when compared to the boring high-rises with their turquoise inserts which we have erected all around it." A grin illuminated his angular face. "But, then, my opinion is suspect. I've been corrupted and undermined."

"By what?"

"By a pair of antique limbs," he said.

"They're not antique. A bit Art Deco, maybe." She looked again at her watch. "Well, Caleb, I'm sure it's been a tough day for both of us and I . . ."

"Just a minute and I'll go. I've been terribly upset since that night in the Rib Cage two weeks ago. I want to apologize for my behavior."

"Unnecessary but accepted. It wasn't fair for me to blind-side you like I did. On our reunion, as it were," she said.

"And I would like to say that if you would see me again, I would be awfully glad. I find that I'd like to ply you with French food, wine, and concerts. Or barbecue, beer, and stock car racing. I — "

"Either way would be nice," she said. "I'll think about it. We can decide . . ."

The doorbell rang.

"Well, Caleb, I do have these plans for tonight," she said, faintly shrill. She pushed the button by the door with apparent unease. "Now, Caleb, just be cool about this and remember I have promised we'll talk about things."

"Be cool about what?"

Granville Zebulon walked through the parlor door.

"Oh," Dr. Old said.

I took advantage of the few moments of stilted greetings that ensued, and made an unobserved running dive into Miss Tebell's purse. From there I heard Dr. Old clumping down the stairs.

"I hadn't heard that house calls were coming back," Mr. Zebulon said.

"If you must know, we were discussing furniture types. Now fix yourself a drink while I get dressed."

As we walked through the square to Main Street and the church I began to feel pangs of unease, if not of active guilt.

Miss Tebell and Mr. Zebulon were going over to investigate the Phantom of the Organ, but the phantom would not play tonight. A full third of him now bounced and swayed against the gentle curve of Miss Tebell's right hip. I began regretting my timidity in not departing earlier. And now, although the problem of crossing the square in safety had been solved, once on the sidewalk near the church how could I bail out? I had failed to consider that.

"Gee, there must be a hundred people there," Miss Tebell said. "Look. Two prowl cars. Three television vans. The smell of pot in the air. It's an event."

Confused snatches of conversation now penetrated the purse.

". . . ain't gon' play tonight."

"Crowd scairt him away."

Another voice seemed to direct itself to Miss Tebell.

"Aren't you with Historic Byrdport?"

"Yes."

"Alton Pannebacker, from the *Byrdport Enquirer*. I wonder if you're aware that it's being suggested this is a publicity stunt to get attention for the church."

"Who's saying that?" Miss Tebell asked.

"Some doctors at the medical college, I believe."

"Well, if it's a publicity stunt, it sure has worked, hasn't it?"

The reporter had a flat, stubborn persistence.

"Did your organization have anything to do with this organ story?" he demanded.

"No," Miss Tebell said. "We might have, if we'd thought of it first. Have you actually heard it?"

"Heard what?" the reporter asked.

"The organ, for crying out loud," she said.

"Personally, no. I have interviewed some who have claimed to. They say he's not very good."

I gritted my teeth.

"Well, there you are," Miss Tebell said. "If we'd engaged an organist, he would have been a good one."

We paced slowly on the sidewalk for some fifteen minutes more. I could feel Miss Tebell trembling with cold.

"It must be ten above, Granzeb," she quavered. "Let's go into the Rib Cage and warm up."

"Excellent. Wouldn't you know we'd come on the phantom's night off?"

The restaurant's familiar odors rolled upon me. We bumped into a seat, and Miss Tebell searched the purse for a tissue. A finger brushed my coat, sparking mixed shivers of danger and pleasure that traveled along my spine. The latch was open; I could, and should, have made my silent departure and returned to the church, but I saw no harm in lingering a few minutes. I might overhear some pertinent information.

"Viola da Gamba's on tonight," Mr. Zebulon said. "See? That brunette waitress with the great bones?"

"And great pectoral development," Miss Tebell said. "So. A personal friend of yours?"

"Not of mine. Nooo, indeedy. She belongs to Mr. Junior."

"Oh, come on Granzeb. The scion of Byrdport's leading industry slumming with a dago waitress? Though I will admit she is a dish, if you're impressed by spectacular carriage, perfect teeth, hair like onyx, flawless skin, and mountainous chest. Me, I loathe her," Miss Tebell said.

"Waitress she may be, but not a dago," Mr. Zebulon said. "Her real name is Viola Lipschitz and she's an aspiring actress. So far, her only roles have been ingenues in local dinner theater productions, Byrdport not being exactly Broadway south. She works here between jobs. Actually, I hear she's not half bad as an actress."

"Here comes the paragon now," Miss Tebell said archly.

"Heighdy, Viola," Mr. Zebulon said cheerfully. "What's new in the footlight set?"

"Hey, Granzeb. Nothin' much. I read for *Glass Menagerie* at the Horse Barn last week, but I didn't score. I thought I read pretty well," the waitress said.

"*The Glass Menagerie*? Good God, Vi, no wonder. Of two women in the play, one is middle-aged and the young one is a homely pathetic creature, a dog, a cripple. I really don't think that's your play," Mr. Zebulon said.

"Maybe not. They all but promised me Roxanne in *Cyrano*, though. That's up next."

Miss Tebell and Mr. Zebulon ordered beer and sandwiches.

"She's made for Roxanne," Miss Tebell said. "All those looks and a brain the size of a walnut. Lord, how depressing for me. I must be fourteen or fifteen years older than Viola. I'm literally old enough to be her mother. How old are you, Granzeb?"

"Is that important?"

"Depends."

"I'm twenty-eight," he said.

"I'm pushing thirty-seven," Miss Tebell said.

"So who's counting?"

"Everybody. 'The immortal gods alone have neither age nor death. All other things almighty time disquiets,' " she said.

"Sophocles, right?" Mr. Zebulon said. "But it should not matter. I promise I have never once thought about it."

"Thanks, Granzeb."

She fished for her wallet, and clinked some change into the jukebox.

"Playing . . . ?" he asked.

"B-Seventeen. 'The Song Nobody Knows.' Funny how I didn't like it at first. It seemed terribly sad. But lately I love it. It occurs to me that if you took away the modern arrangement, it would have the dearest antique sound. I really can't explain why. I don't know enough about music. But something in that song reminds me of the Civil War era music. Or Stephen Foster's later work, like 'Beautiful Dreamer.' "

"What are you, some kind of time traveler?" Mr. Zebulon laughed.

"You should know better," she said gently. "I'm very much a modern woman."

I certainly knew, and I found it disquieting.

The hour grew late. I had to return to Serena and Grandpa, and with great care I emerged from the open mouth of Miss Tebell's purse. Far above me she soared, like a goddess painted on a palace ceiling, her golden head bathed in light from the Rib Cage's fly-specked fluorescent tubes. Her expression was sweet and vulnerable and ineffably sad. Below the table, I noted that one of Mr. Zebulon's well-polished wingtip shoes insistently pushed against one of her brown pumps. She did not withdraw, nor did she seem to be pushing back.

The jukebox cried as I left the booth.

Now someone sing again the song
That only lovers hear,
The one that put the world in tune
Whenever she was near,
I can't recall a single word,
Or how the music goes,
Won't someone play once more for me
The Song Nobody Knows.

I encountered Sidney in the walls. It was good to see his swarthy, worried face.

"Charles. Do not think I am prying. But how is Serena? Is everything still okay between you?"

I assured him Serena was fine and that our relationship was satisfactory. "I'm on my way home right now," I said.

"Good. The reason I asked is as follows. That mouse Earl, remember him? The one that lives in the Mercedes? He has been unhappy since Serena left him for you. He still hangs around here a lot, and he asked about her. I have not told him she's living in the church next door."

"Thanks, Sidney. Do you think he might try to make trouble for us?"

"Who can say. My advice to you is to make sure Serena is happy and well looked after," Sidney said.

I gave my assurances. Then I crossed the alley to the church. Toward the street, I could see the remnant of a motley crowd of sensation-seekers on the sidewalk. They would be disappointed. The darkened sanctuary was quiet as I entered through a cellar window. Upward through the great stuccoed walls I advanced to the choir loft and home.

Serena lay on our paper nest. Grandpa sat beside her, holding her paw. Their expressions were grave.

"About time," he said softly. "We about gave you up.

Look." He pointed to Serena's right flank, which was darkened and matted with dried blood. A long gash was the source of the blood.

"What happened?" I cried.

"Alabama Ruby," Grandpa said. "Serena's lucky to be alive."

"I was just careless," she said. "But I was so worried about you that I couldn't keep still in the organ. I was up in the window behind the choir, looking at the crowd out in the street, and I didn't see the cat until she was almost there."

"Ruby caught her with one swipe. Serena was able to jump for the window sash hole," Grandpa said.

"The cut's not very deep," Serena said. "I'll be fine."

"When did this happen?"

"About an hour ago," she said.

An hour. I was relaxing in the Rib Cage with Miss Tebell and Mr. Zebulon. Had I returned when I should, this would not have happened. Dr. Christie once said in a sermon that no witness is so dreadful, no accuser so terrible as the conscience that dwells in the heart of every man. But was a mouse required to feel this badly?

"How can I make this up to you?" I blurted.

"Don't be so melodramatic," Serena said. "I'll tell you how. By not going off and leaving me."

"I promise."

"And you might make yourself useful by fixing the nest. Look what a mess it is. Blood everywhere."

Grateful for the opportunity to do something helpful and physical, I hauled away clumps of soiled shredded paper, while relating the day's activities to Serena and Grandpa. I described the meeting at the Canal Boat, as well as indications of an incipient triangle formed by Miss Tebell, Mr. Zebulon, and Dr. Old.

"What's going to come of it?" Grandpa asked.

"Nobody really knows. Some concede a chance the church may be saved, but there would remain the question of what to do with it."

"I think we better start considering a new place to light," Grandpa said. "Even if the church ain't destroyed, there'd probly be nothing to eat for a mighty long time. It's getting bad enough as it is."

"We can go to the Rib Cage," Serena said. "Sidney and Rebecca would be glad to have us."

I could not feel that our permanent happiness lay at the Rib Cage. "After all," I said, "we're churchmice. We might consider going to the new church, out in the suburbs."

"Not me," Grandpa said. "It'll be too fancy. I'd rather go to one of the black churches a few blocks from here. There at least we'd have plenty food and good music." He paused. "Of course, we could do a sight worse than moving over to the Capitol. Except when the Assembly's in session, it's a good place. They'll be gone in a few weeks."

I thought of Miss Tebell's apartment as a permanent home. Something prevented me from suggesting it.

As we talked, I pulled to the nest several large sheets of paper. They came from a stack which, as I have explained, rested on the organ floor just inside one of the case's doors.

"Everything about this place is ancient," I mused, studying one of the sheets. "Look at this old music. Here is one that doesn't look like organ music. I wonder what it's doing in here?"

"You mean it couldn't be played on an organ?" Serena asked.

"I guess it could be played on an organ, but it was not intended to be. It's like the stuff Mr. Hudson refers to as secular." I returned to the pile and looked at other sheets. "In fact, most of this is secular. It all looks very old. I wish we could read the printed words."

I remembered Miss Tebell and the young archaeologist, and how they said the different artifacts forged a link with the long ago.

"Look," I said. "These appear to be original manuscripts, not printed scores." I pulled one from the pile. It was wrinkled, yellow, and partially eaten by the bugs called silverfish. I studied the faded pen writing on the score, and the inked-in notes that marched and jumped across the five-line staffs.

"I believe that with a little more practice, we could learn to read music," I said.

"Right now, Charles, I'm more interested in lying on it than in reading it," Serena said.

"Sorry." I began shredding one of the better-preserved papers. In a few minutes I had produced a comfortable new nest. With a relieved sigh, Serena eased into it. Grandpa retired to his own chaotic quarters.

I sat by Serena until I thought she was asleep. Then I lay down beside her.

"I meant it, Charles," she said. "Don't leave me anymore."

"I won't. I promised, didn't I?"

Serena's injury healed faster than anticipated. By Friday afternoon she was walking about the organ with only a slight limp, and her recovery seemed assured. But she was plainly unable to forage for food, so Grandpa and I had to provide for her. We worried about the supply until we discovered a mound of freshly delivered loaves of bread in the church kitchen.

"Communion Sunday coming!" Grandpa whooped. We tore open a wrapper, ate our fill of bread, and returned to Serena with great snowy chunks dangling from our mouths. For the first time in my life I learned the satisfaction that flows from supplying food to a loved one. I almost resented Grandpa's presence, and his relentless, confident, bustling about. I needed to work and serve and expiate the guilt still nagging me from Serena's accident.

Does a martyr always lurk in the shadows of generosity?

CHAPTER 10

"LET'S GO TO PREACHIN'," GRANDPA SAID. IT WAS SUN-day morning and the church thumped and buzzed with human occupants.

"You two go along," Serena said. "That's still too much walking for me."

"Promise you won't leave the Erben?" I said.

"Don't worry. Besides, I can hear everything from here almost as well as you can from that hole in the attic. The view just isn't as good."

"It's hard to believe this is the next-to-last meeting in the old church," Grandpa said while we trudged across the attic floor. Only Grandpa would still use the archaic expression "meeting." The more I observed him, the more he seemed a living link with some vanished era. I promised myself to encourage his oral reminiscences, and commit them to study.

We took our places at the rim of the hole above the pulpit. Far below, the old sanctuary never looked better. Either on stern instructions from Dr. Christie, or from pride stirred by a need to send the battered theological liner off on a final cruise with all flags flying, Jackson Ward had polished brass until its reflections stung the eyes. And Mr. Hudson was in exceptional form on the electronic organ. To my delight he played Bach's "Prelude and Fugue in E Flat."

But Dr. Christie's sermon faltered in its trajectory, and fell wobbling to earth. He appeared tired and excessively cautious. I concluded he was preoccupied, for when he completed his sermon he neglected to manipulate the hidden control panel. Normally, he would have switched off the spotlight that played from above our observation hole, and he would have brought up the sanctuary lights. But he did not, and the dramatic pulpit lighting remained in place.

It was time for church announcements.

"I would like to express regret for the recent melodramatic publicity about the so-called Phantom of the Organ," Dr. Christie said. "Each of us suffers embarrassment from these sensationalized reports in the media. I wish I could tell you we had settled the matter."

"I don't think he likes our playin', Charles," Grandpa said.

"Through a trick we have not fathomed," Dr. Christie continued, "someone has simulated the sounds of a pipe organ."

"Simulated, eh?" Grandpa muttered.

"As to whether it has any connection with the sudden campaign to preser-rr-ve this building, for whatever tentative purposes someone may have in mind, I simply do not know. Some of the more impressionable are even claiming the phantom music to be a supernatural sign. On that, my feeling is emphatically in the negative. I think we have passed the day of signs. I think of this still-inexplicable 'phantom' as just a noisy nuisance."

Grandpa pulled himself back from the edge of the hole. He reached to the old nest I had constructed nearby, and filled both forepaws with shredded paper. Then he moved back to the hole, and with a wink at me, hurled the litter into the void. Then he went back for another load.

We looked down as the trash fluttered in slow motion along the brilliant shaft of light. Like confetti tossed from a skyscraper, the nest rubbish shimmered and swirled downward until it filled the vertical beam with majestic refulgence. And like some melancholy hero discomfited by his own parade, Dr. Christie looked up as the mess came down. He did not flinch. When the last scrap had settled on his black-robed shoulders, as he still stared up into the light, I saw his lips form the words, "Why, Lord?"

Back in the Erben, Serena listened in high spirits as I described Grandpa's shocking exploit.

"I've heard of pennies from Heaven, Grandpa, but really! Shame on you."

"Ezekiel saw the wheel, these humans say," Grandpa chortled. "I figured, poor old Doc Christie, he probly never got a heavenly sign before. So I give him one."

Grandpa was so buouyant from the experience that he did not object, late that Sunday night, when I suggested a brief concert.

"We've laid off for a while now. Let's wait until around 2:00 A.M. and play a few bars. Just a few," I said.

"Why the hell not?" Grandpa said.

"I won't be too frisky," Serena said, "but it would be good to hear a few honks and squeaks."

"Since we're in such an irreverent mood anyway, let's try something different," I said. I ran to the stack of ancient sheet music and pulled out a torn, decayed specimen, one which I had noted earlier as probably a rather simple secular melody.

Thus it happened, with Grandpa on lookout, that Serena and I worked on a strange new musical routine. Doubtless we made a ruin of the old melody. For a time we despaired of forming anything at all of the notes. But ultimately they began to make some sense.

We played from a score.

The title had been partially eaten away by bugs, and anyway, we could not have read it.

But somehow the refrain sounded familiar.

By Tuesday the communion bread remnants were gone. A solitary Sunday remained before the last pious exercises at Main Street Presbyterian passed into memory. It was reasonable to assume that additional rations would not be stocked.

"We have a choice," I reported after a careful kitchen search. "Bathroom soap, or glue from the hymnal bindings. Most of the hymnals are so old that the glue retains nothing of its original flavor."

"At best, glue tastes like mildew," Grandpa said. "Now the soap I don't mind at all. You can count on Presbyterians to have good, traditional soap. None of that stuff with cold cream in it, and sissy smells."

There is no accounting for taste, I thought.

Serena, exercising her leg, reacted with disgust. "I'm dying for some knockwurst," she said. "I think I can make it to the Rib Cage."

"No, no, no," I said. "The alley is dangerous. You know what's often out there: cats, dogs, winos. You may really have to sprint. Can you do that?"

Serena was silent.

"I thought not. Look, I'll go over and bring something back. I've made that run so many times, I know exactly what to do," I said.

Serena argued halfheartedly. But finally she said, "With a little Dijon mustard, please," and I dropped into the walls.

It was almost midafternoon. A good time; in the Rib Cage, many lunches would have been consumed, with many leftovers scraped into galvanized cans or piled on stainless steel carts. It was safer to raid the wasted food first. No excitable cook with a cleaver watched the garbage. I could not afford to lose any more of my tail.

Surveying the alley from a basement window of the church, I saw straightaway an unexpected aggravation: the Mercedes convertible of Mr. Flemmons R. Slemp, Jr. I did not care that he had parked in a restricted zone, but the car was an obstacle impeding my path and vision. I studied the alley with extra care, but saw no dangers. And indeed I shot easily across the alley, fancying myself as a sleek, implacable, food-seeking missile.

The food-gathering instinct, routinely constant in all of us, undergoes some bizarre transformation under the stress of love. And I did love Serena. If our relationship then did not quite sustain the level of ecstasy of those early days together in the Rib Cage, I can only aver that the fury of a new love affair cannot endure for long. It is tempered by the strains and bumblings and misunderstandings of life. If it subsides into deep happiness together, that is the most that can be asked. And there are individual complications, such as the ill-advised, ill-starred fascination for Miss Tebell which intruded itself into the idyll which Serena and I should have been living.

But my point is the compulsion to provide for one's lover. In human terms, you might say I itched to grow vegetables. I longed to heap them, musty-smelling from the earth, in a rumbling jumble on her kitchen table. I yearned to carry a rifle into the forest, bring down wild game, and drop it limp and sinuous at her feet. Scavenging at the Rib Cage was a pallid substitute, but it was all I had.

My dash across the alley ended in a bravura leap into the Rib Cage cellar, almost at the feet of Sidney and Rebecca.

"Love," Sidney said disgustedly. "What fools it makes."

"I beg your pardon, Sidney," I said.

"Oh, he didn't mean you, Charles," Rebecca said. "He was referring to the relationship between Viola the waitress and that little man who always comes around."

"Mr. Junior," I said.

"Who else?" Sidney said. "She's up there sitting with him right now when she should be cleaning up. At this moment, cleaning up. She may be fired. She should be fired."

"They do not as a usual rule fire waitresses who look like Viola," Rebecca said tartly.

"You think it's possible she is pursuing Mr. Junior for his money, Sidney?" I asked.

The swarthy mouse rolled his eyes upward. "Your innocence is always refreshing, Charles."

"No, Sidney," I said. "It's not that simple between those two."

"Hah. Come and watch the way she works on him," Rebecca said.

I was curious. It would hurt nothing to delay a few minutes. I followed Sidney and Rebecca to the booth occupied by Viola da Gamba and Mr. Junior.

By now the two females whom I had observed with obsessive curiosity, Serena and Miss Tebell, had humbled me by the power of beauty. Earlier in my story, I referred to points of consensus by which any creature's looks may be judged. But consensus is an imperfect and superficial apparatus. Despite all our striving to analyze beauty, its finer points remain ineffable. If you want to advance to a philosophical level of maddening opacity, try to fathom the impact of beautiful features upon

107

those who fall in love with them. Thus do beauty and attraction get mixed up together. Try grasping the collective impact of a certain tilt of nose, curve of eyebrow, flash of dimple. Their appeal is undefinable.

Why do we fall in love with some, but not others? Was there someone who loved us in brief and misty babyhood, leaving us programmed with adoring response to a full mouth, or wide hazel eyes, or soft line of cheek? The reminders of such a person, such a ghost, may account for much of what we call attraction, translated by our subconcious into a perception of beauty. Beauty is a terrible complication. It drives us mad. Yet, looking at some we acknowledge beautiful, the seismic needle on our desire gauge does not flicker.

Even that oversimplifies the matter, for it implies we are either attracted or not. Maybe it would be well that love were that uncomplicated. While one love may set off a huge detonation and bounce the needle off the gauge, others may create lesser blasts.

I thought about all that as I gazed through the jukebox control at Viola da Gamba. Soon I got down to basics, and recognized one of the few absolutes of beauty. While flawless skin and hair, an exemplary smile, and superlative eyes may point to beauty, they will be wasted if arranged on an imperfect structure. You must start with the bones.

Viola da Gamba's bones would have agitated the dreams of an orthopedic surgeon.

She did not project the lusty strength of Serena, or the carefree blonde verve of Miss Tebell, but Miss da Gamba was a smoky genetic masterpiece with the conformation of a yearling thoroughbred. Why, indeed, would she tolerate such a gnome as Mr. Junior? Was Sidney correct? Was money that important?

I learned that apparently, it was not. Sidney was wrong.

"I'm doing fine, Junior," she was saying. "Look. You've always been very generous, hon, and I appreciate it. In fact your gifts have been excessive." She smiled. Imagine an explosion in a pearl diver's treasure chest.

"Aw, Viola, they haven't either. I like to make you happy," Mr. Junior said.

"And you do. It's just that you must understand my raw ambition to succeed as an actress."

Every softly chiseled plane of that slender head seemed crafted by some Olympian stage manager for maximum effect under lights.

"But there's no need for you to keep on hustling pizzas and knockwurst," Mr. Junior said. "Let me take care of you to that extent. Or, if you just gotta work while you're not acting, I'll give you something to do with the basketball team. I'm going to have lots of jobs open."

"That's sweet, Junior, but I don't know anything about the game."

"You wouldn't have to. I — "

"Don't you see? I'm learning about life. I'm suffering a little as meanwhile I hustle pizzas. And I'm meeting all kinds of people, which is important for an actress. Besides, I like to be independent. I'm not quite ready to be a kept woman yet. Maybe someday I won't mind. But now I must keep trying. I'm only nineteen, Junior, after all."

Flemmons R. Slemp, Jr., sighed heavily.

"Sometimes I wish I'd met you before I started in the basketball business," he said. "That's taking too much of my time."

"But how's it going, Junior?"

"Fine. I've just about hired a general manager who knows all the ins and outs of the draft and stuff."

"Do you have lots of good players?"

"I don't have any players. It's a new team in a new league. The action starts next winter for the first time. I became one of the league's charter members when I outbid some guys down in Tidewater for the franchise. Boy, were they disappointed."

"Why don't they just start their own team?"

"Because nobody would play them. They wouldn't belong to any league."

Beyond my appreciation for Miss da Gamba the conversation had proved of scant interest to me, and I knew if I dallied longer Serena would worry and grow hungrier. I searched through some unscraped dishes on the busboy's table, found a juicy portion of knockwurst, clamped it firmly in my jaws, and headed for home.

I do not believe I was careless. What happened was an accident beyond my control.

Camouflaged by the light and shadow of midafternoon, Alabama Ruby lay on the cobblestones in the alley, under the Mercedes.

We saw each other simultaneously when I was midway in the alley. Far quicker than I, she cut off my line of progress in a few liquid steps. I started back toward the Rib Cage, but I knew she would overtake me before I could reach it. My only hope was to find cover somewhere under the car. Circling to its rear, I leaped to the back axle and bounded onto the big round bulge in its middle.

But I was not safe there. Almost languidly, Alabama Ruby pulled herself onto the axle. It was a tight squeeze for her. But she began wriggling toward me.

"Oh, *Chawles*," she purred. "I almost think you're avoidin' me. Come on, Sweetie, just a little *touch*."

She was within inches of my face. By now, my eyes had adjusted to the dim light that reached the dark, convoluted inner recesses of the chassis. I saw a horizontal crack, a space of about one inch, opening just above me into total darkness. Aiming carefully at the space, I jumped from the axle.

I was now on the fuel tank, slung close under the trunk floor. I had ample clearance, and safety from the cat, though it was unpleasant enough when her face appeared at the opening. She shot one saberlike claw into the space, but could not reach me.

"Do you have plenty of time, Chuckie?" she taunted, eyes glowing into the crack. "I sure do. Guess we'll just have to see who las' the longest, seein' as how you play so hawd to get."

"I have all the time in the world," I said, hoping my voice did not shake.

But the wait was neither long nor affected by patience. As we glared at each other, a car door opened. The vehicle rocked as someone entered it; the door slammed, and the sound of the starter came grinding through the chassis in loud amplification. The cat looked around uneasily.

Then the car moved.

"Bye-bye for now, Chawles," Alabama Ruby hissed. She dropped from the axle and disappeared. At least I was free of the cat. Yet what remained was threatening, too: if I clung to the immediate safety of the car, what then? Where would I go with Mr. Junior's Mercedes? I looked down from the edge of the tank. Already we were moving too fast to drop out safely. There was a quick pause at the street, but before I could steel myself for a jump, the car shot forward into traffic.

No creature ever began an automobile journey in greater wretchedness. I was an unwilling chip on a mechanical wave. Strange mutterings in the chassis, the hiss of tires, the background roar of wind, the random harsh Babel from surrounding traffic: they combined in syncretized terror. What could I do but persevere? We did stop briefly at intersections, but the thought of swinging down to a congested city street at midafternoon, far from home, was even less appealing than the ride.

Thus I stayed with the car. I wondered what Serena was thinking — that I had abandoned her, hurt and hungry?

We rode for about twenty minutes. The noise of traffic subsided; the car made several turns; its tires crunched into gravel. The car's engine was extinguished. I heard the sounds of Mr. Junior exiting the car and walking away. And then I heard a form of rare and beautiful music: the cheeping of songbirds. Even in the dead of winter, Byrdport retained a sizable ornithic population.

Apart from their songs, there was no sound.

I dropped to the smooth orange gravel and reconnoitered.

For a city mouse, it was a scene of unimaginable beauty. The car rested in a courtyard behind a mansion. I have learned since that the architectural style was Georgian. Picture a central structure of three full stories and a high slate roof, surmounted by a white pineapple. On either end, two-story wings completed a composition of classic symmetry.

Facing each other across the courtyard were two buildings of smaller scale but similar architecture. Beyond them, at the far end of the courtyard, was a four-car garage. To either side of that I could see the beginning of a formal garden. Plump dark green boxwoods marched in rows and circles, and pyracantha berries flamed against salmon-hued brick walls.

Yet this was no country estate, for through the bare trees of February I could see the rooftops of similar houses.

I considered my options. There would probably be an op-

111

portunity to return downtown, but when? Meanwhile, I was cold and hungry. Several times I had thought of Earl, Serena's former friend, who reputedly had lived in the Mercedes. Was he still there, in the upholstery? If so, could he advise me? I decided to hold that possibility as a last resort, and explore on my own. I made for the great house.

The rich fortify themselves well. I searched for chinks in the structural fabric, found none, and almost despaired when I discovered the kitchen venting system. There, I was able to enter through a partly open duct.

The kitchen was as big as the one in Main Street Presbyterian, but brighter and better equipped. A tray of leftover sandwiches sat on a counter in the butler's pantry. Gooseliver! I ate voraciously, despite my worry over the aborted mission to provide food — not half this good — for Serena. By now she must be frantic.

What I needed now was information on the occupants, to help plan my return downtown. The best source would be resident mice. I entered the walls and searched for telltale signs: a bit of loose hair here, a dropping there. Soon I came to what I was looking for, a mouse nest. It was the most grandiose I had ever seen.

"Anyone home?" I called.

"Is that you, Earl?" said a voice from inside.

"No," I said. "My name is Charles Churchmouse."

She was called Lianne, the mouse who lived in that extraordinary production. Lianne had little else to do in her pampered life but plan additions. The structure went on for yards in the south wall of the home of Flemmons R. Slemp. For it was he, Lianne was proud to confirm, who owned the wonderful house.

"How did you get here?" she asked.

"I rode with Mr. Junior," I said. "In the Mercedes."

"Oh. He lives out back in one of the smaller houses. Did you, ah, see anything of a mouse named Earl?"

"No. Does he live here? I mean, are you and he . . ."

Lianne had a way of looking at you for a long time before answering a question.

"He did, and we did. But Earl is not the kind to stay for long."

I said that neither was I. There was no need to explain that circumstances, not a rambling nature, accounted for my case. "What I have to do is get back downtown. Do you know anything about the Slemps' schedules?"

"Mr. Slemp goes to his factory every morning, but it's across the river in South Byrdport. Junior is unpredictable. He goes lots of places. So does the old man. Does that help?"

"It seems my best hope is to take off with Mr. Junior again and hope he returns to the Rib Cage. That's a restaurant where we are habitues," I said.

"What happpened to your tail?" Lianne asked. "It's kinda cute, bobbed like that."

"I lost most of it in a revival service, and the rest in a juke-box," I explained.

"You do get around, Charles. Hey, it's cocktail time. Why don't we go down?"

Lianne came close and took my forepaw. She certainly did smell nice.

CHAPTER 11

FROM A WALL IN THE SLEMP LIBRARY, WE ENTERED A bookcase filled with volumes bound in leather. I could see most of the walnut-paneled room, where a seated woman was reading a magazine with big yellow letters on its front. The woman appeared to be tall, and her white hair gleamed slightly blue. "That's Mrs. Slemp," Lianne said. "She says *Southern Living* is the finest magazine in the world."

Outside the house, gravel crunched under car wheels. Mrs. Slemp put down her magazine and drummed her fingers on a table. Just as Mr. Slemp entered one door, an elderly black man entered through another, carrying a small silver tray with a single glass and a dew-dampened pitcher.

"Thank you, Alonzo," Mr. Slemp said, plucking off the glass with a stubby hand. "Sure you won't have a little something, Mama?"

"Flemmons, for forty years you have asked me that, and for forty years my response has been the same. No. I just can't understand why you use that awful stuff."

"I don't use it, Mama, I drink it," Mr. Slemp said. "Well, Alonzo, up to the lips, over the gums; look out guts, here it comes."

"Yes, sir," Alonzo said.

"Leave the pitcher and go pour something for yourself," Mr. Slemp told the butler.

"Oh, Flemmons," Mrs. Slemp said. "One of these days."

"There was one teetotaling Episcopalian in Byrdport, and I had to marry her," Mr. Slemp said.

"My daddy was a Methodist, don't forget," Mrs. Slemp said. "Well! Speaking of churches, I heard all about the plans to save Main Street Presbyterian today. Imagine my surprise, when I had to learn of your involvement from Ditty Randolph at the garden club."

"My involvement?"

"Don't be coy with me, Flemmons. Ditty told all. About how you're giving three hundred thousand dollars, and how the preservation movement must scratch up the rest. Honestly, the way you give money away. But I must say it made me proud to hear about it."

Mrs. Slemp's eyes were a surprising china blue. I felt certain she had never been beautiful, but she must have once possessed a certain coltish appeal, which was not altogether destroyed by the sardonic work of time.

"Anything you'd like me to tell the governor tomorrow morning, Florine?" Mr. Slemp asked.

"That awful man? Just that I hope he decides not to run for the Senate in two years."

"I never tell a politician what to do," Mr. Slemp said. "I just try to work 'em so they don't realize it. Same technique they use. Sometimes I think there ain't anybody as gullible as a cynic."

"Er, how are things going with him, anyway?" she asked with an odd mixture of embarrassment and intrigue. "Not that I care, but the whole affair is rather interesting. I presume that what you're going to see him about pertains to . . . that special research."

"Yep. The answer is, it's going mighty good. Much better than we had ever dared hope. It's so amazing I can hardly believe it myself. Just look at what we've done. Florine, Hygeia is going to burn the barn with this product, when it comes to market."

"I'm so glad, Flemmons," she said.

I could make no sense of most of the conversation, except for the news that Mr. Slemp was going to the governor's office. The Capitol! That was almost as good as home for me. But not quite. I did not relish dropping from a car in broad daylight in the congested, crowded parking area of Capitol Square with the legislature in session.

"Flem Junior out tonight?" Mr. Slemp asked.

"I suppose. Honestly, since he moved out to the quarters and got interested in that basketball . . ."

"Mama, please, I asked you and asked you. Don't call it the quarters. It's like we were living back in slave times."

"But that's what it is. I mean the building. It was copied after slave quarters, even if it was built in 1940," she said.

"I just don't want to embarrass Alonzo and Novella."

"Flemmons, you'll never think like a Byrdporter, will you?"

"I hope to God not."

When the Slemps went in to dinner, Lianne turned close to me in the bookcase and whispered: "This is the best part. Come on."

Puzzled, I followed her to the small library table where Mr. Slemp's cocktail pitcher and glass remained on the silver tray.

"He usually leaves some in the glass," she said, pointing to about half an inch of clear liquid, cooled by the remains of an ice cube. "It's a good thing he likes them on the rocks, in a short, wide glass. If he ever went to straight-up, I don't know what I'd do."

"I haven't the faintest idea what you're talking about," I said.

"Martinis, of course. Don't tell me you don't like martinis."

"Oh, sure," I lied. I had never tasted hard liquor, though occasionally I had enjoyed a sip of wine in the Rib Cage.

"See how easy?" she said, jumping to the rim of the squat, heavy glass. "You couldn't do this with stemware. Come on." She carefully eased her upper body down the inside of the glass, and began sipping the martini.

"Perfect," she sighed. "Ah, that Alonzo."

At my first lapping, the martini was a disappointment:

cold, distant, far too subtle for my simple taste. But I was willing to persevere. Lianne certainly seemed to enjoy it. After several more gulps I was about to give up, when to my surprise I seemed to hear a faint arpeggio from the Erben's bell-like flute pipes. A hint of warm tingling played over my skin. Suddenly, a great chorusing of major pipes rocked my brain. I felt wonderful.

"This is — *hoop* — like being in love," I hiccuped.

"You got it, C. C.," said Lianne with a smile I can only describe as lascivious.

I slipped entirely to the bottom of the glass. The cold splash, which I scarcely felt, convulsed us with unaccountable laughter. I pulled Lianne in with me. We roared still more hilariously.

"This is unshanitary," I brayed between slurps.

"Next time, wash your — *wheep* — feet first," she guffawed.

When we finished the martini there was the problem of climbing from the glass, although it seemed anything but serious at the time. Lianne first tried climbing up on the olive, but it rolled, and her feet slipped off. Then she stuck one foot in the pimiento hole, as we wheezed uproariously. At length, by climbing on my back, she was able to pull herself over the rim. Then she reached in with a boost for me.

I recall little about our walk back to Lianne's place. According to her, I bellowed the complete lyrics of "The Song Nobody Knows" as we staggered across the table and through the bookcase, and then I roared the melodic theme of Purcell's "Toccata in A" as we traversed the walls.

As to the climax of that raucous, disgraceful episode, I cannot say. It will always remain a blur in my memory. I can only relate that in the morning, Lianne — despite what she described as the worst hangover of her life — was touchingly warm and appreciative. "I'm grateful, Charles," she said, caressing me softly. "I don't get much company these days. Why don't you stay for a day or so? Rest up. God, you look worn out."

The invitation was appealing, but even the hammers crashing in my skull could not deter me from journeying downtown as quickly as possible. I pondered what to do. Should I try to enter one of the Slemp cars? Should I again ride under-neath? The climate was growing colder. Suppose I became numb, and fell to the street?

"Mr. Slemp said he was going to the Capitol this morning," I said. "I wonder if that means he'll go there first, and not to the factory?"

Lianne did not know. "You'll just have to chance it. I'll tell you what. The thing to do is get in his briefcase, if it's there."

"What do you mean?"

Sometimes, she explained, Mr. Slemp carried important papers home at night, and returned them to the office next day. On those occasions he placed his briefcase on a hall table at night after reading the papers, and took it away in the morn-ing.

"Let's have a look," I said.

The briefcase was there. The device had no zipper, but its giant mouth was restrained by a kind of built-in spring. I found I could climb in and out with effort.

"It must be almost seven-thirty," Lianne said. "He'll be here soon."

She looked forlorn and not a little blowzy, but I liked her. She gave me a soft kiss. "You could always wait until tomor-row," she said. "But I know you won't."

I entered the leather case to wait for Mr. Slemp. Time dragged as I tried to flatten myself and not make a suspicious bulge in the soft, light leather. Then, with an instant's warn-ing from the sound of rapidly approaching feet, I was roughly jerked off the table. In short, jarring strides, nothing like the smooth pace of Miss Tebell, Mr. Slemp marched to his automo-bile, and we were on our way.

My fear was that we would go directly to Hygeia Pharma-ceuticals, where Mr. Slemp might discard the case before trav-eling to the Capitol. I could be left behind at the plant. And in-deed, my heart plunged when the "Good mornings" barked by gate guards, receptionists, and secretaries made it clear that Mr. Slemp's first call this morning was at his place of business. In his style of rough jollity he asked questions, issued orders, teased, and bantered. Soon we entered his private office.

"Please find Dr. McIntosh and send him in," Mr. Slemp

said to someone. The tyooon rustled papers impatiently as he hummed a country song.

"Ah, Mac," he said in a few minutes. "Come in and close the door." Then in a lower voice: "I need about twenty more capsules of undercoat. It's for . . . you know who it's for."

"Okay, Flem," the man said. "But personally, I'm starting to worry a little. We may get by with it this time. Maybe a little longer. But the case may grow chancy when the FDA really starts monitoring this project closely. So far, we've stuck to animals and just a handful of preliminary human tests. But you know that. I just want to avoid any run-ins."

"I ain't worried, Mac. We'll keep our tits out of the wringer. The product is super good, and super safe. And I can promise the subject won't talk. Matter of fact, we're gonna find all the test group on this one about as gabby as clams."

"True," said the man called Mac. "Even finding them in the first place will be a problem."

"Yeah. Funny how I hit one right off. I guess I better warn him, though. One of these days, once the project gits into the next official testing phase, we'll have to do this through a doctor."

"Warning him might be best, Flem."

"But I ain't sure I'm going to do that this morning," Mr. Slemp said.

"You know what you're doing."

"I try, Mac, I try. But I'm getting old. Now get me the stuff, huh?"

For perhaps five minutes there was silence. Then the scientist returned.

"Here you go, Chief. Hot stuff. In a plain, unmarked, brown bottle."

"Obliged."

I heard the man leave. My predicament now was at a crisis point. Should I take the desperate risk of transferring to Mr. Slemp's pocket? He snatched up the briefcase while I cringed at its bottom. There came a soft *plop* as a small bottle dropped into the case. Good! He would carry the case to the Capitol. Again I felt the sharp, powerful stride of Flemmons R. Slemp as he marched back to his car.

The journey from South Byrdport required about ten minutes. When we stopped, I heard squirrels. Some familiar scents registered in my nose. We were in Capitol Square! So close to home! I knew, as Mr. Slemp slammed the car door, that we were probably within sight of the church. But I dared not risk bailing out now. Somehow, from inside the Capitol, I could make a break for the walls. There I would remain safe until nightfall.

Grandpa had described the Capitol to me in some detail. He said certain inner walls had hollow cores, while others, mainly the outside ones, were solid masonry. The latter offered no thoroughfare. But Grandpa had talked of his own visits to the governor's office, and I felt I could find my way out.

Mr. Slemp's staccato footfalls echoed now from marble floors. Then there was a humming which I took to be an elevator to the second floor. There the gentle bumpings of massive doors ushered us into the governor's suite.

"Why Misteh Slay-ump," a woman's voice crooned. "Aren't you the prompt one. The governor was just asking about you, and I said, 'Why, sir, that man is always on time. Don't you worry,' I said. The governor always does so look forward to your visits. He must value your advice very highly."

"I like to be of service any way I can," Mr. Slemp said.

"Yes," she said sententiously, "service is what it's all about, isn't it? The public life. How grand a calling. You know what Churchill said: Politics is almost as exciting as war, and quite as dangerous. Well. Just come right with me."

More heavy doors whispered. Then a man's voice, pitched too high, with a strange resonance, squeaked a greeting.

"Flem, you rascal."

"Heighdy, Jack," Mr. Slemp said.

The two men shifted from opening banter into polite queries. The governor asked considerately about Mr. Slemp's manufacturing pursuits. Soon his voice grew quieter and more sincere.

"Of all the things that have happened to me in public life, Flem, this is the damnedest. To think that you and I would ever get together. That you would help me like this."

"Yep. We never was in the same pew politically, Jack. Same church, different pew."

"You supported the other side last primary. You were his biggest contributor. And I beat thunder out of him. Still, you came around to my side by November's election," Governor Pine said.

"I come around. You're a party man, or you ain't," Mr. Slemp said. "I'm a party man."

"But I just wish you felt the same way I do on the issues. Public employee bargaining. Repealing the right-to-work law. Those are the things dear to me, but not to you. And I don't know why. Sometimes I think you and I are just backwards. I started out in the privileged class, with a silver spoon in my mouth . . ."

"And my dad worked in the mines," Mr. Slemp said. "All my life it's been a case of bottom rail tryin' to git on top. Well, Jack, it don't matter. We just see things different." The manufacturer's voice dropped a notch; became confidential. "The important thing is, how you comin' on? Everything still as good as it was?"

"Gawdamighty, Flem, I still can't believe it. You've changed my life. That woman, Mrs. Archer, who brought you in? I wish you could ask her."

"That's great, Jack. Don't reckon I'll ask, though. I'll just leave this new bottle of undercoat with you." He picked up the briefcase, popped it open, and grabbed for the bottle. My heart pounded, but his thick fingers went straight for the small container and pulled it out. He closed the case again and put it down. It was time for me to make a move. I crawled slowly to the mouth of the case and looked around. Fortunately, Mr. Slemp had placed it on the floor beside his chair. It was unlikely that he or the governor would see me emerge.

Floor-length draperies bracketed the room's tall windows. I raced for the nearest one, and reached it unseen.

"I was just thinking, Jack, not that I want you to feel obligated by this little confidential business at all, but I was just wondering if you were still so dead-set to repeal the labor law. I would just plumb hate to see compulsory unionism come to the state," Mr. Slemp said.

"Heck, Flem. Why should you care? You pay top wages; give the best benefits. The few times a union organizer came around Hygeia, I know what happened. The union finished up like the past of pea time. I mean, whipped. As long as Flem Slemp's in charge, you're never going to have a union at Hygeia, right-to-work law or no," the governor said.

"But if we did get a union, then everybody'd have to join, if it wasn't for the labor law. I just couldn't stand that," Mr. Slemp said.

The governor's voice took on a slightly different, pontifical edge. "The truth is, Flem, I am not all that certain I have the votes for repeal. This is a conservative state these days. I'm not including you, mind — "

"As conservative? Maybe I am, Jack. But maybe I'm just stubborn."

"Anyway," Governor Pine said, "you and I are friends, Flem. Friendship transcends such artificial barriers as political positions."

"That's what I say. Well, I'll be gittin'. Time to light a rag out of here, as we say back home."

"You mountaineers," the governor said. "We flatlanders'll never figure you out. You're inscrutable."

"Maybe that's how we manage to stay free," Mr. Slemp said. "Inscrutable and free. Haw, haw. Good seeing you, Jack. I'll be checking you out in a few weeks."

"God bless you, Flem," Governor Jack Pine said.

Mr. Slemp picked up his leather case and stumped from the room. The governor, whom I could see from my spot behind the drapery, sat reflectively at his desk. He looked to be around sixty, but his hair was untouched by gray and it grew low on his forehead. His skin seemed faintly yellowish. He possessed a fleshy, triangular nose of unusual breadth across the bridge. He lit a cigar and picked up the telephone, and dialed.

"Randy, have you counted heads lately on the labor law repeal?" he asked. There was a long silence. "Still the same, then. Well, that pesky s-o-b Flem Slemp is messing around here today. Look sharp to see if he talks to any of the fence-sitters, okay?"

It seemed a strange reaction for a friend to have, but the ways of politics were unknown to me. I began searching for an entry to the walls.

Mr. Robert Adam designed a lovely State Capitol, but lesser men had tampered with it since the first plaster dried. Grandpa was correct; the outer walls were solid masonry, and impenetrable. But certain of the inner walls, too, were either solid brick originally or had been filled in during remodelings. Passages that seemed promising ended abruptly. My best discovery was an ancient, unused chimney, which led straight from the governor's office on the second floor down to a subbasement, with various escapes along the way. I learned where to exit at the ground level and leave the building through a ventilator.

But I had to wait many hours before it would be safe enough to strike out for the church. Already twenty-four hours had elapsed since I left Serena and Grandpa. What would they be thinking? Surely they could never believe I would willingly desert them. Therefore, they had decided I encountered trouble. They would check with Sidney and Rebecca, who would be as mystified as they. The one creature around home who knew the truth — or a part of it — was Alabama Ruby.

All I could do was wait until dark.

Around the time the Bell Tower clanged four times, the legislators and lobbyists and staff administrators began leaving the old Capitol, amid strident laughter. Soon the building was almost empty save for its custodians. I wandered back through the walls and entered the governor's office. His duplicity concerning his supposed friend, Mr. Slemp, had surprised me and aroused my curiosity as to what kind of man he was. I remembered Grandpa's analysis of the governor's character.

On my visit with Mr. Slemp that morning, I had been unable to see the various anterooms of the gubernatorial offices. Now I could see their spacious proportions, their fine antique furniture, their massive carved woodwork painted off-white.

Two women were covering typewriters, snapping off lights, and bundling themselves into woolen coats.

"Leave Archer's light on; she's still here. She and the Old Man are working a little late."

The other woman's eyebrows rose. Then the two exchanged blank glances, shrugged, and walked out the door.

I passed through a ventilator into the chief executive's inner office.

There, on a green leather-covered Chippendale sofa, Governor Pine and Mrs. Archer were embracing strenuously. It surprised me completely — after all, the man was about sixty; the woman at least fifty — and I did not realize persons of that age could harbor passions of such magnitude. Judging by the gasps and sighs and, indeed, certain visual evidence as the scene unfolded, Governor Pine and his inamorata operated under high romantic pressure.

I need only tell you that the affair on the green sofa moved inexorably to its logical conclusion.

In about fifteen minutes, they began composing themselves.

"Mercy, Governor Pine," Mrs. Archer said. "When you said your administration would give full service to the state, I didn't know that would include *me*. I just don't know what to say. All this passion. I suppose I should be ashamed, but I feel so *proud!*"

"A good executive attends to the fringe benefits as well as the big picture, Mrs. Archer," the governor squeaked.

CHAPTER 12

I SHALL PUT THIS AS DIPLOMATICALLY AS POSSIBLE: AD-vancing age does nothing to enhance the human form. Other mammals are more fortunate in that regard. We mice may have our problems, but aesthetically speaking we age rather well. We suffer nothing comparable to the downhill slide of human morphology. I had now observed, at close hand, hairless expanses of drooping flesh, mounded with wormlike veins and studded with moles, warts, and keratoses. The entire production added up to a pasty white, sagging cover for swelling stomachs and shriveling limbs. It depressed me to think that Miss Tebell, in just a few more years, might suffer the same fate. I supposed it was almost inevitable. I had sensed in Miss Tebell a fierce urgency, an impatience, in her personal life. Maybe I understood it better now.

Age was all around me as I waited for deep night. The antique furniture and ancient pictures spoke of ages past. One of the gubernatorial reception rooms was a virtual gallery of old prints and photographs. I assumed they were quite historical, but I did not understand their period or significance.

In that room, hung with the old pictures, was a window giving the best view of Main Street and the evening traffic load. From the window I could see the church quite clearly. There seemed less than half a dozen people who might be orbiting the sidewalk there, in early hope of hearing the phantom organist. Our two-day layoff at the Erben, plus the deepening damp cold of February, was discouraging the turnout. That suited me perfectly, for I dreaded the run across that broad thoroughfare. The incident of the dog, and my encounter with Alabama Ruby in the alley, had undermined my confidence as a street mouse.

The church windows, I saw, were totally dark. The old building's silhouette was framed by a wall of high-rises behind it: Byrdport University Medical Center. A galaxy of lights shimmered from the BUSM complex. The great medical center was too far away for me to discern humans behind those windows, but I decided thousands of them must be there: doctors, technicians, students, nurses, interns, patients. All those buildings and people overwhelmed the dark, empty church. What chance did it have? The medical center was so entirely a creature of today, as was medicine itself. How frivolous, even dangerous, it would be for medicine to look back, to become even conscious of tradition, except on occasional commemorative events. Science, I decided, was entirely and properly of today. The old church was yesterday. I could almost understand the doctors' point of view. They just did not care.

Then I remembered something in Dr. Cotesworth Stirling's speech a week and a half before. He said the church was a hospital during the Civil War, and its floor still showed the bloodstains. That vivid image caused me to focus on the past with more intensity. I tried to blank out the high-rises from what I saw across the street, and imagine the scene as it was when the church became a hospital, long before there was a medical center.

With an almost audible click, the image made an important connection. I had just seen a real picture of the very tableau!

Main Street Presbyterian Church was featured prominently in several of the ancient illustrations displayed in the governor's suite. I looked at them again, and discerned the reason I had not recognized the church. Small and insignificant it might be against its modern neighbors, but the building had dominated the street in the days of its youth. On the wall before me was a remarkably clear photograph from that long-ago time, a view that could have been made from this very window. It revealed almost the entire block. I saw dignified three-story residences. Other buildings, judging by the goods they displayed, were stores. A new-looking four-story stucco building, with tall windows and a sign with a picture of an eagle, might have been a hotel. Next to that was another building with an ornate entrance, equipped with lanterns and billboards displaying large notices. On the sidewalk was a substantial crowd of well-dressed humans: men in strange floppy coats, and women in long conical skirts that dragged the ground.

Having studied an archaic image of the very block where I lived, I looked again at the other pictures on the governor's wall. Some made no sense to me, but I recognized one as a close view of the building with the billboards. Somehow it reminded me of a modern motion picture house, like some I had seen traveling with the evangelist. Had I only been able to read, I could have interpreted the words on the billboards in the picture. Even so, as I studied them, I could tell that some of the words looked familiar. Where had I seen them before?

I remembered. Of course: the same inscription — or something close to it — was on one of the pieces of sheet music inside the Erben!

I puzzled over the significance while I waited for the traffic to subside.

At last, conditions seemed tolerably safe. When I made my long passage down through the Capitol, and out across the street to the church, the trip was so easy and hazard-free that I regretted my timidity in waiting so long.

Safe in familiar quarters, I began yelling for Serena and Grandpa as I raced up the inner walls of the church. I shot into the Erben. "I'm back!" I cried. "Hey, it's me, Charles!"

No one responded. I ran to our nest, Serena's and mine. It was empty and cold.

Then I checked Grandpa's, a few feet away. It was so untidy that I could not see if he was there. In the absence of any sound, I thought that his nest, too, was empty. But it was not.

"Hello, Charles," said Grandpa.

"Grandpa! Is everything all right? Where's Serena?"

"Sit down, Charles. Don't make such a commotion," he said.

"Why are you talking like that, Grandpa? I can scarcely hear you. Where's Serena?"

From the rubble of his nest, Grandpa raised one paw, which waggled at me in an unmistakable gesture: *shut up.*

"Serena went looking for you. Around sundown yesterday when you hadn't come home."

"Did she go to the Rib Cage, Grandpa?"

"Said she was. Never came back." Grandpa's voice was a scratchy whisper.

"Grandpa. What's happened?" I leaned into his nest, to hear better.

"Aw, I got careless. Couple of hours ago. Thought I'd look around, maybe go to the Rib Cage myself. Worried about you two. I reckon I warn't watching too close, or maybe I just can't see so good anymore, Charles."

"It was the cat?" I asked.

"Alabama Ruby. My old friend. She hit me just as I come out of the organ. But I got away from her, just like I done before, a long time ago on that Communion Sunday."

"And you'll be all right again, Grandpa. Just like you were after that episode," I said.

"No. I done rung the knell this time. Now be quiet and let me finish. Two things I need to say, Charles. First is, find Serena. And when you find her, for pity's sake stay with her. You keep running off with some excuse that sounds good when you give it, all persuasive like, but somehow the project don't work out."

Grandpa was finding it difficult to breathe. I reached down and grasped his forepaw.

"What's the second thing, Grandpa?"

His voice came very softly.

"When you play 'The Old Rugged Cross,' don't drag the beat. You ought to speed it up a little. It ain't a sad hymn. It's confident," the old mouse said.

"Soon you'll be playing it again yourself," I said. "You can show me what you mean."

"No. Now get out of here and let me rest a spell." He made a strangled sound.

128

"Grandpa!" I cried. I kneaded his scrawny paw. It was as limp and thin as a tangle of worn-out twine.

He was gone.

There was such a stillness, such an infinity of discontinued time. Had I been outside, I was sure the traffic, the bare branches of the trees, the clouds, the very planets were frozen in fixed position to mark his departure, and etch his monument on the sky. Until I saw the void he left behind, I did not understand how much space the old fellow occupied in life. I had failed to appreciate his uncritical loyalty. I had not known how much I would miss his experience, wisdom, and balance. What a horror the death of a loved one is; what a desperate legacy to know that by my heedless absence, I might have contributed to this calamity.

In any case, Grandpa was gone. His troubles were over.

I wept bitterly beside his squalid nest.

Then I carried him to a high place in the walls, above the organ. He was remarkably light and frail.

I fixed the blower wire and climbed to the console. There, where we had frolicked so recently with hardly a care, the keys seemed battered and weary, the stops massive and immovable. The theme of lifelessness pervaded everything. I had difficulty commencing. I had never played alone before, and I shrank from the prospect now. But I had to do it. I threw the blower switch and jumped onto the great manual. The pipes spoke.

Grandpa was correct. "The Old Rugged Cross" went better with a bit more *brio*.

Despite my grief, the mystery of Serena's disappearance never completely left my mind, and my concern for her intensified. Clearly, I should first seek her in the Rib Cage. Yet, if she were there, why had she not returned to the church? I dreaded the answer from Sidney and Rebecca. Despite what I saw as my best efforts to fulfill my promises, it was undeniable that my performance had failed in the clutch. All my good intentions paraded mockingly through my conscience.

It's what you do that counts, I decided, not what you think, or what you say. Thoughts and talk may be pleasant, and even stirring, but when life's final accounts are entered, words count only as self-indulgent luxury if the speaker did not perform as advertised. I had failed to appear once; Serena was injured. I had failed again; Serena was gone. And Grandpa was dead.

In both cases, a trivial distraction had diverted my attention just long enough to trap me in a ruinous rendezvous. Clearly, some imp of the perverse had set up a sinister pattern of disruption. Now that I understood it, I knew what to do. I vowed that never again would I stray from my determined course. There, alone in the silent church, I resolved to be a mouse of iron.

That was just as well, for the news at the Rib Cage was bad.

Sidney was agitated.

"Charles, Charles, what can I tell you. For hours she hung around here, waiting, wondering, all last night. Nobody knew where you had gone. You say some cat drove you under the Mercedes and you motored off. We didn't know that. Today Serena said she was returning to the church. That is all Rebecca and I know about it."

"She never came back to the church," I said. "Did the car return to the alley?"

"I don't know," he said. "Maybe."

"I think it did," Rebecca said. "That man, Mr. Junior Slemp, was in here today."

"Then Serena could have gone with Earl," I said.

"She could have gone with Sammy Davis, Jr., for all we know," Rebecca said. "But yes, Charles, I think she went with Earl. And if she did, I must say this to you — who could blame her? You have disappointed her grievously."

"But I couldn't help it," I said.

"We girls like somebody to count on," Rebecca sniffed.

It hurt, but I deserved it. "Well, I'm convinced that if she went with Earl, it was against her will, and when Mr. Junior returns tomorrow, she will be back. I will deal with Earl appropriately at that time," I said.

"Mr. Junior Slemp won't be coming in tomorrow," Rebecca said smugly. "Because I heard the Rib Cage manager, Mr. Stern, giving Viola the waitress off until Saturday. That's two days. She was accompanying Mr. Junior Slemp to Tidewater for basketball."

So. Serena was now a hostage in another city.

"But don't worry, Charles," Rebecca said with increasing sharpness. "Your other lady friend is still in town. She's sitting right here in the restaurant, in fact."

"I don't have another lady friend, Rebecca," I said.

"Well excuse me. Then Serena must have been wrong. She burst out crying and said she thought you liked a human better than her. She referred to a woman named Miss Tebell."

"Oh, Rebecca," Sidney said in discomfort.

"Miss Tebell and I are partners in historic preservation," I said. "Beyond that, I owe nobody an explanation."

I found some blueberry cheesecake, but scarcely enjoyed it in my profound depression. Grandpa dead; Serena gone. What more could happen?

It was now past midnight on Thursday morning. Wondering if Miss Tebell was truly in the Rib Cage at such an hour, I found a useful crack in the baseboard and studied the customers' feet. Instantly I saw, above a narrow pair shod in mahogany leather, unmistakably familiar ankles and calves. Opposite them were scuffed but expensive-looking male brogans.

"You couldn't have heard it," the voice of Dr. Caleb Old said. "You can't believe that hysterical nonsense, Tayloe."

"I didn't believe it until tonight," she said. "Oh, I guess it's my imagination, Caleb, but just as we were coming in, there was a sort of whisper in the wind. I know it's crazy."

"Describe it."

"A hymn. 'The Old Rugged Cross.' "

"Tayloe, there was nobody else out there tonight on the sidewalk. If the phantom had been playing, wouldn't the usual crowd have gathered? You must have imagined it."

"There's been no report of the organist since Sunday. It's late, and it's cold. That's why there was no crowd," Miss Tebell said.

"You're hardly an impartial observer, Tayloe. All this is getting to you."

"Maybe I want to believe. Damn, Caleb, hasn't it been great, though? All the publicity! Main Street Presbyterian is a national cause now. We're starting to get offers of help from the top preservation societies. Not that we mightn't have stirred

131

'em up anyway, but the phantom sure gave us an extra dimension of drama. Bless him, I say. Or her. Or the collective imaginations of everyone who says they've heard the organ."

"I can't play the organ, Tayloe, but I'm doing all I can for you at the university. I'm probably a better doctor than politician."

"Caleb, is there the slightest chance the BUSM administration may change its mind? Accept one of the other sites, and let the church alone?"

"I doubt it. They just don't speak your language. To my colleagues, it's an old junk pile the city will be well rid of."

"How about you, Caleb? Do you speak my language? You say you're helping all you can, but why?" Miss Tebell asked.

"I have noticed there is a critical stage in learning any new language," Dr. Old said, speaking slowly as if to find the precise words. "It is where, despite your best efforts, all seems hopeless. None of it makes sense. One despairs. Yet that is usually the point where one more big effort creates a breakthrough. When that happens, the language becomes understandable."

"So? Have you had a personal breakthrough in the preservation language?"

"No. But I may be approaching the point of desperation."

"Then you're not helping me because of any conviction that the church should be saved," Miss Tebell said.

"Does the reason matter, Tayloe?"

"Well, if you're doing it just for me, personally . . ."

"Anything wrong with that?" Dr. Old asked.

"It . . . well, of course not. Unless it complicates things."

"Things usually are complicated. But it seems perfectly natural and good that I help you. That much is clear-cut and simple. Even if it arises from something far profounder." Dr. Old's feet twitched and shuffled.

"And that is?" Miss Tebell asked.

"That I never stopped thinking about you in those fourteen years."

Miss Tebell's right foot suddenly churned the air.

"All that time," Dr. Old continued, "life has gone on with its usual complexity. A fourteen-year span where you and I have racked up millions of thoughts and reactions and deeds. Everything is different. Yet here I am, knowing that as far as I'm concerned, nothing has really changed. Some things are simply immutable."

"Caleb." Her foot waggled vigorously. Her voice became gentler than I had ever heard it. "Do you mean you still love me?"

He may have nodded. They were silent for a moment.

"There is something so right about you," he said. "I suppose every man has his idea of perfection. You happen to be mine. You are like a clipper ship, a Ferrari roadster. When I am with you — to make the metaphors still more ridiculous — I am like a mighty Baldwin steam locomotive, thundering and clanking and whistling across prairies. I feel like swaggering into the woods and chopping down a tree, just because it's there."

Tell her about food-gathering, I thought.

"I fantasize myself killing a wild boar, and then returning to the cabin where you are cooking biscuits on a huge black wood-burning stove, with fancy nickel trim. That is the sort of absurd effect you always had on me. All it took was one look, three weeks ago, to make me realize I never changed. God in Heaven, Tayloe, I must have been born to love you," Dr. Old said.

"Caleb . . . well, I honestly didn't realize. I have certainly thought about you, too, but I haven't pictured myself at a wood range."

"Women are always more practical about these things," he sighed.

"It had seemed to me that love was just a bit out of style for a while there," Miss Tebell said. "I had made up my mind to get along without any grandiose, long-term commitment. Do you mean to tell me that all these fourteen years, you've pined away . . ."

"No no no," Dr. Old said. "After all, I got married, was successful in my career, enjoyed life. I have not pined away. You had nothing to do with my marriage failing. Normal people don't collapse with broken hearts. We can find many people with whom we can enjoy life, marry, raise children. It's just that for some of us there may be one person beyond all others who becomes an obsession. When we see them, we know. There are no games or doubts. I suppose you think I'm being melodramatic."

"Caleb, I don't know if that's terribly adolescent or terribly mature. I do know that in my experience, love was more trouble than it was worth."

Seconds passed. Her foot described parabolas. Dishes clinked in the Rib Cage.

Miss Tebell continued. "You are certainly right, Caleb, that things are complicated. And boy, you have just made them considerably worse. Would you take me home now, please? I have a lot to think about. And I have an important meeting tomorrow."

"How important?"

"Remember I told you about the old lady the cops hauled off when they demolished the ironfronts? She's a legend in the preservation movement. I've been wanting to meet her for years, but she's reclusive. So I just called up and invited myself over, and she agreed to see me. I hope she can help me get some things in perspective."

"For instance."

"For instance, why I am really making all this big effort for the church. Don't tell anyone, but there are times when I wonder. See, Caleb, I honestly think I'm going to win this one, but instead of feeling triumphant I start getting cold feet. Have I picked the right battleground this time? I look at what I've stirred up, I read the newspaper articles, and I realize that my motives are not altogether clear. Not impure," she laughed, "just not clear."

"That surprises me," Dr. Old said. "I had not expected an uncertain trumpet at this stage."

Again I faced a quick decision. Serena would be gone for two more days. I reasoned that if I went to Live Oak Row, I could return to the church or the Rib Cage in relative safety at the appropriate time. Nobody needed me in the meantime. So, I crawled up the scratched and blackened booth beside Miss Tebell, hoping her purse would be ajar. I was not disappointed.

The night was bitterly cold as we strolled through Capitol

Square. Curiously, Miss Tebell and Dr. Old made a wandering, irregular promenade, not the direct path suggested for sensible creatures by the freezing climate. They collided lightly, veered apart, and crashed together again. It was a highly inefficient method of walking in ten-degree weather.

"Know what, Caleb?"

We had reached the door of Twelve Live Oak Row.

"What, Tayloe?"

"I would like very much to ask you in. I think you would like to come in."

"Exactly so."

"And I could raise some frivolous objection, like, 'it's almost two A.M., and we both have big days tomorrow.' And then we could get over that and play around, and then we might say the hell with it all, and you would come in anyway," Miss Tebell said.

"Yes. All that might happen," Dr. Old said.

"But the real reason I'm not going to ask you in is that I am at present keeping company with another very decent gentleman, and as long as that's going on, I am old-fashioned enough to entertain only one man at a time. You might counter that by observing that for people with our age and experience, such naiveté is inappropriate. But it matters, Caleb. I want to make it clear you have given me a lot to think about tonight. Now let me get to the door, please."

With a hollow, bumping sigh, the old heavy door with its carved panels opened, admitting Miss Tebell and me.

But then she unexpectedly stepped back outside, and attached herself more firmly than ever to Dr. Old. Assorted sighs and whispers filtered sibilantly inside the purse, which suddenly took a jolting drop as the long strap slipped from her shoulder. She then concluded this odd performance by reopening the door, and going back inside.

"Whew," she said. Then we walked slowly up the stairs.

Mr. Granville Zebulon arrived at 9:30 that Thusday morning.

"Hi. Busy?" he asked Miss Tebell.

"Not terribly at the instant. I do have to leave this morning to go visit someone."

"Tried to call you last night. Everything okay?"

"Sure, Granzeb. Just a late meeting," Miss Tebell said.

"Until eleven-thirty? That's when I stopped calling."

"Well, it did seem important. What's up?"

"I was just on my way to the Capitol and thought I'd give you a bit of news. Remember I told you about the Reverend Mott Gooch, the pioneer black missionary?"

"Sure."

"I made some contacts with friends in the black church orbit. It seems Mott Gooch is even more a hero than I thought. And there's some sentiment forming that, since Main Street Presbyterian was where he started, the black religious community might throw in with preserving the church."

"Terrific!" Miss Tebell's reaction was sincere, if tentative. "But . . . what would they do, exactly? I don't quite understand."

"Seems to me the moral support alone would be good, especially if you remember that Byrdport has a four-to-three black majority on city council. We do have a black mayor, in case you forgot. Significant?"

"I'll say. They might influence the governor and the university."

"It's even possible they may chip in a little money. It wouldn't be much, but even a token amount would be a major breakthrough. Blacks have customarily had other things to do with their cause money than pour it into the preservation movement."

"That's good news, Granzeb. I can't tell you how grateful I am," Miss Tebell said.

He looked at her questioningly. "No need. See you tonight?"

"Of course. You asked me days ago."

"Just making sure. Well, 'bye."

I did not know when Miss Tebell would depart, so by midmorning I was positioned in her purse. Around 11:00 A.M. she said to Thelma: "I'm off to see Judith McGuire. Wish me success."

"Tayloe, she never sees anybody," the secretary said. "Even preservationists. How did you manage it?"

"Told her I was a member of NOW," Miss Tebell said. "As an old suffragist, that sorta got to her, I think."

"A suffragist? You mean, one of the originals? Getting the vote and all?"

"Getting the vote and all. One of The Few. From our own Battle of Britain, except from more than sixty years ago. I think she wants to hear about the ERA from me more than any old-building chitchat."

"Well, have a good time, Boss. One sister to another," Thelma said.

CHAPTER 13

I ENJOYED SOME TEN MINUTES' WORTH OF PLEASANT, bouncy walking. Then I heard Miss Tebell grinding a doorbell, which emitted a clatter like the antique fixture on Live Oak Row. I heard the door open, and the voice of Miss Tebell identifying herself.

"This way, if you please," said a female voice of enormous dignity and resonance. I heard a starched, rustling sound. The door closed behind us, drawing a screen on modern Byrdport. Old smells filtered in upon me. They were clean and pleasant, but alien to the world outside.

Then came another voice, husky, flawed with cracks and wheezes, but still vibrant. "Tayloe, my dear. How good of you to come." She turned to the maid. "Thank you, Mrs. Pickett. I'll call if we need anything." The rustling sound faded away.

"Sit there, please. Good. Jefferson Davis found that chair comfortable, I'm told," Mrs. McGuire said. "Well, Tayloe, you have just encountered a vanished institution. Mrs. Pickett is the last mammy in Byrdport. Or anywhere else, perhaps. I doubt that even in Charleston or New Orleans is there a surviving mammy. They went out around 1930. Don't ask me how it is I still have her; I don't know. She came with us in 1918, when my daughter was born. Somehow she never left. She is now ninety-one, which is two years older than I. Well, what do you think of this place?"

"It's wonderful," Miss Tebell said. "I'm sure there's nothing in Byrdport to equal it."

"That is accurate," the old woman said. "Everything is just as it was when my grandfather built and furnished it in 1859. Even the wallpaper. Sporting house wallpaper, my father called it. Both of them were in the War. Grandfather was a political general. My father, Bushrod Mosby, was a fifteen-year-old cavalryman. We were no relation to the other Mosby of the cavalry.

"After the War," Mrs. McGuire continued, "when Grandfather and Father got rich making cigarettes, they could have replaced the house, with something more stylish and grandiose. But they liked things as they were before the War. This house, these furnishings, reminded them of some ideal Old South. It never quite existed, if they had been totally honest with themselves. We went through a long period of exalting the Lost Cause. We enhanced and gilded a defective though lovable picture. Now, what was it you wanted to see me about?"

I peered from the purse mouth. We were in a grand, high-ceilinged parlor with a chandelier similar to Miss Tebell's. Dark furniture, heavy drapes, gleaming mirrors, and bronze and silver lamps filled the room. A coal fire glinted orange from the grate in a marble fireplace. Everything seemed immaculate and polished. Mrs. McGuire's house seemed even nicer to me than the Slemps'.

"I wondered if you'd been following the Main Street Presbyterian controversy," Miss Tebell said.

"How could I miss it?" the woman said.

I wriggled carefully into a position from which I could see her. Judith Mosby McGuire was not quite what I had expected. She was old, to be sure, but she was not dressed like other old ladies I had observed. She wore a tweed suit with a simple gold chain at her throat. A gold bracelet richly caparisoned with charms jangled at one wrist. She was thin to gauntness, and her skin was ravaged by wrinkles. No pink, plump sweetness softened the looks of Mrs. McGuire. Yet she had something better: the same thoroughbred conformation of Miss Tebell and Miss da Gamba. She had the inviolate beauty of magnificent bones.

139

"One would have to be on Mars to miss it," Mrs. McGuire continued. "The newspapers and airwaves have been chockablock. The *Enquirer* has even editorialized. Clumsily, as always."

"Yes," Miss Tebell said. "They tried to be funny about the Phantom of the Organ. Accused us of reincarnating Lon Chaney to help save the church."

"Revolting. How can I help you?" Mrs. McGuire asked.

"I was hoping . . . well, for some moral support and for some advice. You have been such a pioneer in preservation; I guess you know more about old Byrdport buildings than anyone else."

"Not necessarily. I just happen to own more of them," Mrs. McGuire said.

"But you pioneered the idea of finding some useful modern purpose for an endangered structure. Adaptive use, as it's come to be called."

"I just stumbled into that stuff," the old woman said. "I decided we had enough struggling museums and memorials in our historic buildings. We can't support any more. The alternative? Give me a branch bank, or wine bar, or shoe repair shop, any day."

"Correct. But what do you do with a church?" Miss Tebell asked.

"Actually, the best solution was one that apparently was ignored. The university could have used it for an auditorium. God knows, universities always seem to need them. Hmm. Some large old buildings can be adapted for boutiques and restaurants. There's a former bakery in Louisville. An ex-brewery in Denver," Mrs. McGuire said.

"That might work, but . . ."

"Hardly up to the nobility of the structure, eh? See here, Tayloe, don't let that worry you. Save the building first; that's the important thing. The future will unfold in due time. This is a game of stalls and delays. You have to live almost as long as I have to appreciate two things: the random capriciousness of life, and the pathetic record of humans as prophets. We simply do not know what will happen. Don't spend too much time thinking about the future. Forget about it."

"That's hard to live by," Miss Tebell said.

"Of course."

"But you don't seem to have lived that way. Your life has obviously been well organized. You have participated in successful causes that changed the future, starting back with the suffrage movement. Your whole life refutes any sort of carelessness about the future," Miss Tebell said.

"Who said anything about carelessness? We must always plan and work while hoping for the best. But we must recognize that it may all blow up in our face with shocking suddenness. Life has a way of making us humble. That is what we really need to prepare for," Mrs. McGuire said. "My life is a testament to that."

Miss Tebell looked at her questioningly.

"I'll give you a sample. In 1918, when I was just twenty-one and therefore, it seemed to me, of proper voting age but unable to cast a ballot, I marched in the great suffrage demonstrations down Pennsylvania Avenue in Washington. Then I made countless speeches. Attended a thousand sidewalk rallies. And finally we won. Women got the vote. We endured ridicule and abuse you cannot imagine today. But through it all, my husband, Branch McGuire, was an absolute saint. At first he didn't quite understand, but he tolerated. Gradually, he came to see the injustice of women not having the vote. So he supported us. That traditional man, imbued with all the Victorian claptrap of old Byrdport. Do you have any idea what the male-female relationship was like in those days, Tayloe?"

"I don't think my generation could ever really understand," Miss Tebell said.

"It is a tribute to the indomitability of the species," Mrs. McGuire said, "that all of us weren't hopeless neurotics. And yet I think that on balance we were at least as happy as people today. The saving grace was discipline and order. There was no doubt as to the God-given roles of men and women. Things were carved on stone in those days. In matters of intellect, finance, politics, business, and law, women were deemed inferior. In matters of the home she was supreme.

"I must say," she continued, "it wasn't altogether a case of seeing to the dirty socks. Women truly were on a pedestal.

When the system was working at its idiotic best, straight from Sir Walter Scott, we were adored, worshiped, treated as precious flowers. So you see what a jump it was for my man to admit the injustice of it all. But he did. He came through. He even made speeches for female suffrage."

"And you got the vote . . . let's see, in 1920?" Miss Tebell said.

"Correct. The Nineteenth Amendment finally passed. Our state, I emphasize with shame and disgust, did not ratify it until decades later, and reluctantly even then. But in 1921 we were preparing to vote for the first time. I cannot describe the sense of jubilation.

"Then, three days before the election of 1921, my dearest Branch died. He bled to death from a simple, undetected stomach ulcer, while the surgeons at Byrdport University pondered what the trouble might be. The president of the state medical society was at his side. That worthy physician had spent more time mobilizing doctors against woman suffrage than he had spent staying abreast of modern medicine. So my husband died."

"Oh, God," Miss Tebell exclaimed. "And with that, voting was probably the last thing on your mind."

"We buried him on election day. But no, my dear. Late that afternoon I went to the polls. And I cast my vote."

A mantel clock ticked. In the fireplace grate, a flare of burning coal gas hissed with a bluish orange flame.

"You see," the old woman said softly, "why I refer to the capriciousness of life."

"In 1921 you were a very young woman," Miss Tebell said.

"Twenty-four. But Branch left me well fixed. And I had something from my father's estate. I have had more than enough."

"You never remarried?"

"No." The clock, clacking with infinite patience, scattered a few more seconds of Byrdport history. Was it doing that when Confederate soldiers bled on the floor of Main Street Presbyterian? "Perhaps I should have married again, yet somehow I held back. I had the feeling that one such commitment was enough. I did consider it, at least twice. For a woman who feels secure, and who had loved someone as I loved Branch McGuire, it would have taken a truly exceptional passion for me to have married again. Oh, I felt attraction, but there was never the obsession, the long looking into eyes."

"Lots of us talk about liberation," Miss Tebell said, "but you lived it."

"Well, I did get the money from men. But I always tried to go my own way. That's the reason I never had much to do with conventional women's activities. I dropped out of the Pocahontas Garden Club thirty years ago. Most clubwomen had been horrified at the suffrage movement, just as they are horrified by the ERA campaign today. And as for NOW, Tayloe, which you said is an affiliation of yours, why, if you wore a scarlet 'A' on your chest you would enjoy a better reception in the women's clubs."

"But I must tell you," Miss Tebell said, "that the Pocahontas Club is supporting the preservation of Main Street Presbyterian."

"Lord help you," the old woman laughed. "As if you hadn't troubles enough."

"Let's go back a moment, please," Miss Tebell said. "You were talking about remarriage, and if it was worth it. The subject was love. Correct?"

"Of course!"

"And it seemed that you made two well-considered decisions not to remarry, and that you had no regrets. My question is, how could you be so sure?"

"But Tayloe, you just *know*! The other party is an obsession, or he isn't. How do you feel while contemplating life without him? Is there a hint of devastating loss? Do lights, stars, whole galaxies silently twinkle off? Does the pavement grow grittier and the wind colder? Do such simple acts as pushing down the car's accelerator become burdensome? Or can you say, gracious, old girl, he's quite something in the short term, but I really couldn't stand listening to him eat for the next thirty years. Really, how long can two people spend under the counterpane? Living with someone is apt to include heavy doses of boredom, confusion, and bathroom stenches. Overcoming those requires major perseverance. With Branch and me, the negatives were not just overcome, but overwhelmed. Perhaps I was unlucky that the two subsequent men in my life didn't affect me as strongly. But if you don't care, why, you don't care! Do you?" Mrs. McGuire said.

Her ravaged face was gentle but serious. "Yet I must add . . . Yes, I must say this, Tayloe. In remembering how love could be, at its best, I do believe that whatever it costs, it is worth it. We clutter life with many contrived meanings, but love is one of the few things no one can contrive. It is at the heart of life."

"Then those who can't feel it . . ." Miss Tebell began.

"Are certainly diminished, although they sometimes overcompensate in other pursuits. There's just something lacking in them. Take our own esteemed governor. Just look at the success achieved by that impotent, driveling dotard."

"You don't mean literally impotent, I assume," Miss Tebell said.

"But I do. Literally."

"How on earth do you know?"

"I've known him all his life. His mother was an acquaintance, a rather stupid, horrible woman, but one I saw occasionally. Little Jack was in and out of my daughter's set. He was considered . . . rather strange."

"Gay, you mean?"

"No, more like . . . just neuter. I remember hearing my daughter and her friends talking about him. One of the, er, wilder girls was quite explicit. Jack was just never interested in *anybody*. He was incapable," the old lady said.

Wait a minute, I cried silently. *That can't be, Mrs. McGuire; your information cannot be accurate.* This perception of Governor Pine was intensely puzzling.

"He never married?"

"Never. He's the first bachelor governor in two centuries. I think he spread some story about having been heartbroken by an early love affair, et cetera. But those who knew him knew there was no early love."

It couldn't be, I thought, recalling yesterday's energetic scene in the governor's office. If that man was uninterested in women, then I was a three-hundred-pound Central American ground sloth.

"I don't know what there is about him that I don't like, but there's something," Miss Tebell said. "I thought it was just his political views."

"He is the perfect example of the Hobbesian theory that a democracy is an aristocracy of orators. If there is one thing Jack Pine can do, despite his squeaky voice, it's make a speech. He plays the rabble like a violin. My, Tayloe, we have wandered far afield. I don't think I have helped you any. I have no brilliant suggestions about what to do with this church. But I promise you something will turn up. So go ahead full tilt."

"I feel a little better," Miss Tebell said. "But I'm curious: why have you spent so much money and effort in a solitary crusade to save old buildings? You have gone your own way. You are unique. The rest of us band together in organizations."

The old woman pondered.

"I never analyzed my reasons. It was just a hobby, a minor passion, a caprice. A lesser obsession. I suppose I think of old buildings as time capsules. They grip me because they were conceived and built by people. An empty site, however historic, is not the same. An old building is terribly vulnerable. Nature herself conspires to destroy it, through decay, fire, earthquake, probing roots and branches, and the gnawings of insects and animals. It's as though anything humans build is an affront to nature's blind force. But buildings are among our noblest works. It pleases me that man has built the Pyramids, the Parthenon, the cathedrals of Europe. And the World Trade Center and the Sears Tower.

"That doesn't quite explain the passion," Mrs. McGuire continued. "I think it comes down to this. By preserving these buildings, we are preserving ourselves. If the buildings have meaning in our culture — the world that formed us — then by preserving them we are affirming ourselves."

"Would you say," Miss Tebell asked, "that in a more simple and selfish manner, we're trying to stop the clock from robbing our lives?"

"My, but you ask awkward questions, dear. Put it that way if you like. It certainly hasn't worked for me, has it?"

Their conclusions seemed faintly depressing, if I followed them correctly. Was intellect always the dupe of feeling? Was simple vanity the hidden heart of the preservation movement? Was it true that passions may sleep, but vanity never rests?

"You asked about organizations," Mrs. McGuire said. "I do know that Historic Byrdport is well run, and does a lot of good. I'm going to give you a donation."

"I didn't . . ." Miss Tebell began.

The old woman cheerfully waved off the objection. "I always preferred doing things my way, and I have been able to afford it, which makes a difference. Most organizations put together for common causes become boring and self-centered. Unions. Manufacturers' associations. Chambers of commerce, the bottom of the barrel. But I have been remiss in not supporting Historic Byrdport, and I shall make amends. I may even join NOW. By the way, when you return to your office, will you be walking up Madison? Good. Then you'll pass the Pocahontas Club. When you get there, I want you to look at what some juvenile delinquent recently scratched into wet cement, right in front."

"What on earth is it?"

"Just look," Judith McGuire said.

Amid mutual assurances, the ancient mammy, Mrs. Pickett, showed us out.

We walked two blocks, and Miss Tebell suddenly stopped. She was, I decided, reading the message on the sidewalk concrete. Then she laughed loudly in delighted hoots.

"Beaver power," I heard her say.

CHAPTER 14

ON THAT WALK WITH MISS TEBELL I PONDERED MRS. McGuire's observations about love. I was struck by the ageless practicality of women, and by the absurdity of men who treated them as frivolous creatures who lived by impulse. Nothing could be more inaccurate.

Mice indulged in no such delusions. But had I not lived a delusion of another kind? And should I not be big enough to confront it now? I, Charles Churchmouse, had come perilously close to being captivated by a human. How could I feel smug and superior to human males, with such self-deception on my own conscience? *Enough is enough,* I told myself, and as I did, Serena's dear face rushed back into my thoughts. When, if ever, would I see her again? Mrs. McGuire had talked of a terrible sense of loss as one of the sure signs of love. I felt loss for Serena. And I knew that Serena loved me, or had loved me, before my last fast food mission aborted beneath the Mercedes.

To be loved again by Serena, I resolved, would be worth monogamy.

Meanwhile, the familiar door at Live Oak Row bumped open, and we were inside.

"Granzeb! You're early," Miss Tebell said.

"I finished up at the Senate before I thought. Rather, the Senate finished ahead of schedule. So I came on over. That zoo finally did something right," Mr. Zebulon said. "It decided not to repeal the right-to-work law. That was our big issue, and we won. I would have to add that neither their motives nor ours were totally pure. You could hardly say that either side was acting on high social impulse. Which is probably a sign that the decision was the correct one."

"That seems terribly cynical, Granzeb. What if everybody acted just on their selfish motives?" Miss Tebell asked.

"But everybody who is sane does. It's only when the real reason is cloaked by hypocrisy that the resulting pretense hurts the naive and innocent. And causes a heap o' trouble in general."

"C'mon, Zebulon. Some people are genuinely altruistic, don't you think?"

He hesitated. "Most people do pretend to some degree of altruism. But when you scratch deep enough, you find that what passes for charity is really the satisfied feeling of power in helping others, and thus controlling them. Power is a basic appetite. Fear is a basic aversion. Pity is imagining our own future calamities. All impulses . . ."

"Oh, Granzeb!" Miss Tebell almost exploded. "Have a heart. I just walked in the door."

That's what I said too. I needed to get out of that purse, breathe, and pilfer dinner.

"Sorry," Mr. Zebulon said. "I didn't mean to sound like Philosophy 101. I get carried away when I view the degenerate vestiges of the democratic process."

"Tell me about it after I've been to the bathroom," she said. "Timing is everything. Now, go up and fix yourself a drink. I'll just see if anything's happened in the office while I was gone."

Thelma was switching off the lights and closing up. "You've had calls from Dr. Old, a newspaper reporter, and that awful woman from Channel Seven. No messages, though."

"Thanks. Oh, Thel, wait a minute. You know more people over at the Capitol than I. What do you, er, hear about the governor?"

"That he wants to be a U.S. senator so bad he can taste it."

"Yeah, but that isn't what I mean. I mean about his personal life. He's a bachelor, right? It must be kinda tough to have any romantic life, the way a governor has to live in a goldfish bowl, and all," Miss Tebell said.

"Gosh, Tayloe, Jack Pine doesn't let that stop him. The Capitol girls say he's the one guy you don't want to be alone with in the elevator. They tell me he's in a terminal state of lechery. The staff of authority, they call him," Thelma said.

"Really?"

"Why so surprised, Tayloe? Governors have glands too. Or so I hear."

"Sure. But . . . oh, never mind. Good night, Thel."

We ran upstairs. Granville Zebulon was standing by a front window, gazing out at the Capitol and clinking ice cubes in two glasses. "Don't worry," he said. "I'm not about to resume the lecture."

"But I want you to," Miss Tebell said charmingly. "Is that my drink? Thanks. It looks divine. Now, as you were saying . . ."

I exited the purse and hid in the draperies.

"I don't want to bore you," Mr. Zebulon said.

"You have never bored me, Granzeb. I get impatient sometimes when you talk high-flown philosophy and politics. What did you mean by, 'degenerate vestiges of the democratic process?' "

"That's just one of those snide cracks offhanded by lobbyists with guilty consciences," Mr. Zebulon said.

"Oh. Do you have a guilty conscience?"

"Did you know that in this light, your hair matches the color of the antique gold leaf on that picture frame?"

"You do have a guilty conscience. And stop trying to get so close," Miss Tebell said.

"I always was a late afternoon man."

"Come on, Granzeb, what about the democratic process? You probably know more about government than anybody I've met."

Mr. Zebulon focused intently on the Capitol, glowing a pale oyster gray as the first lights came on.

"I try not to be cynical. But I look over there and think of the geniuses who started it all, who worked and talked in that

149

old building almost two hundred years ago, and then look at the bungalow brains there today, why ... need I continue? It's a wonder the system works as well as it does."

"But you haven't given up on the system, have you?"

"No. I have been disillusioned by the narrow selfishness of many politicians. Especially by some who have preached the loudest for some of the causes I used to hold the most dear."

"Is that why you went to work for big business?"

"Not entirely. I went to work for a particular business and a particular man. Hygeia and Slemp. Both honest institutions."

"You have a master's in political science, and experience as a lobbyist. Ever think of having a shot at politics yourself?"

He did not respond directly. "A democracy is mostly a game for talkers, which makes it a set-up for lawyers. King Ferdinand II of Spain forbade any lawyers going to his American colonies, lest they multiply disputes among the Indians. I should add that he also regretted doctors had been allowed to go, because they were making new ailments with their cures. Ferdinand thought the worse-off countries were those with the most laws. He could see nothing humane in the law. He doubted that any savagery could be found among the barbarians to equal that of the highly legalized, so-called civilized societies. Lawyers like to keep hostilities churning as long as possible. A democracy is the perfect place to do that."

"Do you mean you'd prefer another government?" Miss Tebell asked.

"Personally, I would prefer no government. In a sort of passive way, I am a born subversive. But a practical one. In the real world, government is a necessity. Not because man is naturally bad, but because he is just awkwardly individualistic. Society is a war of each against all. Man is greedy, pugnacious, and erotic, qualities that always threaten to disorder society, and flat wreck utopias."

"So, I'm puzzled," Miss Tebell said. "Is democracy the least-flawed system we've devised?"

"Not necessarily. Maybe it's best in the long run," Mr. Zebulon said.

"If you could choose, what kind of government would you have?"

"Maybe a monarchy where the sovereign would provide enough law and order to let us peacefully study, play, and do business," Mr. Zebulon said. "Meanwhile, I cope with the system as it is."

"And you enjoy that? Lobbying among those pygmies?"

"Sure. I'm pretty good at it. I'm good in the battle of us against them. Mostly it's pretty drab: fighting for a little advantage on one bill; trying to yank the rug out from another. Horsetrading and wining and dining for the sake of one small phrase in pending legislation. And all the time, I follow La Rochefoucauld's advice: 'The art of life lies in concealing our self-love sufficiently to avoid antagonizing the self-love of others,' " Mr. Zebulon said.

"Okay," Miss Tebell said. "Now that you've cleared all that up, I'm going to the kitchen to start supper. You can fix me another drink, and clear up something else."

"Like what?" Mr. Zebulon asked, above the clatter of pans.

"Like Governor Pine. I have stumbled onto a mystery, Granzeb, a massive contradiction. I have heard today that the elected leader of the Commonwealth is (a) some kind of neuter, an asexual zero, with no romantic life at all — and that he is (b) a raging billygoat who tears off women's garments with his false teeth. I know you can hear all kinds of rumors about politicians, but these two are so out of joint . . ."

The strangling noise I heard was Mr. Zebulon laughing. He laughed so hard that liquid sloshed from his glass onto Miss Tebell's kitchen floor.

"What's so hilarious?" she asked.

"Whee-*yooo*. 'Be sure your sins will find you out.' Oh, God, the irony is too much. That the most personal, intimate details of that old pretender's life would be dragged out at last, and the ridiculous thing is . . . oh, *haw, haw, haw.*"

"Come on, Granzeb. Obviously you know plenty. What's so ridiculous?"

"*That both stories are completely true.*"

"That's impossible."

"No. It's a case of before and after. He once was as libidinous as a harem eunuch. Now he's the hottest thing in pants."

"Boy, what a Freudian turnaround. The governor's psychiatrist should receive a knighthood," Miss Tebell said.

151

"He never saw a psychiatrist in his life."

"Then what happened? Don't tell me he prayed his way into lubricity."

"Tayloe, can I swear you to secrecy on something?"

She held up three fingers. "Girl Scout's honor."

"Mr. Slemp, unlikely as it may seem, is a real-life Eros," Mr. Zebulon said.

"Mr. *Slemp?*"

"Picture him with wings, a loincloth, and a little bow and arrow. Picture him dipping his arrow into a small phial labeled, 'Hygeia Pharmaceuticals.'"

"I don't get it," Miss Tebell wailed.

"I'll explain. You know that lots of problems once thought psychological have turned out to be chemical. The shrinks would spend years finding out why some poor guy was messed up. They might claim he resented his toilet training, or he was frightened by a duck in the park at age two. But it still wouldn't help. Then, just as the patient is about to open a vein, it turns out all he needed was a daily lithium pill. He had a chemical imbalance. He'd spent a fortune and gone through hell exposing every guilty secret he owned, but all he needed was a few cents' worth of daily chemical supplement."

"Yes, I've heard of that. Chemistry has helped many schizophrenics," Miss Tebell said.

"That's it. About five years ago, Mr. Slemp began studying hormone replacement therapy. There had always been the problem that in administering either male or female natural hormones to correct a patient's deficiencies, it wasn't very successful because they were soon destroyed in the bloodstream. Mr. Slemp had a hunch the problem could be solved. So he put two of his best research scientists to work on synthetic hormones. They came up with something called estradiole decanoate for women, and testosterone undecanoate for men.

"Mr. Slemp, who had trouble pronouncing the words, dubbed the male hormone 'undercoat.' That's what we call it informally. In testing the drug on men with abnormally low hormone production, somehow undercoat triggered a natural production of testosterone and other male-linked hormones, like the luteinizing hormone, and the follicle-stimulating hormone. This takes about nine weeks. In a test group of twenty men, almost all reported a gratifying improvement in overall mental and physical tone. Some grew their first facial hair. Most electrifying, though, was that fifteen reported their libidos and sexual activity zoomed. Some, ah, became capable of that for the first time."

"Hmmm-hmmm!" Miss Tebell said in mock provocativeness.

"We can hardly believe it works as well as it does," Mr. Zebulon continued. "It's easy to administer: dissolved in ethyl decanoate, placed in capsules. Absolutely zero unpleasant side effects."

"How about the women? Does their version work as well?"

"It's dynamite. Women who never entertained a sexy feeling before have been turned on. It restores the menstrual cycle where it has lapsed, and gets it going in women who never menstruated. Amenorrhea, or not menstruating, is . . ."

"Hah. I wouldn't mind having that problem for a while," Miss Tebell said.

"Oh, yes you would. You'd mind. You'd feel terrible physically, as well as sinking into depression. The estradiole decanoate jazzes up the production of brain chemicals that regulate the female mood. In women whose ovaries have been removed, it restores production of plasma estrone and estradiole, plus prolactin and the luteinizers."

"But . . . is this stuff in drugstores yet?" Miss Tebell asked.

"Oh, no, no, no. We've been testing it for about two years under the strictest clinical control. That's going to continue for another five years. It takes seven or eight years of testing before the Federal Drug Administration lets us market a drug. We'll probably spend fifteen million dollars in research and testing. This country has the toughest rules on earth for bringing out new drugs. It's a good system from the safety aspect, but it makes drugs very expensive."

"You can't just have human guinea pigs sitting around the Hygeia lab for seven or eight years. Who's taking these pills?" she asked.

"All drug companies have retainer agreements with doctors around the country, mostly at medical schools. The doctors pick the patients for testing. The FDA monitors all this very closely under its drug application program. With some drugs, they test on prisoners. Not in this case."

"But it's incredible that a governor . . . yet you must be saying Governor Pine is taking the stuff. You mean he volunteered for the program? Come on, Granzeb. That's hard to believe."

Granville Zebulon studied his ice cubes.

"Well, he sure volunteered. But he's not exactly in the program."

"He's in it on the q.t.?"

Mr. Zebulon nodded. "That's the part I had to swear you to secrecy about. No governor would go down to a clinic, have his name on charts, submit to all sorts of embarrassing tests, particularly on something this sensitive. No way. I'm not quite sure how it happened, but Mr. Slemp, for all his rough edges, is a subtle and perceptive man. As well as brilliant. Somehow he sensed the governor had a problem. Somehow he dropped a few key words into a conversation with old Jack. The bottom line is that for almost two years, he's been slipping the governor enough undercoat to keep him hotter than a boardinghouse range."

"But why? Are they friends?"

"Businessmen are tough, practical people. The bigger the business, the more government control. The drug business is absolutely dripping with government control. Most of it's federal, to be sure. But Mr. Slemp figured that a little leverage with the governor might come in handy. Or maybe he did it just for the hell of it. He never explained, even though I'm one of only two at Hygeia who know about this. Dr. McIntosh is the other. Now you know."

"It's the hottest piece of gossip I ever heard in my life, and I can't tell anybody," Miss Tebell moaned.

"You sure can't. If you do, I'll have to go back to being a TV weatherman."

I could not empathize with Governor's Pine's problem. Indeed, I never heard of a mouse whose interest in sex was impeded by anything. But I was interested in the clarification of that odd scene at the Capitol between Mr. Slemp and the governor. Moreover, I now could reconcile the riddle posed by Mrs. McGuire's characterization of the chief executive as an impotent, driveling dotard. Driveling and dotard he might still be, but certainly not impotent.

Yet having heard with my own ears the governor's perfidy toward Mr. Slemp, whom he claimed as a friend, it seemed to me the drugmaker's plan had failed. He had achieved no apparent advantage, personal or political, from his role as secret pusher of testosterone undecanoate, or undercoat for short. I felt Mr. Slemp was risking a great deal with little hope of any return. But that was his problem. I was weary of human problems.

Miss Tebell and Mr. Zebulon dined elegantly, leaving a feast of wild rice and snow peas for me in the kitchen. In about an hour they returned to the living room from the dining room, small glasses in hand. She sat gracefully on a sofa and curled her long legs beneath her.

"Bring the Hennessy's, Granzeb, and let's read the paper," she said.

Soon they were sharing sections of the day's *Enquirer*.

"Good Lord," she burst out.

"What?"

" 'CHURCH ORGANIST REVEALED AS HIT COMPOSER,' " Miss Tebell read aloud. "Oh, Granzeb, this is the day for exposing secrets. Listen. 'Arthur P. Hudson, organist at Main Street Presbyterian Church for almost forty years, has been identified as the author of several of the biggest popular music hits from the 1960s to the present.

" 'Currently riding high in the national charts is Hudson's latest, "The Song Nobody Knows," recorded by Southern Cross.

" 'The connection between Hudson and the world of popular music might never have been known had it not been for recent events focusing attention on Main Street Presbyterian.

" 'Reports of mysterious, late-night organ music at the church, giving rise to alleged Phantom of the Organ stories, brought Hudson's name to prominence, although he steadfastly denied he is the so-called Phantom. The *Enquirer*'s music critic, however, noting the identical name of the church organist and the composer of hit songs, called the National Association of Song Authors and Composers (NASAC) in New York. NASAC confirmed the author was Arthur P. Hudson of 33 Riverside Gardens, Byrdport, which is the residence of the church organist.

" 'Today Hudson reluctantly confirmed that he has been leading a double life as pop composer and church organist. Church officials expressed astonishment that the sixtyish organist had produced a string of hit songs, including five gold records. One church elder said there might be some sentiment that Hudson's secular success was undignified, but others said they could see no cause for criticism.

" 'The church's minister, the Reverend Angus Christie, was unavailable for comment.' "

I could scarcely believe my ears. Mr. Hudson? That gentle, retiring, person?

"Really!" Miss Tebell crowed. "Main Street Presbyterian just can't stay out of the news."

"The more the better," Mr. Zebulon said. "Luck is running with you, Tayloe. You could have hired the best flacks in the country, and they couldn't have concocted anything better than what's happened spontaneously."

I had observed Mr. Hudson as closely as anyone. How could that feckless, absentminded musician have been creating a series of hit songs?

It made no sense.

Exhausted, crammed with wild rice and a sip or two of Riesling, I trudged to my quarters in Miss Tebell's walls and fell asleep.

I dreamed of Mr. Hudson playing lead guitar in a rock band. He wore a floppy long vest, and his upper arms were bare. A frayed, yellow manuscript rested on a music rack before him. Serena was dancing with a burly mouse I knew was Earl. I tried to dance with Miss Tebell, but Dr. Old and Mr. Zebulon ran onto the floor and tried to step on me. I jumped into an amplifier as Miss Tebell's suitors began a furious fist fight.

CHAPTER 15

IT IS ONE OF THE PENALTIES AFFLICTING MY SPECIES that when Aurora flings her fair, fresh-quilted colors through the air, we are rarely in a position to see them. Occasionally, I have had the pleasure of viewing a nice sunrise. I envy humans who, warm in their beds, receive the blessing of dawn through sparkling glass. As for mice, we awake to the eternal gloom of the walls.

The term "oversleep" is moreover nonexistent in the world of mice. We do not have to report for work. But my absorption in human culture was by now so intense that when I finally awoke on Friday, March 4, my first agitated thought was that I was late for the office. Historic Byrdport opened for business promptly at 9:00. It was 9:30 when I arrived in the baseboard behind Miss Tebell's desk, aware — through the combined agencies of memory, concentration, and the subtle capacity of the subconscious for sorting things out — that perhaps I could make an interesting contribution toward Miss Tebell's sum of knowledge about the history of Main Street Presbyterian Church.

"Caleb!" she exclaimed as Dr. Old walked through her office door. "How come you're walking around loose this hour of the day?"

"My morning lecture was canceled. We have a distinguished visitor from the Mayo Clinic, and the dean laid on an assembly for him. I should have stuck around, but my feet were drawn by some inexorable force to the Historic Byrdport Foundation."

"I'm glad. I was just going over to the church. How about coming along?"

"Sure. Any special reason?"

"Day after tomorrow the congregation holds its last service within those dingy walls. I was just wondering if Dr. Christie might have had a change of heart about throwing some moral weight behind saving the building. The matter is still so far in the air that I'm not sure where it will come down. Has anything happened on the BUSM side?"

Dr. Old's angular face was difficult to read. "The chairman of the board of visitors said to me yesterday that as far as the administration was concerned, demolition should proceed on schedule. That nothing in the recent publicity, or the opposition of the preservation movement, had made any difference. Furthermore, that in his opinion, it was all a rank, steaming mass of sentimentalism. Furthermore, and I quote precisely, 'That old pile of junk is an eyesore on Main Street anyway, disrupting the medical center's architectural flow.' "

"I see, Caleb. And you said . . .?"

"I said that speaking personally and as assistant provost of BUSM, I disagreed. I said that while medicine, as an objective science, could hardly make common cause with historic preservation, neither should medicine oppose it. I said the least we could do was listen to those with special knowledge, and consider their views as we made our plans."

"Thanks, Caleb. I really appreciate that."

Dr. Old sighed. "But then he said, 'Hell, no.' "

"So they're going ahead," Miss Tebell said.

"The chairman said, 'We need the new building and we're going to get it.' We hashed over the whole affair, and the availability of the two other sites. But he's totally intransigent, Tayloe. We're not going to get any help there."

"We?"

"Sure. We."

"Can't you get in trouble?" she asked.

"From the BUSM organization, I can take some flak. But as a doctor? I've practiced a rather arcane specialty for fifteen years, and I've done it well. I'm not worried about my career. The school needs a good thyroid specialist more than I need BUSM."

"I hope you know what you're doing. Okay, let's go over and scrutinize the old pile of junk," Miss Tebell said.

I had crept into her waiting purse.

As we strode through Capitol Square I reflected on the vein of irony that permeated this affair of three males and Miss Tebell. Mr. Zebulon and I each knew different things that might pass ammunition to Miss Tebell's cause, but we were unable to take action. Dr. Old, a fresher recruit, appeared free to act and speak, yet he had nothing special to do or say.

Well, we would see. I resolved that as for me, I would do my very best, though precious little preferment lay in it for Charles Churchmouse.

After four days in exile, it was good to inhale the smells of the old church. Some places are so drenched in emotion-triggering scents that regardless of any lapse of time, in spite of whatever battering our senses have absorbed in however long a journey, they rush upon us with effect undimmed. In one way or another, those places are home.

"Ever been inside before? No? I'll show you around. I can see Dr. Christie later," Miss Tebell said.

"I haven't been inside any church in twenty-five years. Except to get married and attend funerals."

"I used to feel that way," she said. "Then I went on a trip to England. Every day there was a fresh cathedral or historic church on the tour. At first they all looked alike and were a bore. When I started noticing differences, they were like snowflakes, Caleb. St. Paul's, Canterbury, Salisbury, Winchester, Exeter, Wells, Chester, Durham, York. I was hooked. I remember, when we reached Ely, there was a boys' choir performing at evensong. It was like hearing angels. I stood there against an ancient pillar, still bearing traces of blue Norman paint. What I finally realized was, while hardly anyone takes religion seriously there anymore, such places are still used and cherished because of what they mean culturally. They go through the motions of religion, and nobody minds, because of all the good stuff that comes in the fallout. So when I got home from that trip, I surprised my friends and myself when I joined a church. Main Street Presbyterian. This is my church, Caleb."

"I understand the appeal," Dr. Old said. "But there's quite a difference between a major medieval cathedral and a middle nineteenth-century church."

"Mainly matters of degree," she argued. "Main Street Presbyterian is a serene, top-of-the-line statement. And 1842 is not exactly yesterday. One problem, though, is that we haven't any historical star quality. No big names. If General Lee or Andy Jackson or Sam Houston or anybody big had only been associated with it . . . but no. Of course, it was used as a Civil War hospital, but so was almost every other large building in Byrdport, and lots of them are still standing."

"So the Phantom of the Organ is our chief asset," Dr. Old said. "Where's he been lately?"

"Beats me, Caleb. Nobody's reported anything for a couple days."

"Mass hysteria is amazing," he said.

"You think that's what it was?"

"Of course. Oh, there may have been some real basis of sound, approximating organ music, to get the first impressionable person started."

"But I think I heard him, Caleb. Playing 'The Old Rugged Cross.' "

"Let's see this ghostly instrument."

We clumped up the narrow stairwell to the choir loft. There was nothing grand about either of the church's matching stairways to the organ loft and gallery. The builders had boxed them in with simple wooden paneling, considerably less elegant than the rest of the interior. With doors at bottom and top, the effect was almost like entering a large closet.

"Almost nobody has the original stairwells anymore," Miss Tebell said as we approached the top. "They were made like this for heat economy. But they weren't fancy enough for the late Victorians, who usually tore them out and rebuilt grander stairs. Well, here we are. The Erben organ. Can you imagine throwing that out for the trashmen?"

"It's a handsome thing, and seems in better shape than I'd imagined. Sure it won't play?" Dr. Old asked.

Miss Tebell slid onto the bench and flicked the switch. With the short circuit blocking the connection, nothing happened. "I understand it's some minor electrical problem they just didn't think worth spending money on," she said. "Actually, I think the action and the pipes are in pretty good shape. I played it once. Like all Erbens it has a soft, lovely tone. Very sensitive."

"I remember you played the piano, but I didn't know you could handle an organ."

"Oh, I really can't. Hey, let's walk up front in the gallery. I want you to get the interior perspective from there."

It was the same scene that occurred so long ago between her and Mr. Zebulon. She left her purse on the organ bench and I heard them walk away.

Here was the opportunity I had hoped for.

I jumped from the purse and entered the organ.

My objective was the familiar stack of ancient sheet music inside one of the case doors. I had destroyed some of it for nests, and we had scattered several sheets around while examining them last Sunday, just before our first experience in playing from a score. It was that sheet I searched out now. I grasped it in my teeth and dragged it from the organ case. While the weight of the paper was no great problem, the music's cumbersome shape made it awkward to handle. Climbing up the console bench was the hardest part. On my first attempt I dropped the paper halfway up the bench, and started over. The sheet music billowed over my face, blocking my vision. It caught and ripped on one side, but I persevered and tugged it free.

And I placed the score on the bench, right beside Miss Tebell's purse.

I could hear their voices from the front of the gallery. They would soon return. Did I have time to pull out one more paper? There was one I had in mind. It might be of interest too. Possibly it was of surpassing interest. I ran back into the organ case.

Seconds passed while I searched for it. Then I discovered the manuscript was so fragile that it tended to break apart at the edges when I gripped it with my teeth. The dry fragments

161

tasted of concentrated age. I feared I might destroy the brown, spotted paper before I moved it. Yet after several false starts, I had dragged the music, largely intact, out of the organ door when I heard Miss Tebell and Dr. Old approaching. There was no more time. I dropped the music and ran for Miss Tebell's purse.

"The place is a time capsule of the 1840s," she was saying. "I . . . that's funny. I don't remember this old piece of sheet music being here. Do you, Caleb?"

"No, but I wasn't concentrating on the bench. I hardly saw it."

"And look! There's another one on the floor. I don't remember that either. And that little cabinet door is cracked open."

From her purse I heard the door's muffled creak as she opened it wider. "For crying out loud, Caleb. The organ case is crammed with old sheet music. Look at this."

"What a mess. Well, you're going to have to inspect it alone. Look at the time; it's almost eleven. I have two patients scheduled for thyroid scans. Call you late this afternoon?"

"Sure. Oh, Caleb, wait a minute. I wanted to ask you something about drug testing."

"Can it keep till tonight?" His voice echoed in the stairwell.

"I guess," she said. "See you."

"'Bye." I heard his footsteps descending two stairs at a time.

Miss Tebell took the console bench. There were faint rustling sounds, and I knew she was examining the old sheets of music. The church was drenched in silence, save for the distant rumble of Main Street traffic.

In her astonishingly rich contralto, she began to hum.

She was perfect in all other ways. Why should she not have perfect pitch?

Without significant hesitation she hummed the first of the two songs I had dragged from the organ. Then she gasped.

"Good Lord," she said.

She hummed through the other melody, *con brio*.

"Good *Lord*," she repeated.

Decisively, she slipped off the bench, grabbed the purse,

and ran from the church. Horns honked as she darted across Main Street. Then we trotted through Capitol Square and into the office on Live Oak Row.

"Thelma. What's Billy Manchester's phone number?" she panted.

"That funky archaeologist who cleans out old wells? He's at State Landmarks Division, right? Here, I have it. Want me to dial?"

"Please. I sure hope he's in, and not out in a hole someplace. Ah. Billy? Tayloe Tebell. Hi. Glad you're in. Look, do you know anything about old manuscripts? I know it's a bit out of your line." Pause. "Sure. What you learned in one good graduate course ought to help. Can I slip over to your office? Good. There in five minutes."

"What's going on?" Thelma asked.

"Maybe some star quality at last. Maybe the church had some all along. Get me a good sturdy folder and a big manila envelope. These things are falling apart."

"Here. What's . . ."

Miss Tebell and I were already out the door.

The Capitol Square perimeter was lined with government office buildings. I am not certain to which one we proceeded in Miss Tebell's surging stride, but it does not matter. Soon I heard the voice of the archaeologist who had visited Miss Tebell a week or so before. She dumped the purse roughly.

"Glad you called," the man said. "This time of year I get sick of sorting pottery shards and rustproofing seventeenth-century hoe blades."

Now their voices seemed to come from a distance, and I risked a look around. I saw a large room filled with steel cabinets and boxes. Down one wall was a row of tanks. Floor-to-ceiling shelves held a clutter of rusted, dirty, broken objects. Miss Tebell and the archaeologist were leaning over a desk, inspecting the sheet music.

"Well?" Miss Tebell demanded. "What do you think?"

Mr. Manchester's pleasant expression seemed to mask a mild disappointment.

"Ah, I'd have to say they weren't very old. I was somehow thinking you might be talking about some seventeenth- or eighteenth-century stuff. These are just middle nineteenth century," the man said.

"I know that, or hope that," she said impatiently. "That's the point. Look, both manuscripts have dates written on them. March 3, 1859. What I want to know is, before I do something foolish, are these sheets definitely of that time, or could they be later copies?"

Mr. Manchester studied the documents through a glass device.

"The paper looks right. Fiber, rag content — all checks out. Common, average quality manuscript paper of the time. These lines here — staffs, you call them? — were printed. For composers to write in the notes. And the lyrics underneath. I guess musicians use the same kind of blanks today. These, as you can see by the penmanship and the style of inking in the notes, were done by two different hands. The style of both hands appears to be early to middle nineteenth century."

"There's no chance, then, that these could be some kind of printed reproductions?"

"No way. Both are definitely hand-produced manuscripts. I . . . Jumping Heinrich Schliemann! The title of this one just sank in!"

"I was wondering if you'd ever notice," Miss Tebell said with an enormous grin.

"This . . ." he reverently held up the most tattered of the two sheets of music, ". . . if this signature is authentic . . ."

". . . is at the very least an early copy by the composer . . ." Miss Tebell interrupted.

"And quite possibly the original," Mr. Manchester said.

" 'Dixie,' " Miss Tebell said.

" 'Dixie.' Or as it says here, 'Dixie's Land,' which is how it was introduced," Mr. Manchester said. "Look what a flourish he signed it with. 'Dan D. Emmett of the Virginia Minstrels, the Nonpareil Interpreter of Ethiopian Melodies.' "

So that's what it says, I thought. While I had not been able to read the words, I had recognized them, because they were some of the same ones that appeared on one of the buildings in the ancient photograph of Main Street. I had thought there could be a connection. But I knew nothing about "Dixie" or a Mr. Emmett.

"I can't thank you enough, Billy," Miss Tebell said. "Gotta run now."

She picked up the manuscripts with great gentleness and placed them in the envelope.

"Wait! What's it all about? How'd you get possession of those things?" the man demanded.

I ducked down in the purse.

"I'm really not sure, Billy, but I'll find out, and you'll be among the first to know."

With a lurch I was airborne again.

I rejoiced in Miss Tebell's favorable reaction to the "Dixie" paper. Yet it was the first manuscript, to which she had paid little heed, which had seemed more significant to me. I hoped that later she would find it interesting too.

After a staccato dash through Capitol Square we were back in her office on Live Oak Row, and again she was telephoning.

"Dr. Christie, this is Tayloe Tebell. Fine. No, I haven't given up. Have you? Well, sir, something's come up that I think might be of interest to you and the church, and I would like to slip over and talk about it. Yes, I realize you are very busy, but . . . No, next week sometime would not do, Dr. Christie . . . Well, I can summarize it this way. I have just come into some important historical information regarding the church that will doubtless make further headlines. I think we both might prefer those headlines to be as dignified and constructive as possible. Yes, around five today will be fine. And oh, one more very important thing: could you please arrange to have Mr. Hudson, the organist, on hand too?"

It was now around 1:00 P.M.

Miss Tebell drummed her fingers on the desk. "Thel, I feel as though I've done a day's work in the fields, I'm so hungry. I'm going upstairs and fix a sandwich and look up something in my encyclopedia."

"You said you'd tell me why you went kiting out with those two old pieces of music," Thelma said.

"And I shall. Let us imagine, Thel, a manuscript copy of 'Dixie,' signed by the author and dated at the time the song was known to be composed. Let us further speculate that this manuscript just might be the long-lost original copy, the composer's numero uno. And let us imagine that this old document was found in Main Street Presbyterian. Think that would make news?"

"You mean a copy handwritten by the composer?" Thelma asked cautiously.

"By Daniel Decatur Emmett himself. In 1859."

"I think it would excite antiquarians and music scholars. The AP would probably carry a brief story around the country. Yes, it would make news. The public likes short doses of that kind of Americana," Thelma said.

"Think it would have any effect on saving the church?" Miss Tebell asked.

Thelma thought a moment. "I'm not sure. The effect might be good, or it might be just sort of . . . shrugged off. At least by BUSM."

"That's how I see it," Miss Tebell agreed. "But I think there's something more to this, something I haven't figured out yet."

"Tayloe, did you really find the copy of 'Dixie'? Is that what you're saying?"

"I didn't exactly find it. Thel, it was almost like someone handed it to me."

I was fairly bursting with pride as we climbed the stairs.

She made her sandwich while I, cocky with power, strutted in the parlor. I climbed to one of the front windows. It was a brilliantly clear afternoon in early March. The bare branches of Capitol Square's mighty elms, contorted by wind gusts, scratched harshly into the cerulean void. On the ground, lovers stretching their lunchtimes strolled among the boxwood and holly, hunched against the wind in their winter coats.

And directly below me in the street, a Mercedes roadster cruised.

At the passenger's window I saw distinctly the perfect facial planes and onyx hair of Viola da Gamba.

Mr. Junior had returned a day early! Was Serena down there too? Was this the moment I had waited for, three days' running? Was my honest impulse one of pleased excitement at a reunion with Serena, or was I agitated by the inconvenience of this premature return? What might it do to the schedule now set in motion by Miss Tebell and me?

Apparently, Live Oak Row was the car's destination, for it nearly stopped there in the street, and I saw the driver's stubby hand point past Miss da Gamba toward our front door. But there was no place to park, and the car moved on slowly.

I heard Miss Tebell coming from the kitchen. She went to the bookshelves that covered one end of the parlor, and pulled down a large book. She riffled through its pages. "Emmett," she read aloud. "Yep, it was in 1859, all right."

More minutes passed as she searched through other books. The telephone rang. She picked it up.

"Right, Thel . . . Mr. Junior Slemp is here?" Miss Tebell said in surprise. "I'll be right down."

I melted into the walls. On my way downstairs, I resolved to make every effort to accompany Mr. Junior and Miss da Gamba when they returned to the car, regardless of what I might miss later that afternoon. I could do nothing else. But I confess it was a decision based upon duty and rectitude, rather than my strongest impulse. Call it a victory of probity over passion, for again I was ensorceled by Miss Tebell. Yes, I admit it. But I determined to find Serena. It is important to understand that, and I take some ease of conscience from it.

"Hey, Miss Tebell," Mr. Junior bawled. "Remember me?"

"Of course, Mr. Slemp."

"This is Viola da Gamba. I don't suppose you've met," Mr. Junior said.

"I've seen you in the Rib Cage, Miss Tebell," Miss da Gamba said in a friendly way. "You like your pizza with double anchovies, right?"

"Viola here," Mr. Junior said, "is really an actress." The squat young man beamed at the two women. "And she's mighty good."

"Aw, Junior, she doesn't want to hear about me," Miss da Gamba said, with a wide smile.

"Baby, the whole world's going to hear about you, *haw, haw, haw.*" He was transparently good-natured. I doubted that he would ever have the depth of his father, but he was impossible to dislike.

"Ah, why don't we all sit down? And then you can tell me the reason for this nice call." Miss Tebell seemed baffled by the young couple.

"Sure. We didn't come by just to holler at you. The fact is, Miss Tebell, I've been doing a lot of thinking about the old church. Now, please correct me if I'm wrong, because I want to be certain I understand the situation." He leaned forward in his chair, his expression earnest.

"As I get it, three things must happen for the church to be saved," Mr. Junior said, "and time's running out on all three. First, the medical college has to put its new building somewhere else. And there must be something to make 'em do that. The state owns the church now, and if the state declared it surplus property, it would have to be sold again. Am I right so far?"

"Right as can be," Miss Tebell agreed.

"But if that happened, the right party has to be there ready with the cash to buy. That's the third thing. They're all kind of mixed up together. They interlock," Mr. Junior said. "Well, I can't do anything about the first two pieces of the puzzle, but if you want somebody to buy that building, and make good use of it, Miss Tebell, why, I'm your man."

Miss Tebell extended her arms upon her desk. She meshed her fingers together and contemplated her parallel thumbs with a restrained smile.

"I'm sure that's very good news indeed," she said. "I'm also very curious about . . ."

"About what he's going to do with it, right?" Miss da Gamba said with a gigantic smile. I doubted that any dental chart in the BUSM School of Orthodontistry approached that perfect symmetry and occlusion.

"Well, Mr. Slemp," Miss Tebell said, "I didn't know you were a preacher."

"No, ma'am. What I want to do, Miss Tebell, is make it into a theater."

"A great legitimate theater," Miss da Gamba said.

Miss Tebell thought it over, and shrugged. "Well, why not? The church people don't care; they've already sold it for junk. But I thought . . . I heard somewhere . . . that you were going into professional basketball."

"So did I. Had me the franchise for this area in the new league. But I started figuring, what did I really know about running a professional basketball team? And all I could see ahead was about three years' worth of headaches and hassles before there was even a prayer of breaking even. Contrary to what Daddy may think," he said with some bitterness, "I'm a pretty conservative businessman."

Mr. Junior looked levelly at Miss Tebell. "When I got the franchise in the first place, I slipped in ahead of some Tidewater boys. They wanted the franchise bad, it turned out, and they didn't give up easy. Kept after me to sell. So this week, I just let it be known that Viola and I would be down at the ocean in Daddy's condo, just watching the breakers, and if they had anything more to say, I'd listen."

"I take it they had something to say?"

Mr. Junior hitched a sock up one powerful calf. "They did. They offered me a million and a half. Since I only gave five hundred thousand for the franchise rights a couple of weeks ago, I figured I'd grab the money and run."

"You made a million dollars and you didn't do *anything?*" Miss Tebell demanded incredulously. "You never even organized a team?"

"Never so much as bought the first basketball. Almost sinful, isn't it? In a couple or three years, though, that same franchise will be worth double what I sold it for, at least. Even if the new owners lose a pile of money getting started, which is likely.

"In college," Mr. Junior continued, "I ended up as a drama major. Don't laugh. I wasn't an actor, but I handled the technical and organizational side. I liked it. I was good at it."

Miss Tebell seemed dubious. "Do you think Byrdport will support a legitimate theater? The suburbs already have lots of dinner theaters. They come and go."

"They're pretty amateurish," Miss da Gamba said, more serious and intelligent than before. "The actors are local people having a good time. What Junior wants to do is bring the best to Byrdport. And, occasionally, some historical stuff, like eighteenth-century comedies, and Civil War melodramas."

"Funny thing about that church," Mr. Junior said. "I've

had an architect look it over, and he says the interior dimensions are just perfect for a medium-sized theater. It would take lots of modifications, but nothing that couldn't be handled. He said that because the architectural style was neo . . . neo . . ."

"Neoclassical?" Miss Tebell said.

"That's it. He said if the church had been built ten years later, it wouldn't have been as good."

"Exactly, a Gothic revival church would have had too many features that would have been hard to alter," Miss Tebell explained.

"It would have looked too churchy," Miss da Gamba said. "The architect said we shouldn't change anything on the outside."

Mr. Junior now showed increasing animation. "You asked if Byrdport would support such a theater. My feeling is, the downtown's about to come back. Already we have a restaurant boom. People are restoring whole neighborhoods of old townhouses. There's going to be a new cluster of high-rise condos by the river. People with money are coming back downtown, and they're the kind of people who enjoy good theater. There's no place now, no legitimate theater. The Civic Center gets the big ice shows and rock stars. But you can't have theater there; it seats twelve thousand people."

"You're right," Miss Tebell said with more enthusiasm than before.

Mr. Junior nodded happily.

"It sounds like you've given lots of thought to the project, and you may have the answer. Or part of it," Miss Tebell mused. "I think I like the idea. By the way, can I assume the leading lady for your first production has been already named?"

Miss da Gamba smiled. It was as though a cosmic stage hand turned up the house lights.

"You got it, Miss Tebell," she agreed happily.

Announcing that he had more stops to make, Mr. Junior and Miss da Gamba prepared to end the interview.

I flexed the muscles of my legs.

CHAPTER 16

I HAD TO GO WITH THEM. SERENA WAS PROBABLY IN MR. Junior's car. Throughout the conversation, I had considered every aspect of darting across the office rug to where, with the grace of an ocelot, Miss da Gamba rested in a green leather chair. The run would be difficult, for she was in the center of the room. And instead of flinging her purse on the floor, in the manner of Miss Tebell, Miss da Gamba had stuffed it beside her in the chair. Mr. Junior carried no briefcase. I considered his coat pockets. But he was seated a good ten feet from any wall of the enormous room.

All I could do was make a dash for Miss da Gamba's chair. There was no other answer. I began to run.

She saw me just before I reached the chair.

Mr. Junior already was on his feet, making his goodbyes with Miss Tebell. Miss da Gamba was starting to uncoil from the chair. Even as I sprinted, I could see the sudden alarm in her glorious brown eyes.

"Oh, damn, a mouse," Miss da Gamba said. She did not scream. "Hey, stomp it, Junior. He's . . . oh, hell, he's gone under my chair!"

"Get up and I'll tip it over and see," Mr. Junior said.

I clawed upward into the upholstery. If I could enter the

bag while they were still looking under the chair, on the floor
. . .

Too late. Lost in a maze of springs and cotton batting, I felt the shift of weight as Miss da Gamba raised herself from the chair. Then it tilted giddily as Mr. Junior looked underneath.

"I don't see him," he said.

"These old houses. It's hard to keep mice out," Miss Tebell said.

"I never did see him," Mr. Junior said. "Are you sure you put your contacts in this morning, Vi?"

"Not funny, Junior. I really did see a mouse."

I heard their voices and footfalls fading into the hall; out the front door.

So, you see, I tried. I could not follow them through the streets to wherever they had parked the car. At midafternoon, that would have been almost suicidal. Perhaps, I thought, I could pick up their trail tomorrow evening at the Rib Cage, when Miss da Gamba was expected to return to her waitressing duties. Until then, or some earlier unforseeable opportunity, I could take some comfort in having done my best, even daring a confrontation with Mr. Junior's extra wide brogans.

As I returned to the safety of the walls, Miss Tebell returned to her office with Thelma.

". . . seems like a solid idea," Miss Tebell said. "Making a theater of the building would preserve it in a useful and vital way. It would make the place a lively centerpiece of the downtown's culture. I think it might succeed handsomely."

"That boy Junior might not be as slow as we thought, eh?" Thelma said.

"He's not slow. He does have the misfortune of being a clone of his father in looks. That makes it harder for people to consider him as his own man," Miss Tebell explained.

Late in the afternoon, she carefully placed into her briefcase the manila envelope containing the two antique manuscripts. While she shrugged into her coat, I, tense with excitement, entered her purse.

"I don't know what I'm getting into over there," she announced energetically. "Dr. Christie has always puzzled me.

172

But here goes, Thel. This may be a disaster, but it'll sure as hell be interesting."

Already it was twilight. I heard the rush of evening traffic, and the relative tranquility of Capitol Square. The thrill of beginning a journey with Miss Tebell never palled. With her graceful, athletic stride, her body warming the purse from beneath her arm, and the nearness of her perfect form, an aura of rightness was all around me, and I imbibed it with shameless intoxication.

"Hey, Tayloe!" a familiar voice cried.

"Granzeb!" She stopped walking.

Why did the bliss always end so soon?

"What a day," he said. "I was just coming back to the Capitol after a little heavy lobbying at a hotel cocktail party."

"Isn't the Assembly about to adjourn?" she asked.

"It is, I hope. This was the last scheduled day. But they'll probably stop the clock tonight and keep going through tomorrow at least. Where are you off to?"

"I'm just running over to the church a minute."

"Any chance you'll be in your office tomorrow? I know it's Saturday, but I'd like to come by, with some people I know. I think you'll be interested in meeting them. It's about the church, need I add."

"Sure, Granzeb. If I'm not in the office I'll be upstairs."

"Good. Hey, all that business about the old organist who's been writing pop hits. How does that fit in? Can you use it to your advantage somehow?" Mr. Zebulon asked.

"Maybe, but it's still . . . developing. It'll keep until tomorrow. Look, I do have to run. See you then," Miss Tebell said.

We continued past the Capitol, and soon had crossed Main Street. In a moment I sensed that we had entered a side door of the church. Then we went through an inner door.

"Hello, Mrs. Pope," Miss Tebell said, vibrant with spirit.

"You," Mrs. Pope said in frigid response, "are the young woman who has been stirring up all this preservation business."

"I've been trying pretty hard," Miss Tebell admitted.

"Dr. Christie is working on his final sermon to be delivered in this sanctuary," Mrs. Pope snapped. "I dislike interrupting him."

173

"It's all right," came Dr. Christie's voice from the adjoining office. "I'm expecting her."

We entered the pastor's study, familiar to me by its musty scent of old theological volumes.

"Have you ever met Mr. Hudson?" Dr. Christie asked.

As they murmured greetings, I wished that I could see them all. But the danger of leaving the purse, and the risk of being left behind, was too great.

"I'm a great admirer of your musicianship, Mr. Hudson," Miss Tebell said. "When you play the Erben, it's marvelous. Or was."

"Mr. Hudson's skill at sacred music is well known," Dr. Christie said. "Lately we have lear-rr-rned of his equal gifts at the profane."

"Dr. Christie, I tell you again how embarrassed I am," Mr. Hudson said.

"I suppose there's nothing wrong with being repeatedly in the top for-rr-rty, but you might have told us, Hudson. To learn it in the newspaper. That came as a powerful surprise."

"I think 'The Song Nobody Knows' is just great," Miss Tebell said.

"Someday I must listen to it," Dr. Christie said. Did he never turn on a radio? "Mr. Smeak informed me this morning, with a certain unbecoming glee, that an Oklahoma evangelist claims to have discerned a Satanic message when the recording is played backwards. If theologians of that kidney are preaching against the song, perhaps it has merit. But that is beside the point. As for this gathering, I suppose you have come to regale us again, Miss Tebell, about the necessity for preservation. I do think we know all the arguments by now."

"No, sir. No lectures from me," Miss Tebell said. "The campaign may be about to succeed, anyway."

"Indeed," Dr. Christie said.

"What I have to tell you relates to the musical history of Main Street Presbyterian Church," she said.

Someone shifted suddenly in his chair. From the same place in the room I heard staccato throat-clearing sounds. It sounded like Mr. Hudson.

"This morning," Miss Tebell began, "I found something of

174

extraordinary interest at the Erben organ." She described her visit to the church with Dr. Old, and how she discovered the two old musical scores. Then she recounted her interview with Mr. Manchester, the archaeologist.

"So," Dr. Christie interjected. "You removed those objects from the church. They were not your property."

"Agreed," she said cheerfully. "But they are back in the church now. I have them right here. I'll turn them over to you now, if you wish. I certainly trust you in every way."

"How kind." Dr. Christie's voice was laden with irony. "May I see them, please?"

Miss Tebell unzipped her leather case. I heard gentle rustling.

No one spoke for at least two minutes.

"Indeed," Dr. Christie said at last, "they appear very old. And this one is, as you say, 'Dixie.' It would certainly be remarkable if it were an authentic manuscript by the composer himself."

"An expert on old documents — handwriting and so forth — could tell," Miss Tebell said.

"What about the other one? You haven't said much about that. It seems equally old," the minister said, with obviously increasing interest.

"As you can see here at the top, although part of it has disintegrated — eaten by bugs — the piece is entitled 'Nocturne Triste.' It is only a melody, however; there are no lyrics. There is no composer's signature remaining, either," Miss Tebell said.

"So? What significance can you attach to it?" Dr. Christie asked.

"This," Miss Tebell said. "Just listen."

She began to hum. Her contralto was so vibrant, so resonant, that even at lullaby level it seemed to fill the room.

After two bars, the most tone-deaf auditor should have guessed. Should have known.

It was "The Song Nobody Knows."

She hummed once through the chorus, and stopped.

"Well?" she asked, to no one in particular.

"Oh, dear," Mr. Hudson said.

"What do you mean?" Dr. Christie snapped. "What does each of you mean?"

"That's the melody of Mr. Hudson's current hit song," she said softly. "Right, Mr. Hudson?"

"I should have known this would happen," Mr. Hudson said.

Poor man. His voice seemed intensely agitated.

"That *what* would happen, Hudson?" Dr. Christie asked. He was now firm but sympathetic.

"It's my grandfather's melody," Mr. Hudson croaked. "All of them are. The music to my pop songs, I mean. Grandfather wasn't much of a lyricist. A great melody man, but he just couldn't get the words right."

"Your grandfather?" Dr. Christie said unbelievingly. "But this music seems far too old . . ."

"Grandfather came here in the 1850s," Mr. Hudson continued in a flat and toneless voice. "He was the organist in this church when it was still almost new. But he was very late in marrying, and he was an old man when my father was born. My father, in turn the organist here, also married very, very late. It is unusual, Dr. Christie, but among us Hudsons, a few generations cover a lot of ground. Oh, they would be so ashamed of me now."

"But — Hudson, I think your grandfather might be rather pleased," Dr. Christie said.

"I never meant to seek any glory for it," Mr. Hudson said, in rising accents. "There was no copyright on the melodies. I had to change the time, the beat, to make the music more contemporary. And I wrote all the words. But then I entered words and music in my own name. It was wrong. The first time, I did it just for convenience. I mean, why explain? I thought. I never dreamed the songs would be so popular."

"If anyone was entitled to use those melodies it was you, Mr. Hudson. There's no problem with that," Miss Tebell said soothingly. "Now, what I think we'd like to know is, do you have any idea of how the old manuscript copy of 'Dixie' happened to be in the organ with your grandfather's manuscripts?"

"Why, Mr. Emmett left it there."

"Mr. Emmett. *Dan* Emmett?" Miss Tebell gasped. "The composer? The minstrel man?"

"The same."

"He . . . he was here?"

"Miss Tebell, he wrote 'Dixie' here," Mr. Hudson said.

There was a silence during which Dr. Christie and Miss Tebell assimilated the news. Finally, Dr. Christie spoke.

"Hudson. Are you quite certain of this?"

"Of course, sir. Mr. Emmett and my grandfather were great friends. It happened this way. Mr. Emmett organized the first troupe of Negro minstrels in 1843, as a very young man. He invented the genre, as it were, and called his company the Virginia Minstrels. They were all white men in blackface, and their music was called Ethiopian melodies, all about the happy slaves and so forth down South. He called them the Virginia Minstrels not only because he wanted a Southern name, but — although he was born in Ohio — also because his father had come from Staunton, Virginia, in the Shenandoah Valley. That was the old Emmett family home."

"How did your grandfather happen to meet this Emmett?" Dr. Christie asked.

"In the early 1850s my grandfather was studying music in Philadelphia. Although he was a gifted classical musician, he also had a talent for popular music. He could play the banjo with some virtuosity. Well, one of the Emmett troupe got sick, and my grandfather filled in. Later he traveled with Emmett's Virginia Minstrels for several years. He and Mr. Emmett covered the country with the minstrels. Mr. Emmett wrote the big hits, like 'Zip Coon,' 'Old Dan Tucker,' and 'Jordan Am a Hard Road to Travel.' Grandfather began writing songs too.

"But he grew tired of traveling. In 1856, the troupe was in Byrdport for a performance, actually at a theater just down on the corner of this same block. There was a famous early photograph — a daguerreotype — of the theater building made about that time. It showed the Emmett playbill posted out front. You may have seen it. Anyway, on that visit, he heard about a vacant position at the church. So he got the organist job, and he stayed here the rest of his life."

"What about 'Dixie'?" Miss Tebell asked.

"Oh. About three years later, early in 1859, Mr. Emmett broke up his Virginia Minstrels. They had lost their popularity to newer, more sophisticated minstrel troupes, and he was at a low ebb. But one day, while riding a train north from Charleston, he had an idea for a new musical comedy act. He decided to talk to my father about it, and to seek the advice of Mr. Foster, as well."

"Mr. Foster?" asked Miss Tebell in apparent confusion and surprise.

Mr. Hudson continued talking as though he, lost in the past, did not hear. "It was a rather confused period in Mr. Foster's life. He and his wife Jane were moving from one boarding-house to the next in Pittsburgh and Cincinnati. He was drinking a lot and it seemed to make him want to travel. So when Mr. Emmett telegraphed him to ask if he could meet the other two in Byrdport, he agreed."

"Wait a minute, Hudson," Dr. Christie said. "This Foster. Are you by any chance referring to . . ."

"To Stephen Foster," Mr. Hudson said offhandedly. "He was, as I say, commencing his downhill slide. Most of his great songs already had been written. Although nobody realized it at the time. Well, as I say, Mr. Foster came to Byrdport. He put up at the nearby Eagle House, where Mr. Emmett was staying. For the few days that this get-together lasted, they would join my grandfather over here in the church, at the Erben, where they talked over Mr. Emmett's ideas for a new musical comedy. But with one thing and another, nothing ever came of it. Except the three songs."

"The *three* songs?" Dr. Christie exclaimed.

"The three musicians were all rather playful, and proud of their talents as well," Mr. Hudson continued. "So one day they agreed on a competition. This was a great age for musical contests, you see. Bandleaders were heroes, and they were always challenging each other to public competitions. So my grandfather, Mr. Emmett, and Mr. Foster decided on their own personal competition."

"You mean, playing before an audience?" Dr. Christie asked.

"No, sir. They decided that each composer would take a

two-hour period and, from scratch, write a totally new song. Then they would have them published, and the public's acceptance would determine which was the most popular. So, on March 3, 1859, they had the contest."

"Here in the church?" Miss Tebell asked.

"Right here. Grandfather, as I explained, just didn't have the knack for words, and unfortunately he could never get a publisher to accept his song. That is, until recently, and I think you may agree he was a composer of some talent," Mr. Hudson said.

" 'The Song Nobody Knows,' " Miss Tebell said. "That was his entry in the competition."

"Yes. Dan Emmett's song was the first of the three to get anywhere. He went back to New York, where Firth, Pond and Company published 'Dixie.' He signed on with Bryant's Minstrels, the most popular troupe of the day, and they introduced it. I guess you know it became a secular masterpiece and the national anthem of the Confederacy.

"What happened to Mr. Foster for the next year or so is unclear. He kept traveling a lot, and eventually settled in New York, where he died in 1864. He was also having some contract troubles with his publishers. Anyway, it was more than a year and a half later, in November of 1860, that Firth, Pond brought out his Byrdport song." Mr. Hudson paused. "Can you guess what it was?"

"Tell us, Hudson," said Dr. Christie, obviously caught up in the organist's story.

" 'Old Black Joe.' The odd thing is, critics have often puzzled over how Stephen Foster wrote one of his supreme masterpieces at a time when, frankly, he was far gone in alcoholic decline. Most of the other songs he wrote in his last years were simply not up to his earlier work. People have tried to explain it by saying he experienced a temporary, brilliant regathering of his powers. But the truth is, he wrote the song in Byrdport years earlier than its publication date. As to why it took so long to get published, I have no idea."

Above Dr. Christie's fireplace, a small steeple clock ticked off the precious moments.

" 'Dixie' and 'Old Black Joe.' Both written in this church," Dr. Christie said thoughtfully. "At the Erben."

"As well as 'The Song Nobody Knows,'" Miss Tebell added.

"Thank you, Miss Tebell," Mr. Hudson said.

"What I don't understand, Hudson, is why, in effect, you concealed information like this," Dr. Christie said. "Even I, who ordinarily would have scant interest in such matters, can see the historical significance in what is emerging here. This is important material, Hudson. Could you not recognize that?"

"Of course, Dr. Christie." Mr. Hudson seemed terribly dejected, now that Dr. Christie had articulated the point. "But I was afraid that somehow, if the story on 'Dixie' and 'Old Black Joe' came out, then so would the facts on how I plagiarized my grandfather's work. It was all tied up together. And now it has happened, just as I feared. The nightmare is real. Oh, my. Da – damn. Yes, damn. "What will happen to me?"

"*Nothing*, Hudson," Dr. Christie said. "Compose yourself. You can't plagiarize from your own grandfather, for heaven's sake. Especially when he's been dead for . . . how long?"

"Eighty-three years, sir," Mr. Hudson said.

"There you are. I'm sure he is pleased. My advice to you is to rejoice in the success of this long-range collaboration. Now. I suppose, Miss Tebell, that I should compliment you on the resourcefulness and percipience which led you to this discovery. Indeed, I do. And I gather that you are fairly itching to fling this choice morsel into the ravenous maw of the media."

"It would help the cause, Dr. Christie. I'm quite positive. It may be just what the project needs."

"Then I suggest that you call a reliable, conscientious reporter, if the *Byrdport Enquirer* has one, and give him the basic facts. I am sure he will want to interview Mr. Hudson. You might as well steel yourself to it, Hudson."

"Dr. Christie! Please!" Mr. Hudson sounded increasingly distraught.

"Now I think we should . . . why are you giving me that quizzical look, Miss Tebell?"

"You've changed your mind, Dr. Christie?" she asked.

"About the desirability of preserving the church? Yes, although I was never actively opposed, contrary to what you might think. You must understand something about me. I came from Great Britain, where a church less than two hundred years old is considered to have been built yesterday. And there are far too many old churches there, a huge surplus. Ministers get fed up with forever begging funds to patch leaky roofs and exterminate death watch beetles. So I could see no real historical or practical imperative obtaining here, yet . . . somehow, I had a nagging, guilty feeling which perhaps made me feel resentful.

"You see," he continued, "when the decision was made to sell the church and leave this place, the congregation raised not one voice of regret, or care, or concern for the building which had been its spiritual home for well over a century. It was a case of good riddance. And I . . . I said nothing, either. There was a red warning flag in my conscience, yet I said nothing."

"Therefore you were sensitive when spokesmen from outside the church raised the issue," Miss Tebell said gently.

"Of course. And then, when Dr. Stirling made his speech, I knew that a lapse of ecclesiastical and civic leadership had occurred. That is as close to an apology as you shall have from me, my dear."

"It's closer than I needed, Dr. Christie."

"As to the present business," he continued briskly, "it seems to me that we lack one important artifact. The original manuscript of 'Old Black Joe.' Apparently that one did not fall providentially into your hands as did the other two."

I sensed that both of them were looking at Mr. Hudson.

"I suppose it's still in the organ," he said. "There's a huge pile of old music from my grandfather's day. It's . . . it's always been there."

The four of us climbed the stairs to the organ loft.

"Let's see this treasure trove of yours, Hudson," Dr. Christie said. The Erben's door creaked open. "My word. There must be hundreds of old folios and manuscripts in there."

"It may take me a minute to find 'Old Black Joe,' " Mr. Hudson said. "I'm sure it's right here."

But it wasn't. Together they went through the stack of music twice, and 'Old Black Joe' was not there.

"I can't understand it," Mr. Hudson said. "Where else could it be?"

"How do you know Stephen Foster didn't take it with him?" Miss Tebell asked.

"Oh, certainly he took a copy, as did Mr. Emmett with 'Dixie.' But they left the originals here. It had something to do with the rules they agreed on for the competition. To guarantee the authenticity of every note. Besides, I've seen the manuscript here myself, many times."

"We'll release the news anyway," Dr. Christie said. "Two manuscripts out of three is not bad."

The minister volunteered to lock the original "Dixie" in the church safe, as well as "The Song Nobody Knows," or "Nocturne Triste."

"You're getting famous, Hudson, and very soon, so shall your grandfather. Rest his soul. Tomorrow we'd better go through that entire stack and sort out the ones of substantial value. We certainly can't leave them in the organ after Sunday."

Mr. Hudson was silent.

CHAPTER 17

AT THE HOUSE ON LIVE OAK ROW, DR. CALEB OLD waited for Miss Tebell.

"Caleb! You must be freezing. How long have you been waiting out here in the cold?"

"Almost long enough to abort whatever tiny interest I had developed in preserving a church where nothing ever happened. Of course, if you'd give me a key, so I'd have the run of the place as I richly deserve, I'd have been spared the discomfort."

"Key, pah," Miss Tebell said. She unlocked the door and we climbed the stairs to her apartment.

"You're wrong about one thing, Doc," she laughed as we went inside. "The part about nothing happening."

In a voice charged with excitement, she related the events of that afternoon and evening. "Thanks for bringing me luck," she concluded. "If you hadn't been there I'd never have gone up to the organ loft; never have found the music. The story might never have come out."

"Funny how it was lying there. I guess the organist left it," Dr. Old said.

"But he seemed shocked, Caleb. I guess he could have, but somehow I don't think so. Maybe we'll never know."

A truly great heart, I have heard Dr. Christie say, can perform important service anonymously, and take its only comfort and reward in the consequent glow of virtue that flows from good works. As for my heart, it bellowed for appreciation as Miss Tebell called an *Enquirer* reporter and laid out the known facts.

"The reporter'll have to catch up with Mr. Hudson on his own," she said later to Dr. Old. "That poor old man has undoubtedly headed for cover. In the morning, a photographer will be sent over to the church to make pictures of the manuscripts."

"Anything more you need to do tonight?" Dr. Old asked. He seemed in a very helpful mood.

"Yes. A couple of things, Caleb. The first thing is to get out the two best steaks in the house, fry up some potatoes and onions, toss a peck of salad, and see what those nifty little French varietal hybrid grapes managed to devise in Bordeaux in 1971."

"What an amazing coincidence," Dr. Old said. "I was going to ask you over to my place and volunteer the same menu. Except with Burgundy. But now that you mention it, I feel more like Bordeaux. Yes, definitely."

Like Napoleon on Elba, I paced the shadows of the living room while the homely amalgam of hissing pans, clanking dishes, and human chatter disembogued from the kitchen. In perhaps an hour and a half they had finished. As they entered the parlor, I observed that Miss Tebell seemed flushed and rumpled, and Dr. Old's hair was disheveled. All that took some of the edge off my appetite.

"Your musical taste is certainly Catholic," said Dr. Old, shuffling through phonograph records. "Beethoven, Bach, Vivaldi, Hank Williams, and John Prine."

"You put on the 'Eroica,' " she said. "And I'll put some coal on the fire."

"A coal grate is so much more subtle than a wood fireplace," Dr. Old observed. "No wonder the Victorians were such interesting people. And so frequently depraved."

"Mmmm. Thanks for warming your hands. Don't you doctors ever get tired of feeling somebody else's flab?"

"We're insatiable. Oh, perhaps I should remind you, Tayloe. Before dinner you said there were two things you had to do tonight. What was the second?"

There was no audible response. Then she whispered something to him I could not hear. Laughing softly, they took each other's hands and walked quickly toward the bedroom.

I entered the kitchen and gnawed some French bread, and drank a bit of water. In my dejection I recalled the theme of one of Dr. Christie's sermons, taken from his favorite prophet, Isaiah. He talked of the bread of adversity, and the water of affliction. Such was the essence of my Friday night victory celebration dinner at Miss Tayloe Tebell's.

Sometime around 5:00 A.M., long before Aurora's fresh quilting gyrated through the eastern sky, I heard murmured goodbyes and the gentle bumping of doors. When Dr. Old was gone I went to a window and stared at the unchanging Doric facade of the Capitol. It was so pure, so classical, such an expression of reason, as I had begun to understand the human approach to that faculty. I had learned that the Capitol was, in fact, a symbol of a time called the Age of Reason. I supposed that even then, creatures were driven by passion, but perhaps they tried harder to keep it under control, treating it as an important part of life but not one that dominated other parts. That was an important thought.

Hardly stirring, Miss Tebell slept late. It was long after the Capitol Square Bell Tower had clanged 9:00 that the telephone rang. Four rings were required to awaken her, but ultimately she got the receiver off its hook and to her ear.

"In, uh, half an hour? Gosh, Granzeb, I'll try. Four of you? Yeah, sure I remember. Okay. If I'm a little late just wait for me."

She crawled from the bed groaning, but in much less than half an hour she was presentably dressed and on her way down the broad staircase. I, meanwhile, clambered down the chandelier chain.

Through the office door came Granville Zebulon and three black men. One was young, one was old, and the third occupied some middle ground. I had never seen them before, but something in their bearing was familiar to me. With politeness and a certain reserve they responded to Miss Tebell's welcome, and nodded with dignity through Mr. Zebulon's introductions.

When he introduced each as "the Reverend," I knew why they had seemed familiar. I had instinctively perceived that subtle aura surrounding men of the cloth. As they took seats in Miss Tebell's office, the eldest — a chunky man of asphalt blackness and hair and eyebrows of startling white — drew a New Testament from his coat, and fingered it like a talisman.

"Of all the black preachers in the history of Byrdport," he began, "we most reverence the memory of Mott Gooch. Did you ever hear of him, Miss Tebell?"

"Oh yes. Wasn't he also a pioneer black missionary?"

The old man smiled, happy that Miss Tebell knew. I liked the character of his voice, which alternately rumbled and whispered. "Yas, yas," he said. "In slave times, yonder Main Street Church was a special place, with its large black congregation. And Mott Gooch was the leader. He had bought his own freedom and his family's too. And not only did be become the church's first missionary, he was the first to go from Byrdport to a non-Christian land. So he was a pioneer and a great man. But there has never been a memorial to him. The church itself — the building from which he was sent forth to preach the gospel — is the only trace remaining with any connection to him."

Clearly, he seemed to say, the church was important.

"I think some commemoration would certainly be fitting," Miss Tebell said.

The middle-aged minister was a thin, ascetic-looking, bald man, carelessly dressed in a drab brown suit, contrasting starkly with the stylish immaculateness of the other two.

"We have been so preoccupied with the battles of the present that we have paid scant attention to the battles and successes of the past," he said in dry rattling tones, the voice of an impatient man. "We should like — by 'we' I refer to the Black Ministerial Association of Byrdport — to throw our weight, and perhaps a small amount of money, behind the preservation of the church. Perhaps we can help in the mobilization of opinion."

"I appreciate this deeply," Miss Tebell said. "All the moral force that can be applied is important . . . Ah, Granzeb, anything wrong?"

I was in the chandelier throughout the conversation, with an excellent view of the gathering. Mr. Zebulon had a newspaper in his hand. With an expression of growing consternation, he had been reading a news story in the lower half of the front page.

He looked levelly at Miss Tebell.

"I brought your paper in from the portico," he said. "Perhaps I shouldn't have. Have any of you seen the morning *Enquirer?*"

Nobody had.

"Then before we proceed, I think you should all hear this:

" 'DIXIE,' 'OLD BLACK JOE' COMPOSED
IN MAIN STREET PRESBYTERIAN

" 'In fresh revelations termed "Americana of the front rank," sources close to an embattled Byrdport church said last night that two of the most popular songs of Civil War days were written on a bet in early 1859 at the console of the church organ.

" 'Dr. Angus Christie, pastor of the soon-to-relocate Main Street Presbyterian Church, and Ms. Tayloe Tebell, executive director, Historic Byrdport Foundation, said according to freshly discovered evidence, it was "incontrovertible" that the two historic songs, both of them superhits of the Confederate years, were written in the church.

" 'Famed composer Stephen Foster, a genius at romanticizing the slave South, and minstrel man Dan Emmett, master of the so-called "Ethiopian melodies" popular at the middle of the last century, apparently indulged in friendly competition with a Byrdport church organist to see who could write the most popular song.'

"There's a lot more," Mr. Zebulon continued sternly, "about the church organist, and how his grandson has used melodies more than a century old to write soft rock hits of the 1980s."

The younger minister had sprung to his feet, flailing two long arms.

"Great day in the morning, Zebulon! Lawd, lawd, what

kind of jive is this? You talked us into helping save that old building, and we went along. Now you tell us the biggest thing that ever happened there is some white dudes writing the two biggest nigger songs of all time. 'Dixie'! 'Old Black Joe'! Somebody been eatin' cheese on you, Zebulon. Who gonna think about some Uncle Tom missionary now? Who gonna care about Mott Gooch? No, they all gonna be whistling 'Dixie' and 'Old Black Joe.' This done broke bad on us, men."

"Oh Lord," boomed the old man, "calm this angry spirit. There is always time to add a word, but none to take one back."

"Yes. Settle down, Darnell," the middle-aged preacher said to the young one. "Jeff and I recognize rhetoric when we hear it. Look; I kind of like the subtlety. If we go ahead as we planned, and support this campaign, it will be seen as a generous and forgiving act. Haven't we reached a time when we can be generous and forgiving? You want to get your feathers puffed because three songwriters had a competition in 1859? Let's not get all slanchwise on this, Darnell."

"And don't jump to conclusions," the old preacher said, his voice like tamed thunder. "Maturity may be recognized by the slowness at which a man believes. Besides. I always kind of liked them songs."

"Now you lecture me on maturity," the young preacher said. "No. I don't go along. I move we vote with our feet."

There was an interlude of strained embarrassment. Finally, the brown-suited minister spoke.

"I suppose we'll have to think about it a while more, Miss Tebell. I would like the ministerial association's action to be unanimous."

"Like my father used to say, it's too wet to plow today," the old man said.

"Of course," Miss Tebell said.

The three black preachers rose. The young man stalked out quickly; the others extended formal goodbyes and walked thoughtfully out the door.

"I do wish I'd known about this, Tayloe," Mr. Zebulon said.

"But Granzeb, this just came up last night."

"There was time enough to get in print with it. You could have told me," he argued.

"Granzeb, you're talking as if the discovery of the songs were some big problem, something almost shameful, to be explained or hushed up. Can't you see what a wonderful help it will be? Can't you see the significance of it?"

"What I see is how it blew my little supportive activities out of the water."

"Oh, Granzeb. You can't take seriously the sort of adolescent racial posturing we just heard from that young preacher."

"To the extent that I understand what set him off, yes, I do," Mr. Zebulon said.

Finally, though, his expression relaxed. "Aw, hell. Darnell took it like somebody was hollering 'nigger.' And nobody did; I know that. I guess what's bothering me is to have my little carefully crafted backstage maneuvering get smashed."

"Ah, speaking of backstage, there's something else you may not know about. Have you seen Mr. Junior in the last few days?" she asked.

"No."

She described in detail Mr. Junior's plan for the church, and his ability to buy it.

"A theater!" Mr. Zebulon said. "It might work; I don't know. But I can bet the old man won't like it too well."

"It never occurred to me to wonder," Miss Tebell said. "Why shouldn't Mr. Slemp like the idea?"

"Because he still thinks Mr. Junior is an incompetent dreamer. It's been a great disappointment that his son never showed the slightest interest in coming into Hygeia. Ever since he got out of college, Junior's been involved in one new scheme after another. Curiously, though, he's never lost a nickel on any of them. In fact, he has made quite a bit of money on his own. And each time he tries something new, his father gets furious. Then he usually becomes reconciled to the idea enough to barely tolerate it. He was just coming around to the basketball thing."

"Well, Granzeb, he'll probably have to learn about it soon enough."

"I'm supposed to meet the old man over at the Capitol later today," Mr. Zebulon said. "Maybe I can smooth the way a little."

"Thanks. You've been wonderful through the whole thing," Miss Tebell said.

"Lines with a faint valedictory ring?" Mr. Zebulon's dark face appeared under strain.

Miss Tebell did not answer.

"Tayloe, for the last couple of days the signals I've been getting from you have been rich in ambiguity. Only now they're getting less ambiguous."

"I've had a lot to think about, Granzeb," she said.

"Such as?"

"Such as the church problem, and you, and Caleb. In no particular order."

"Of those, there's room for only two out of three. The church and one other."

"That's the trouble. Oh, let's stop picking around the edges, Granzeb. You know I have a problem between you and Caleb. I'm crazy about both of you. But I came along just too late to be a wholehearted soldier in the sexual revolution. I'm too much of a one-man woman."

"Has anyone been pressing you to choose? I certainly haven't."

"No, but I must choose. There's not only a certain tranquility of life at stake, there's also the matter of patching up my fairly orthodox conscience."

They sat a minute in silence, there in the big office.

"I guess I need to ask you something pretty serious, Granzeb," she said. "It goes as follows. Do you love me?"

"What kind of question is that? It should be obvious that I . . . that we . . ." his declaration fizzled out lamely.

"That you, that we, what?" she asked gently. "I can't read your mind. And you never said."

"You and I have something valuable," he said.

"Very valuable," she nodded reflectively. "But do you think of me as a clipper ship? Do you want to kill wild game for me?"

"*What?* I think of you as a wonderful woman, a sexy lady, dynamite company."

"I guess you've answered my question," she said.

"I can't see that I've answered anything."

"Then try this one. Have you *ever* been in love? Apart from early high school hots. I'm talking long-term, sustained fire. Have you ever had the real obsession, Granzeb? The one people kill for, drink themselves to death over, grovel humiliatingly under, write poetry about?"

It seemed like a fair question to me. Mr. Zebulon did not respond.

"Well?" she prodded.

"No," he said.

"No. Nor have I, Granzeb. I thought I had the feeling when I got married. But it was a big fake."

"Isn't it mostly a big fake?" Mr. Zebulon asked. "Look at the people you know who've been together a while. Are they still writing poetry to each other?"

It was Miss Tebell's turn to be silent. Finally she spoke, unusually subdued.

"But some people do. They must. Suppose there is just an endless, unquenchable stream of love in some people. That's bound to have some effect on the one they love, isn't it?"

"You mean, out of pity, or maybe a misguided or undeserved sense of guilt, they might respond soft-heartedly. Or soft-headedly," he said.

"That's cynical," she said. "And not what I mean. Oh, I admit that some — with a bent toward masochism, maybe — some might allow themselves to be involved deeper than they should. And they'd regret it later. No, I mean that just maybe, being loved — being on the receiving end of the real, rare article — might have a genuine impact. A catalytic effect. Everybody should be capable of loving; it's just that not everybody can be a self-starter. Does that sound absurd?"

"It sounds almost dangerous. It sounds like somebody needs jumper cables," Mr. Zebulon said.

"Maybe some people do," Miss Tebell replied.

191

CHAPTER 18

Mr. Zebulon departed for the Capitol, where the legislature continued churning forth bills designed to further complicate life for the state's human residents. As the forenoon light streamed through the high windows of her office, Miss Tebell sat at her desk and cried for a very long while. Then she pulled up a stack of reports and correspondence, and ferociously went to work.

In something less than an hour, there sounded a vigorous grinding clatter from the old doorbell.

It was the Slemps, father and son.

Only once before had I seen them so close together. Their remarkable resemblance now appeared almost ludicrous: squat, powerful bodies, massive balding skulls, short noses, wide mouths, even the shapes of their ears. All matched up as if Tweedledum were old and Tweedledee were young. And they were furious. Probably that was why they were both unusually flushed.

"Granzeb caught up with me at the Capitol," Mr. Slemp said. "I was fixing to see the governor; never mind why right now. Once Granzeb reported in, I went lookin' for Junior here. It warn't no trouble. He was where he always is, over at yonder greasy spoon sniffing around that dago waitress."

Then Serena should be back! I thought happily.

"Daddy! She's Jewish."

"Oh, Jesus. I never know whether you're gettin' above your raisin' or droppin' below it. Now, Miss Tebell, there ain't nobody mad at you, but I'm sure provoked at this boy, and that means you get drug in on the edges. I thought we had a deal. I offered to pay about half, if the state would sell the church, and then with you kind of saying grace over the whole thing, the history nuts and the garden club blue hair gang and anybody else with a mind to would spring for the rest. That way it would be a community effort. There'd be a foundation set up to handle it all dignified. Was I right, or wrong, in thinking that?"

"That's certainly what we talked about, yes," Miss Tebell said.

"Okay. Then the next thing I know, without saying doodly squat to me, Junior here comes busting in with some freakish money he just picked up and offers to run off with the whole wheel of cheese. Right or wrong?"

"Mr. Junior has indeed made a generous offer," Miss Tebell acknowledged.

The old man turned to his son.

"Why in hell can't you ever stick to anything? You wouldn't come into my business. No, you had to try half a dozen fly-by-night trifles. Sellin' C-B radios. Runnin' a dive shop. Startin' an advertising agency. I forget the rest."

"And I made money on all of 'em, Daddy," Mr. Junior shot back.

"When you got into basketball I figured you was three pickles shy of a barrel for sure. Even then, I finally come around to the idea. Thought you was finally going to settle down. Now this! A thee-ater, for God's sake. A thee-ater! You can't run a thee-ater. You'd screw up a one-car funeral."

"I never yet screwed anything up, Daddy," Mr. Junior said with tight dignity. "I just never could get started in anything you liked."

Mr. Slemp appeared startled by this perspective. "But why? Ain't I been a good father? Are you ashamed of what I done in life?"

"Sure, you've been a good father. And I admire what you've done with Hygeia very much. I just . . . I just wanted to be myself. But I'd like nothing better than for you to stand by me in what I do."

The elder Slemp did not respond so quickly this time. When he did, he spoke in a calmer voice.

"You two can't imagine what it was like, growing up in the coalfields in the 1920s and '30s. Then startin' a business in the Depression. So I was proud of what I done. And a man in my position, he gets used to having people tell him what he wants to hear. Well, son, I guess I always wanted you to say you was itching to get into Hygeia, to prepare to take the reins. Or that you would even consider it. But you never said that."

Mr. Slemp massaged his eyes and brow with a broad, strong hand.

"I recollect my own father," he continued. "He got *his* nose out of joint when I wanted to leave the coal creek. 'What's wrong with coal mining?' he asked me. Can you beat that? You see, it's a different situation entirely. Here I am, able to give you every advantage. Maybe some men just have to make their own way. Kind of pig-headed, if you ask me."

Miss Tebell cleared her throat.

"If I may say so," she volunteered, "Flem Junior seems to have a pretty firm grasp on how to convert the church to a theater, and make it work. In my opinion, Mr. Slemp, while you didn't ask me, the idea is perfectly realistic."

"I was wrong in not telling you myself, right away, Daddy," Mr. Junior said. "I was fixing to, and I'm sorry I waited."

The old man seemed more relaxed now. "Well, son, maybe you'll do, after all. Like I said, I was in the governor's anteroom when Granzeb told me about this. I was going to put the arm on Jack Pine to have the church declared surplus. Then I got so mad on hearing from Granzeb that I decided to forgit the whole thing. But now that you done cleared up matters for me, I guess I'll go back and have a shot at the governor."

"What do you think the chances are, Daddy?"

"I do have one trump card, son. But let me make it clear: I was saving it until they settled the right-to-work thing. If the Assembly had voted to kill right-to-work, I was going to play my trump on that. I was gonna ask Governor Pine to veto that bill. Let that be a lesson to you, Junior, if you want to be a businessman. Business comes first."

"That's what I always say, Daddy," Mr. Junior said.

Alarmingly late, I saw the next step in the drama would occur in the governor's office, and my only chance of getting there was on the person of Mr. Slemp. If I could do that, I could witness negotiations with the governor, then wait until dark and slip across to the Rib Cage, where presumably Mr. Junior would be parked for his nocturnal visit to Miss da Gamba. At that point, I would clear up the mystery of Serena's disappearance.

Clinging to the blind side of the chandelier chain, I rushed up to the ceiling, and down through the walls, emerging from the baseboard at the point nearest to Mr. Slemp's briefcase. The two men were preparing to leave. As I watched from a crack in the baseboard, Mr. Slemp began reaching for the case.

"Oh," Miss Tebell exclaimed. "I nearly forgot. Have you two seen the morning paper?"

They had not. She outlined the entire story of "Dixie" and "Old Black Joe."

"Great God," Mr. Slemp said. "If that don't blow the doors off." With his attention thus diverted, I made it to the case unseen. I heard Mr. Slemp slap his hands together in forceful satisfaction. "Well, that really done it. I'm gonna let Jack Pine have it full strength now."

"Want me to come with you, Daddy?" Mr. Junior asked.

"No, son, this here's sort of private. And too complicated to explain."

They apparently shook hands. Then it sounded as if the old man hugged his son, probably in an embarrassed, ungraceful, but happy way.

As Mr. Slemp and I left the house, I heard Mr. Junior excitedly relating to Miss Tebell his latest plans for creating a theater. It would retain the classic style of the 1840s, but with no expense spared for comfort of the audience and backstage capabilities . . .

The old tycoon's heavy shoes smacked the brick walkways to the Capitol, then echoed through the marble corridors to Governor Pine's office. Soon I recognized the voice of Mrs. Archer.

"Why Misteh Slay-ump! I am so glad you returned," she cooed. "I saw you an hour ago and then you just *vanished*! And I said to myself, I said, Oh, won't Governor Pine be disappointed, for he always has told me that Flemmons Slemp is the one person he'll see without an appointment. The one person!"

"That's a high honor," Mr. Slemp said, "for which I am appropriately grateful."

Exuding a mist of bourbon that almost fuddled me, a cluster of politicians emerged from the inner office.

"I'll take you in now," the woman said. There was silent movement as Mr. Slemp's feet marched across plump carpeting. "Look who's here to see you, Governor," she trilled, closing a massive door to leave Mr. Slemp and me alone in the gubernatorial presence.

"Why, Flem! How you comin' on?"

"Great, Jack. And you?"

"Ready for anything, Flem."

"Pleased with the legislative session?"

"I won some. I lost the big one; the labor law. No need to hash that over. And you didn't come by to crow; that's not your style. Actually, I . . . I hadn't expected to see you for a couple more weeks," the governor said.

"Exactly so, Jack. But there was just one small thing I wanted to talk over. Nothing whatever to do with politics. It's about yonder old church across the street. My boy has this plan . . ." Mr. Slemp laid out the restoration-theater dream with terse clarity, editing out the less important details, homing in on the pivot points. It required only five minutes or so.

"All it would take, as I see it," Mr. Slemp concluded, "is for you to declare the property surplus. Then Engineering and Grounds can negotiate the sale. Under state law it don't require an auction."

"That's right, Flem. It could work that way. But I can't do it. Those BUSM doctors would have my butt on a rusty gurney."

"They'll still get their building, just a block or so away. I've already paid for half of it."

"And mighty generous of you too. But a theater, Flem! Byrdport's not a theater town. Byrdport wouldn't pay four bits to watch the Last Supper staged with the original cast."

I exited the briefcase and positioned myself under a floor-length drapery. The governor's smooth, yellowish face appeared burdened by affairs of state.

"Maybe not," Mr. Slemp said. "But I'd as soon let the boy find out for himself. He may be right. It's been known to happen with that kid."

"Flem, I'd like to help you out on this. Believe me. But as far as I'm concerned it would be borrowing trouble. I'd come out like a one-legged man in an ass-kicking contest. Why don't you find some other old building for your child to play around with? There's plenty around."

A muscle flicked in Mr. Slemp's powerful jaw.

"Yeah," he said. "Okay, Jack, I guess I'll have to do that."

Mr. Slemp began to stir as though to rise from his chair.

"Oh." He snapped his fingers, as though remembering something, and settled back again. "As long as I'm here, Jack, there's one little thing that's come up. I just had this visit from a Federal Food and Drug Authority inspector. Nice old boy. Sort of slow, careful, and conscientious. They've been very interested in our preliminary reports on undercoat."

The governor pushed back in his chair and sat very still.

"This inspector, he thinks that drug is gonna be hotter than a lightard knot. And, well, because it's so sensitive, they gonna be watching what we do. They'll be on us like a guinea hen on a Junebug, Jack. See, we're going into a second and much bigger phase of testing. And it's to be monitored closer than ever. We're supposed to account for every damn pill. Every one's gotta be administered by our test doctors, who have to keep strict records, like who takes 'em and all. A whole bunch of government officials see that information; pass it around, talk it over, evaluate. What a lot of bureaucratic foolishness! Course, in about seven years, when it's cleared for regular prescription use, private doctors'll be able to prescribe it for their patients. There won't be all this folderal then."

"In seven years," Governor Pine said, "I'll be . . . I'll be . . ."

"You and me both will be pretty much on the go-down in seven years, Jack. That's life. We done had our time at bat. Well, I guess I'll be gittin'." He moved again as if to rise.

"Wait a minute, Flem. You'd still be able to get your hands on a few pills, wouldn't you? Hell, you run Hygeia."

"Oh, I might try," he said. "Seems like I'd need to have a pretty strong reason to put myself out, though. Like to help somebody who helped me."

Very slowly, he relaxed again into the deep leather chair.

The governor frowned, drumming his fingers on the massive deck. "Flem," he said at length, "on mature reflection maybe there's no real reason why that new medical building couldn't go on the other location. I'll certainly think about it. Yes, sir, I'll give it some more thought."

Mr. Slemp did not move. "Oh, I forgot, Jack," he said. "That old boy from the FDA, he wants to make sure we done reported all the names of the early bunch who's taken undercoat. Only natural, I'd say. They want to make sure everyone's been monitored proper. Then, too, they might want to come around and ask questions of the test group."

"I'll think about it real carefully," the governor said softly. "Soon as the legislature leaves . . ."

"Why not right now, Jack?" Mr. Slemp said. "Why prolong the agony?"

"But . . ."

"Now."

Governor Pine placed his head in his hands, as if praying above the broad mahogany. Then he snapped a switch.

"Mrs. Archer. Please locate the commissioner of engineering and grounds, and the state auditor. Ask them to come in. And you come too, please; I'm going to dictate an executive order."

Within half an hour, the officials had arrived, conferred, and hammered out the legal outline under which Main Street Presbyterian could be sold. There would be a minor technicality involving the procurement of an appraisal on the property before the sale to Mr. Junior could be consummated. But the state officers foresaw no impediments.

The church was now surplus property and title would be transferred by negotiated sale. Miss Tebell had won. I settled down to wait for evening, when I would cross the street, seeking to pick up the threads of my life with Serena or, at the least, learn what had happened to her. Again I resolved to

quell my hopeless infatuation with Miss Tebell. I considered —
and rejected — vowing to never see her again. Plautus was
right: the wise mouse maintains an alternative refuge.

Sometime after the Bell Tower clock chimed 5:00, hoarse
cheering rose from the Capitol's lower floors. First the House,
then the Senate, were gaveled into adjournment for another
year. Governor Pine and his staff joined tbe pandemonium in
the corridors, as the rancors of six weeks of intemperate debate
dissolved in expressions of sentimental esteem. Then, like a
horde of lemmings, 140 state legislators streamed from the
Capitol in search of closing night frivolity. From conversations
I overheard, the restaurants and hotels of Byrdport would rock
with feasting and romance.

As for me, I climbed to the governor's window overlooking
Main Street, and the church across it, to wait for abating
traffic.

Conditions could hardly be worse, I saw at a glance. Why
was there such a jam of slow-moving vehicles in the street?

Something extraordinary was happening.

It was Saturday; there was no rush hour. The departure of
less than 200 assemblymen could not account for it. The traffic
had halted almost completely. Rows of cars and trucks were
lined bumper to bumper in both directions, a total of eight
lanes.

Then I saw the crowd on the sidewalk in front of the
church. The people were all looking up. At last I saw why.

About one-third of the way up the church's steeple, precisely at the belfry, the louvers that screened the bells — yet
passed their brassy voices across the city — opened above
graceful balconies on each of the belfry's four sides. The balconies were purely ornamental, yet through small doors in the belfry louvers they could be reached from inside.

Mr. Hudson was on the balcony above the street.

He sat on the balustrade, his feet dangling more than a
hundred feet above the broad granite steps of Main Street
Presbyterian.

I was too far away to see the expression on his face, yet his
posture seemed tranquil and reflective. He might have been
taking the evening air from the railing of an old-fashioned
front porch.

Then I saw, performing the cruelest human outrage of my experience, a cluster of young toughs below Mr. Hudson. Though I could not hear, it was plain they were laughing and yelling taunts. Taunting Mr. Hudson to jump! I could not believe it.

I thought of all the happy hours of magnificent organ music Mr. Hudson had given me. I thought of his genius in writing secular music, in collaboration with his grandfather. I knew that I could never live with myself unless I tried to help Mr. Hudson, yet how could I possibly cross the street? But now, I saw, the traffic was blocked and immobile. Not a wheel turned on Main Street.

Everyone was looking up, hypnotized by Mr. Hudson's bizarre action, titillated by expectation. Perhaps I could make it across. Nobody would be looking down!

I raced down the walls and into Capitol Square, now dark and deserted. Across the grass and ivy and herringbone bricks I headed straight for Main Street, and almost reached the ancient fence of tall iron pickets.

A familiar figure stepped from behind the black trunk of a magnolia tree.

My heart thudded sickeningly. My legs, quivering like poorly congealed aspic, refused the command to turn and run away.

"Chawles, dahling!" Alabama Ruby purred. "How long it seems. Did you have a nice motor trip? Was the Mercedes comfy? I always say, there's nothing as smart as a Mercedes roadster. You looked so *cute* pulling out into the alley."

"Please do not detain me," I said in one quick, breathless burst. "I have to save Mr. Hudson."

"Why, I do believe he's beyond helping, Chawles. Just like you, dear heart."

She glided toward me from the magnolia's black shadows. Then she held up one paw, shot forth its claws, and inspected them. She polished the hideous talons on her chest.

"It is really so strange," she said. "I don't come over here every whipstitch. But tonight I got a little restless. It's terrible of me, I know, but I had the old urge. Except, instead of finding a nice tomcat, I found you! And you are no tomcat, are you,

Chawles Churchmouse?" Alabama Ruby tittered obscenely. "No. You just won't do! But I'm eveh so hungry, and you can help me there, can't you? Tell you what, sugar. I'll make it fast, for old times' sake. None of the usual sadistic cat-and-mouse business, don't you know."

"Please," I begged. "This is very important. Let me try to help Mr. Hudson. Then maybe we can work something out."

The vertical pupils of her eyes were the very mirrors of death.

"Let him jump. Who cares what humans do?" she said. Her tail twitched and curled.

"I care, damn you," I said.

"But of course — you're a fool, Chawles. Mice and dogs. I'll never understand you. I . . . what's that?"

"W-what?" I gasped. But I had heard it, too. Faint, high-pitched beeping: an ululating warble.

"Never mind," Alabama Ruby said. "Fumble your rosary, Chawles; say your prayers; ask Allah for the directions to Paradise. Do whatever you feel necessary for the good of your soul. Do mice have souls? You're about to find out, Chawles. Your short and pointless life is now ov . . . *yeow!*"

The cat clutched at her left eye. A leathery missile zoomed off, banked, and flapped for altitude beneath the magnolia.

"Hang in there, hoss!" a jaunty voice cried. "Here comes the second wave!"

Another flyer glided from the shadows, flicked across Alabama Ruby's face, and climbed steeply with a flutter of leather wings.

"Bats!" the cat snarled, rubbing her other eye. Now in quick succession at least five more bats power-dived on my nemesis. She tried to swat them, but her eyes were filling with blood. She struck out with snakelike quickness, but the small furry flyers eluded her.

"We've got her now, chaps," came a voice from high in the magnolia. "Guide on me, one more time. Full Nine-G pull-out and Katy bar the *doo-o-o-oo-r-r* . . ."

"Stoker!" I cried, as the bats attacked in close and murderous phalanx.

Alabama Ruby desperately covered her eyes. Tiny bat claws slashed at her ears and pulled her fur.

The cat turned and ran a few yards toward Main Street. At the iron fence she hesitated; I am not sure that she could see the moving police patrol car which, driving on the sidewalk to avoid the impassable street, already had begun braking to a halt just opposite the church. The cat plunged ahead, and the officer driving the car did not stop quite soon enough. I heard Alabama Ruby scream. A muffled thump came from under the cruiser.

Stoker and his friends lined up on a low branch of the magnolia, and in graceful unison flopped upside down.

"An utterly smashing mission, lads," he said. "And what a nice new trophy to stencil on the old fuselage. Enemy cat, tabby class, heavy cruiser type. Well done, mateys, well done."

"Stoker, I can't tell you how I . . ." I couldn't finish. Relief swelled through me like a benediction. I could not speak further without unmasculine blubbering.

"Chazz, Chazz, spare us. It was a piece of cake. The boys and I were craving a little action, anyway. Holy Orville, when I saw you down there in the clutches of yon feline, may her soul rot, it set the old battle adrenalin coursing for fair. By God, we totaled her, eh?"

"You saved my life, Stoker. How did you happen to be out this early? Don't bats usually fly later than this?"

"Affirmative, but that poor old coot across the street came blundering up through the belfry, and we scrambled. Godfrey Daniel, but he was pathetic, sobbing and talking to himself."

Mr. Hudson! In my own peril and rescue I had forgotten where I was going, and why.

"Stoker, that's Mr. Hudson, the church organist. I was on my way to save him when you gentlemen saved me."

An impolite snicker came from somewhere in the resting bat squadron.

"At ease, there," Stoker said to his colleague. Then he turned back to me. "*Save* him? I love your self-confidence, Charles. How?"

"If I can just get over there, I have a plan that may work. Stoker! Could a bat carry three ounces of cargo in flight?"

"Dream on, Charles. Were we eagles, or even pigeons, one of us might carry you across. 'Fraid you must soldier it out on terra firma. Tell you what, though. We'll fly a recco formation. The traffic's stopped, so cars won't be a problem, but there's a lot of people around. If anybody tries to punch you out, Chazzkins, we'll give him a dose of what Alabama Ruby got."

"Very well. Let's go." I ran to the sidewalk edge, skirting the police cruiser. I looked under it for the flattened cadaver of Alabama Ruby, but all I could see was a confused jumble of black shadows and harsh lights.

The sidewalk swarmed with humans, but because their eyes were fixed high on the church steeple, my chief danger lay in being stepped on accidentally. I zigzagged around dozens of feet, and safely reached the traffic lanes, where I began negotiating across blacktop pavement clotted with vehicles. Idling engines rumbled and clattered above me, and one spewed hot water on my back. Several drivers had emerged from their cars. They stood in the street, gaping at the steeple and Mr. Hudson. Nobody saw me, and I reached the far shore of Main Street still safe and undetected.

By now the crowd's attention was further occupied by the police, barking through bullhorns and waving people back from beneath the steeple. The ensuing shuffle of feet along the northern sidewalk drove me, retreating, back to the gutter, where I rested temporarily in a plastic cup wedged between an automobile wheel and the curbstone. At that moment, the final short leg of my trip across Main Street — negotiating the sidewalk — seemed the most hazardous of all.

And yet: if I could wait a few more nervous minutes in the cup, the police would have the sidewalk cleared. My final gauntlet would be public indeed, yet it should be unimpeded.

More policemen now arrived to aid the two whose cruiser had struck Alabama Ruby.

"Get 'em back past the alley," said one officer. "Where in hell is the rescue van? We gotta get a net under that steeple. If the old man jumps now, he'll be flatter than a cow pile."

The image of Mr. Hudson in that condition gave me the push of courage I needed. Peering over the curbstone, I saw the sidewalk now unoccupied, though brilliantly illuminated by police floodlights. A mob of spectators was being restrained in front of the Rib Cage, but the alley entrance was clear. Two officers stood at the church steps, incandescent in the blinding lights. My best course seemed to lie diagonally toward the alley, where I could enter the church from a basement window.

I moistened my dry mouth with a vestige of banana milk shake from the plastic cup. Then I ran as I never did before. The lights confused me, and I feared I would blunder off course. Across some fifty feet, in plain view of hundreds of onlookers, I dashed like a mouse possessed.

"Look, a rat," a female voice squawked.

"Ain't a rat. He a mouse. Ain't nobody ever learned you the difference between a rat and a mouse?"

Indeed.

"Look at the little dude," an officer at the barricade said. "He must think we cleared the sidewalk just for him. And God, look at those bats flying over him. What kind of zoo is this?"

For a microsecond I knew the glory of an Olympic champion. There was even applause as I reached the alley and ran for my familiar entrance in the cracked basement window. I plunged through it headlong, into the safety of the church's welcoming arms.

I had seen the police rattling at the church doors. It would be only a matter of time, assuming Mr. Hudson delayed his swan dive into eternity, before they either broke open the locks or located someone from the church staff to admit them. In any case, the success of my mission depended on having the sanctuary to myself. I raced desperately up the walls to the choir loft.

The door to the steeple stairs was in a wall behind the Erben. I prayed Mr. Hudson had left it open. For if he had, the sounds from the organ would funnel up the narrow stairwell to the belfry some thirty feet higher.

The door was closed. Yet by half an inch it was ajar: Mr. Hudson had failed to pull it tightly enough to engage the latch. Could I open it? I had no idea. I squeezed through the crack to the other side; put my shoulder to the wood and shoved. My feet slipped on the slick, uncarpeted flooring. I tried again. The door budged a fraction. I locked my rear toes in a chink between the floor planks, took a deep breath, and strained. With a faint grunt of surprise the seldom-used old door swung softly open. There was now a clear channel to the belfry. The maximum sound would now be funneled upward.

Panting from my exertions I ran inside the Erben and dislodged the short-circuiting wire on the blower motor. Then I jumped to the manual and threw the switch. Deep in the organ's recesses the wind chest filled.

I was ready. It was the second time in my life that I approached the manuals without a partner. And like the night I played at Grandpa's funeral, the task seemed enormous. Saving Mr. Hudson was exclusively on my shoulders. Yet the big things in life must always be done alone.

But what should I play? For that was my plan, to play him down from the belfry. What selections would best be calculated to touch Mr. Hudson's tormented soul, and terminate his impulse toward self-destruction?

I chose Bach's "Prelude and Fugue in D Minor," and jumped onto the keys. A rush of adrenalin sent me dancing through the themes, working all three manuals, shifting surefootedly from a blustery fortissimo to a serene pianissimo. As I concluded, I was confident the rendition was my best work ever.

As the final echoes faded through the darkened church, Stoker flew from the belfry door and joined me at the console.

"I heard you honking away," the bat said. "Is *this* how you propose to get the geezer down?"

"Exactly," I replied. "His faculties are temporarily deranged. The noble, familiar organ passages should calm him. What's happening outside?"

"Just after you sprinted across to the church, some rescue squad guys came. They have a round canvas thing they'll try to catch him in if he jumps. Tough job to handle it on the steps, though. What's wrong with the old bugger, anyway?"

"I'll explain later. Could you tell me how he reacted to my playing?"

"He looked around and muttered something, but I couldn't make it out," Stoker said.

"Stoker, would you please fly back up there, and observe what happens while I play the 'Toccata in C Minor'? It contains a serene adagio which may soothe Mr. Hudson better than my opening selection."

"Check."

The bat flapped off toward the belfry door. I kneaded my toes and began, trying to play the toccata like Mr. Hudson himself would play it, with dignity, yet softened by a touch of warm romanticism.

The last diapasons were still humming when Stoker returned.

"I oughta get combat pay for this mission," he complained. "I went blasting out of the belfry, looking back at your fruitcake friend, not watching where I was going, and flew right into a fireman's face. I stalled out and he took a swipe at me. Almost bought the farm, Chazz. With all this noise in the air, the old sonar goes on the fritz."

"A fireman? On the belfry?"

"He's up on a big ladder, trying to talk the old coot down."

"Could you tell how he liked the toccata, Stoker?"

"No," he said sourly, "I couldn't. Ah, maybe you better let the experts handle this."

Then the answer revealed itself to me.

"I've got it, Stoker, I know what will reach Mr. Hudson. Please return to the belfry one last time, will you?"

Weariness was robbing Stoker's habitual panache, and the gap-toothed smile had faded.

"Roger, Chuckles," he said. "But the next time I get mixed up with mice and suicidal organists, I'm taking early retirement." He flapped toward the belfry door.

I had played "The Song Nobody Knows" just once before, the day I found Mr. Hudson's grandfather's score from the competition. But I knew I could manage the simple, haunting melody. Beginning with the verse, I tried to remember the words from the times I heard them on the jukebox. I sang them to myself as I pressed the keys:

> There was a song somebody played
> When I was young, before I paid
> For all the scores, and all the strings;
> Before the silence heartache brings;
> I can't remember how it goes,
> It's just a song nobody knows.

Then I linked up the major stops for maximum volume on the chorus, being unable to reach the swell pedal:

Oh, someone sing again the song
that only lovers hear,
The one that put the world in tune
whenever she was near,
I can't recall a single word,
or how the music goes,
Won't someone play once more for me
The Song Nobody Knows.

There. That should do it, I thought.

Half a minute passed.

Stoker glided out of the tower door, executed a smart bar-rel roll, and perched on the Erben's music rack upside down.

"Charles. Sometimes it is the duty of friends to bring sad tidings. In those cases we must steel ourselves to unpleasant duty, and perform it unflinchingly," Stoker said.

"Oh no!" I cried. "Stoker, he . . . he did it? Mr. Hudson jumped?"

Stoker stared at me without expression.

"Jumped?" His eyes began to glitter maliciously. "Nega-tive, Chuckaluck. Mercy, no. He didn't jump. He merely men-tioned that he was coming down here to get the son of a bitch who's making all that discordant racket on his organ."

There was a thumping of feet on the belfry stairs.

"If I were you, Charley-o, I'd hit the clouds," Stoker whooped.

He launched himself, laughing shrilly.

I dove into the Erben case as Mr. Hudson burst through the belfry door.

Descending a small, restricted staircase in total darkness apparently is no great problem for a human. But once through the door, Mr. Hudson had difficulty. It was dark in the choir loft, and he had just returned from a scene of brilliant illumi-nation outside the front of the church.

First he crashed into the rear of the organ case. Then he groped clumsily along its rear wall, reached a corner, and fell to the floor in tumultuous thudding.

"Who's in here?" he demanded. "Who's playing this organ?"

He crawled clumsily on hands and knees around the end of

the case, and felt his way down the long, ornate front to the console. One of Mr. Hudson's hands struck a key on the pedal organ, and a sixteen-foot diapason honked in the darkness.

"It plays," he said in wonder. "It really does." His voice rose to a bellow. "Who's here? Who made those screwed-up sounds, Goddamn it!"

Poor Mr. Hudson. I understood his consternation. Certainly, I was disappointed by his reaction to my musicianship. Yet I knew that in his agitated state up on the belfry balcony, blasted by all the noise from the street — the rabble shouting, police and firemen pleading through loudspeakers — there was no way he could have heard my renditions clearly. Therefore, his distorted perception of my three numbers was easily explained.

Mr. Hudson pulled himself to the console bench and, unhindered now by the dark, ran through a graceful arpeggio.

"It plays," he repeated.

The lights of the sanctuary came on with stunning force.

"Hudson! Hudson! Are you up there?" thundered the voice of Dr. Christie from the main floor.

"Fan out and check under them benches," a policeman said.

Dr. Christie clattered up the choir loft stairs.

"Hudson! Oh, thank God. You came to your senses. Whatever possessed you to . . . never mind. But who was playing the organ? I could hear it distinctly out in the street. Coming out the belfry." Dr. Christie looked about him in confusion. "B-but . . . you're the only one here?"

Mr. Hudson riffed a few bars of "The Song Nobody Knows." His gentle features beamed a euphoric smile.

"Nobody here but us organists, Dr. Christie," he said.

An hour or so of anticlimactic dithering filled the wake of Mr. Hudson's aborted suicide. A police physician insisted that the organist be hospitalized for a thorough examination, a course he resisted mildly but in which Dr. Christie concurred. The mob outside, enraged by the forfeiture of its spectacle, re-

208

taliated by stripping eight nearby automobiles of their tape decks.

One of the cars was Mr. Junior's.

When I made my final sprint down the alley to the basement window of the church, the car's presence there had registered faintly. Now, with the church again darkened and empty some two hours after the saving of Mr. Hudson, I remembered.

CHAPTER   19

MY ATTITUDE TOWARD THE MERCEDES CAR BY NOW
was complex indeed. I still found it sinister as the reputed
home of the mysterious mouse, Earl. But I further perceived
the vehicle as an extension of Mr. Junior, one of the church's
strongest allies. That was a favorable association. I, myself,
had ridden in that car, or under it, on a trip that started poorly,
yet as it unfolded became a satisfactory adventure.

But most important of all, the Mercedes was deeply en-
meshed in my relationship with Serena.

I had not seen her in five days. What had happened? How
would she act toward me? Now that the church problem was resolved, I felt a swelling urge to see her. I waited until the last
stragglers had disappeared from the alley, bearing their plundered automotive accessories, before I crossed over to the Rib
Cage.

The first mouse I encountered was Rebecca.

"So! The soldier of fortune finally returns. He concedes a
short visit to his friends and to his *former* lady. What's the
matter, Charles, is there a temporary slackness on the adventure travel scene? Well, let me tell you something. Your next
journey should be to get your gray pelt out of here and never
come back."

Rebecca's message was plainly unacceptable.

"Really, Rebecca," I replied, "I know you may think I have not treated Serena correctly, but that is really none of your business. I . . ."

"Charles!" It was Sidney. He lumbered up and rubbed his paws together. "Rebecca! Oh, you two."

"I was just looking for Serena, Sidney," I said. "Is she here?"

"She's here. I think she's up in one of the jukebox controls, playing music."

I looked in three booths before I found her. Serena lay on her stomach, cradling her chin in her paws. She looked at me with no change in her inscrutable expression.

"I'm back, Serena," I said.

"Got lonesome, huh?" she finally said. "Miss Tayloe Tebell kicked you out, perhaps? Cleaned out her purse? So here you are, as you say with your usual gift of the obvious at crucial times. And I'm supposed to be glad? Go find yourself some other mouse."

"Serena, I tried to get back to you. I honestly did. But so much has happened. You'll never believe it all."

"You're right. I wouldn't."

"I came back once and you were gone. *You,* Serena. I heard you went to the seashore with Earl in Mr. Junior's car."

For the first time she appeared slightly unsure of herself.

"Yes. I did. Why shouldn't I? You had deserted me, after promising not to go away again."

"Please, Serena. Leave Earl and come back to me."

"I've already left Earl. But I'm not coming back to you."

The sudden, crushing weight of imminent loss was overwhelming. *Sense of loss: one of the big signs . . .*

"B-but . . ."

"Earl decided to stay at the beach. At a big seafood restaurant, where there's always a lot of fresh young mice. A new class all the time. Earl becomes more like an overage lifeguard every day. But certainly not without his charms."

She looked at me. Her chin was firm, but her eyes were damp.

"Not . . . without his charms," she repeated in a faint voice. "Earl wasn't so bad. And he turned the car over to me, so to speak."

"It's really all over between you, then?" I asked, relieved that Earl's menacing, unseen presence, which I had worried about frequently, had evaporated. Like most worries it had never materialized. Authentic troubles, on the other hand, came unforeseen, in ambuscade.

Yet what had I gained? Would the reality of Serena's return be a chilling and permanent rejection?

"Don't get ideas, Charles," Serena continued. "The next mouse I take up with is going to approach me on my terms at least half the time. He's going to understand that I've got a brain, as well as the other end. And he's going to know how to approach both of them with some care and finesse. Obviously that lets you out, Charles, but you might work on those qualities. For the benefit of some other mouse."

Sidney's melancholy face appeared in the control box.

"Excuse me," he said. "But I was sure you would want to know. Or perhaps you have heard already."

"What, for heaven's sake?" I asked.

"The church is on fire," Sidney said.

We scrambled to a window sill overlooking the alley.

The church had two rows of windows on each of its vast slab sides. The lower windows, illuminating the main sanctuary floor, were very tall. High above, a row of shallow windows gave light to the gallery. Several small upper windows were ablaze with inner orange light.

"It's back where the organ is," I cried.

"Junior, Junior." Below us, in the restaurant, Miss da Gamba ran to the booth where Mr. Junior was eating pizza. She pointed to the church. He jumped to his feet. His mouth flew open and a line of tomato paste dribbled down his broad chin.

"Turn in the alarm," he yelled. "For God's sake, Viola, get to the phone. Dial nine-one-one. I'm going over."

I could not wait for Mr. Junior. As I started for the alley Serena called something to me, but I was already too far away to hear.

Inside the church I climbed the walls straight to the choir loft. Racing to the Erben, I found one side of the case covered by a flickering tongue of flames. The fire seemed confined to the organ. Then it must have started there!

There was nothing I could do about the fire, but I resolved to save more of the old musical scores. Perhaps some would be of value. The flames had not reached that side of the case, but when I pulled open the cabinet door a mass of vile-smelling smoke enveloped me. A sudden draft cleared it away, and I began pulling out the sheets, two and three at a time. Soon the floor outside the Erben was littered with them.

If only someone came soon and extinguished the flames before they could spread to the gallery floor, the music would be salvaged. There was nothing more for me to do save retire to a safe position. Yet why, I wondered, had this calamity occurred? What had started the fire? I picked my way through the bottom of the organ toward the side that was blazing. In the hellish glow of flames from Mr. Erben's walnut case, the answer revealed itself.

In my haste to fix the blower wire before playing Mr. Hudson down from the belfry, I had failed to move it far enough from its metal ground on the motor housing, where it had short-circuited and caused the original breakdown. Then, when I finished playing, I had failed to restore the permanent short circuit. I left the wire in an in-between state. The current had begun to spark, showering fire onto one of Grandpa's old dry nests. The mass of shredded paper had become a torch of catastrophe.

What should I do with the wire now? As I studied the frayed strand with its deadly inch or two of exposed copper, something moved beside the wind chest. Perhaps it was just a shadow caused by the spreading fire. But as I looked to make sure, it moved again, gliding out of the thickening smoke, glowing in reflected flames.

"Oh Chawles," Alabama Ruby said, "Somehow I always knew our destiny lay here."

In the awful heat of the burning organ, a glacial chill froze my spine and legs.

"But you — you were — I heard the car . . ."

She came closer, and I saw she was dragging her right hindquarters.

"Your naughty friends, Chawles, those disgusting bats, they almost finished me, didn't they? I was unlucky. And when I ran, the car hit me. But then I was lucky. It didn't kill me."

She pulled herself forward. I glanced around for escape routes. Behind and to my right were walls of fire, and to my left the blower blocked the way with a sheer metal wall too high to jump. I could go nowhere. The cat glided closer, and I could see dried blood clotted in the fur beneath her eyes, where the bats had struck. She winced as if in pain. The rear leg appeared useless, and her ability to spring was thus reduced. I assumed a crouch on my own hindquarters.

"There is a sort of divine inevitability in our relationship, don't you agree, Chawles?" the cat purred. "It is truly destiny. One does not trifle with destiny, Chawles. Your disgusting friends tried, but gracious, they merely caused a minor diversion, don't you know. And they made you ever so overconfident. When push comes to shove, you see, friends really can't help."

The fire behind me crackled hotter. In moments it would burn the end of my already truncated tail. I could ill afford to lose any more of it.

Alabama Ruby's face was within four inches of my own. I could smell stale sardines on her breath. Was this the way it ended, to be co-digested with sardines? No, by heaven. I had one last trick to play.

"And I'm not going to hurry it up this time, Chawles," she said. "It's going to be nice and easy. After all, I still have eight more lives, and this is your only one. So why hurry, is what I say."

As if yawning lazily, she opened her mouth. The sardine stench was overpowering even in the smoke. From outside the church came a faint howl of sirens. Somewhere above me in the organ there was a cracking of wood, as if something heavy was coming loose.

I waited for an expression of anticipatory rapture to spread across my great enemy's face. Then, from my crouch, with both forepaws I grasped the blower wire as close to the exposed copper as I dared. I prayed the brittle insulation beneath my grip would hold. Then I jammed the wire with all my strength directly into Alabama Ruby's gaping mouth, and leaped back to the very edge of the fire.

My thrust was satisfactory. The fanged mouth snapped shut wetly on exposed copper. There was a blinding blue flash, and a deafening *pop!* audible above the fire.

Then from somewhere came another, greater explosion. Something struck my head with a burst of cosmic fireworks. The lights were beautiful, but they died soon against an inky sky.

I dreamed of a room that seemed terribly hot, even for the kitchen that it was.

The decor was rustic: whitewashed, square-cut log walls, vegetables and herbs drying on strings, well-oiled long rifles and powder horns hung at the ready on pegs. At the chimney end, a female figure worked at an enormous stove, a piano-sized monstrosity of black iron and nickel plate, baroquely ornamented.

The female figure was all but obscured by smoke and steam, but there was something familiar about the carefree shock of wheat-colored hair, the strong and graceful taper of neck, the set of shoulder, the incomparable long-legged, high-rumped lower half. It was Miss Tebell, in a dress styled in some long-ago time. Among a cluster of iron pots and pans she stirred and sliced and turned, stopping only to hurl a fresh chunk of wood into the firebox, and to mop her damp forehead.

Another female, similarly dressed, entered the kitchen. Serena! It did not seem at all curious that they were the same size, nor that they were friends.

"God, I'm glad you're here," said Miss Tebell. "I've got to get back over to my place and do my own cooking. Ready to take over?"

"I don't know," Serena said. "It's so hard to get up for it again. Pretty soon he'll be coming in here with his damn bag full of wild game, and another wheelbarrow of vegetables. Then he'll dump them out on the floor, and strut around like he was Daniel Boone. Then he'll get romantic, right on the kitchen floor. Is this all there is?"

"Is it indeed?" Miss Tebell echoed. "I wonder too. And I'm not even sure which man I love."

"Love. It is so elusive and undependable," Serena said. "It can start off as hot as this range. And then it can cool down, so fast that it's gone before you know it. On the other hand, it may endure forever. But you can't tell. The question is, do you take the chance?"

215

"What if you don't?" Miss Tebell asked. "You aren't as alive, I think. But I've gotta make up my mind. I'm almost thirty-seven."

"I'm not sure that time or age is all that important," Serena said.

"But it is," Miss Tebell said. "And it can force you to make a decision. I think I've already made it. As yet it is painful and not completely wholehearted. Look there, Serena, out beyond the clearing, at the forest. One of them, if I let him into my cabin, will come in from the woods to stay. And I'll always think of the other one out there prowling, lonely and unsatisfied, dangerous and in danger."

"He'll find another cabin, maybe," Serena said. "Nothing is certain."

"The male of the species!" Miss Tebell blared. "Do you know the nicest compliment I ever got from Caleb? He compared me to a clipper ship. He said I made him feel like a Baldwin steam locomotive thundering across prairies. Sometimes it's enough to make you join the Pocahontas Garden Club and tint your hair blue. Those old gals, they know the real meaning of beaver power."

Serena picked up a wooden spoon. "I don't think that I ever got the first compliment from Charles. Actually . . . actually I always had the feeling he was crazy about you."

Miss Tebell relaxed at last, laughing.

"Charles? He has an exaggerated susceptibility to the forbidden. And a conscience to keep him in agony about it. No, Serena. I'm sure. Charles loves you."

"How do you know?"

"For one thing," Miss Tebell said, looking out Serena's cabin window, "here he comes across the fields. Loaded down with wild game and vegetables."

Serena sighed, and threw fresh wood into the firebox.

"Charles! Charles!" It was Serena, fanning my face with a fragment of music score. "Charles, say something!"

"It's pretty damned hot. I'm burning up. I'm roasting alive."

"No, the fire's out now. It's still hot in here, but the fire's out. You were singed on your back, and you have a terrible bump on your head, where a falling piece of wood hit you, but that's all the damage I can find. Do you feel like anything's broken?"

Her dear face, close to mine, was filled with concern. Tears streamed down either side of her adorable pink nose.

Carefully, I activated my extremities.

"Everything seems okay. Where are we, Serena?" I asked.

"In the walls. Safe."

"How'd I get in the walls? Out of the Erben?"

"I pulled you out," she said. "Who else would rescue a mouse?"

"You came in there after me? Oh, Serena. But . . . the last thing I remember is Alabama Ruby! Did you see the cat?"

Serena nodded. "What was left of her. The cat is dead, Charles."

We heard muffled shouts and the clump of heavy boots.

"It's the firemen," Serena said. "They got here in time. Mr. Junior had put out the fire in the organ, but it had spread to the belfry. You wouldn't believe how fast it went up that staircase behind the organ. I think almost the whole tower was burning, Charles, but they put it out."

"Is Mr. Junior all right?"

"He will recover. You should have seen him. He was like a wild man, running up the steps with a fire extinguisher under each arm. The firemen had to pull him away; he was burned on the face, but he wouldn't quit. And he saved the organ, or most of it. He says he'll have it rebuilt."

The fire-ravaged steeple was removed, a step that made the church more than ever like a Greek temple, a development that pleased Dr. Christie. "It was a providential touch, desanctifying the church," we heard him say. "Now let the shows begin."

One evening in early May, when dogwoods flared across the street in Capitol Square, Miss Tebell and Dr. Old settled into a booth in the Rib Cage as Serena and I watched. Her purse lay beside her, its mouth firmly shut.

"I only wish we'd been able to find the 'Old Black Joe'

manuscript," Miss Tebell said. "I guess we'll never know what happened to it."

I looked at Serena. "I wish we could tell her that I probably shredded it for our nest," I said.

"Is that the only loose end?" Dr. Old asked.

"Let's see. The black ministers are coming through with a bas-relief memorial tablet to Mott Gooch. Boxwood Week cleared enough money to landscape the grounds and convert the alley into a sculpture garden. The building was designated a National Landmark. I guess that does it," Miss Tebell said.

"Ah, and your friend, uh, Mr. Zebulon . . ."

"Off campaigning," Miss Tebell said rather quickly. "Entering the primary for State Senate. It's about time we had some good representation. I hope he'll be governor, someday."

They sat quietly for a moment.

"How about you, Doctor?" she asked. "Any loose ends?"

"When I look at you across a candle, I am reminded of all kinds of unfinished business."

"Hmm. It may remain unfinished, Caleb, unless you promise to renounce any visions of large cookstoves, hunting expeditions, and wild game and vegetables tumbling to the kitchen floor. That's one of many things we need to talk about in the days ahead," she said.

Their feet collided under the table and seemed to cling together, pushing.

"It's the pressure that makes it nice," she mused. "See? Note that when you push, I push back. An elicited response from some mutual psychic interplay. It's possible I may push first sometimes . . ."

"I hope so, Tayloe. Even a Baldwin locomotive can't do it all," Dr. Old said.

"A clipper ship can," she laughed wickedly. "Now play B-Seventeen, and then walk me home. Through the Square."